GRIFFIN HAYES

DARK PASSAGE

Trebor Books

TREBOR BOOKS

ISBN: 978-0-9878068-6-4
eISBN: 978-0-9878068-5-7

Cover design by Griffin Hayes

Also by Griffin Hayes

Novels
Malice
Dark Passage
Hive Omnibus
Primal Shift (Season 1)

Novellas
Hive I
Hive II
Hive III
Bird of Prey
The Neighbors
Primal Shift

Short Stories
The Second Coming
The Grip
Fatherland

Collections
Night Terror
Nightfall

Chapter 1

Five-year-old Tyson Barrett sat on a plastic covered couch, watching a plastic covered TV, in a plastic covered house. He was a smart boy. Smart enough to know the show he was watching was called *Looney Tunes* and perhaps even smarter still because he knew that Bugs Bunny was about to get the better of that dim-witted Elmer Fudd again. Elmer had made the silly mistake of taking a nap in the woods and a big billowing dream cloud was floating serenely above his head. Bugs saw the cloud and crawled into it with a giant can of paint in his hand.

Nightmare paint.

He was going to turn the pudgy hunter's nice dreams into awful ugly dreams filled with monsters with claws and long pointed teeth. Of course none of this happened yet. But he knew it would. He'd seen this episode three times already.

Tyson shifted and the plastic covered couch let out a groan, one that sounded an awful lot like the groan in his tummy. His usual breakfast was waiting for him in the fridge. His mother had prepared it before leaving to take care of Mr. Tanner for the day. Mr. Tanner, she'd told him, had something called cancer. In six months he would be dead. She'd taken him by the shoulders and told him that most important of all, the disease eating away at Mr. Tanner's body was not contagious. When Mr. Tanner died, so too would the disease.

Tyson's father had also gone to work, but even when he was home he was something of a ghost, floating from room to room, like Casper. Invisible and powerless.

The boy was almost halfway to the kitchen when he stopped and skittered to the wall, pressing his back against the cold wood paneling. There were rules about where you could and couldn't walk in the house, and the middle of the living room was a big no-no. He had a vague idea that it had something to do with the "germs" Mommy was always talking about.

Hugging the wall, Tyson slowly made his way to the fridge where his breakfast waited, covered three times over with Saran Wrap: a piece of boiled ham, cold bread, and a glass of grapefruit juice. The taste of all three was so awful that he had once thrown them into the trash. Stuffed them right to the bottom so she wouldn't know what he had done. But somehow she knew, the way she knew lots of things. When she was through with him, he'd never done it again.

"Maybe one day when you have children of your own, you'll understand how much I love you," she'd told him. But before he could promise he would never do it again, the pain had made the world go black.

After he'd finished eating and set his dishes aside to be sterilized, Tyson returned—hugging the wall like a good boy—to the living room. His cartoon was over and in its place was a boring-looking show where a man in a gray suit was talking about how some people called the Russians were doing bad things in a country called Afghanistan.

The smell of pine trees hit him and pulled his attention toward the impossibly long hallway and the room nestled at the end of it. The room that was locked and OFF LIMITS. The one he was never to enter under any circumstance. The room that would make Mommy very upset if she ever saw him go inside. The room where the monster lived.

She kept the key in the top drawer of her dresser and must have thought that was a secret enough place that he'd never find it. But Tyson had found it, by accident. He was looking for his Han Solo and Chewbacca action figures. The ones she'd taken away to punish him for walking in the middle of the living room. When he had started crying, she'd torn Han's left arm off, just to let him know how serious she was.

The tears had stopped.

He'd opened the drawer and although he hadn't found a single sign of Han or Chewy, he did find a key. A long, thin, old looking metal key with two teeth and a large gap that looked an awful lot like the gap in Goofy's smile.

The smell of pine trees became stronger. A smell similar to when Mommy cleaned the kitchen floor, but somehow different. The smell was coming from that room, and it was as though a whole forest was growing in there. He imagined opening the door and finding himself at the base of hundred-foot trees that sprawled through the ceiling and stretched up into the clouds. He wondered what he might find when he climbed to the top.

But Tyson knew well enough there weren't really hundred-foot trees growing in that room. Because that was where the monster lived. His mother would tell him about it every night as she put him to bed. How she had to keep the door locked tight because the creature was always scratching to get out. How his claws were long and sharp, and she swore that on the quietest nights, if he held his breath, he might just hear nails scrapping against the door.

"Does he eat little boys?" Tyson had asked.

"Oh yes."

"Would he eat me?"

"Certainly."

"And you would let him?"

"Boys who listen to their mothers have nothing to worry about. Boys who misbehave… well, that's another story."

"Have you seen him?"

"Many times."

Tyson's mouth fell open. "What does he look like?"

His mother's face darkened. "I'll tell you. He has smooth skin like worn leather and eyes the deepest black you've ever seen. His arms are spindly but strong, and he uses the claws at the end of them to drag himself along the floor."

"His legs?"

"He doesn't have any. Not the way you and I have legs. All he has is a short fleshy tail."

He cowered beneath the covers. "No more, please."

"But I haven't told you about his teeth yet." Her eyes were shining.

Tyson left the couch, shivering at the memory. He started toward his mother's room and the temptation of the hidden key but stopped dead. He blinked long and hard, more than once just to be sure he wasn't seeing things.

The door at the end of the hallway was open. Not much more than a sliver, but it was open and the boy was suddenly gripped with fear.

He watched for a long time, but the door didn't move. Not even a little bit. It looked like there was something on the floor in front of it, two objects lying just inside the crack. He took a step closer to get a better look. Then another.

From here, those shapes looked an awful lot like Han and Chewy. Maybe there wasn't a monster in that room after all. Maybe this was where his mother kept all the toys she'd taken from him. Maybe it was all make believe, so he wouldn't go inside and find all of his favorite things.

Tyson tiptoed down the hallway, feeling the rough carpet biting into the balls of his feet like hundreds of little knives. He made sure to watch the door. Any sign of movement, he told himself, even the slightest sway, and he would run.

The wooden door was tall and brown, with chips of paint peeling off it. The knob was metallic and dull; not polished to a brilliant shine the way the rest of the house seemed to shine.

Suddenly the door moved and Tyson's whole body froze. Icy fingers crawled up his spine, leaving his hands cold and tingly. The breath caught in his throat and now he was sucking in air. Lungful after lungful and yet it still didn't quite feel like enough. Dangling around his neck from a piece of frayed packing rope was his asthma pump. Tyson brought it to his lips, depressed the button and all at once his face began to relax.

The door before him stood motionless. But by now he'd already made up his mind. He wasn't going in.

He reached out to shut the door and then stopped himself.

Han and Chewy weren't there anymore. But what if they were inside, waiting to be rescued? The thought was almost too much to ignore and the more he entertained the possibility, the more sense it seemed to make. And with that, he placed his little hand against the peeling paint and pushed at the door until it creaked open.

Inside, the monster stirred.

Chapter 2

Present Day

Self-righteous prick. That was thirty-eight-year-old Tyson Barrett's first impression upon shaking Dr. Charles Stevens' hand; a limp and pale thing that Stevens had left dangling between them like a length of loose rope. Even the walls of his spacious office made the man look like a name-dropping bore. A diploma from Harvard Medical School. Behind Stevens, a picture of him and Bill Clinton shaking hands. Another with Benjamin Netanyahu.

Tyson wished he could say he didn't care what Stevens thought of him. Wished he could even say he didn't care if he made it through what was turning out to be a bitch of a screening process. He had a hard time identifying with prissy little men like Charles Stevens, and as much as he hated being made to feel somehow inferior, he knew he needed the man. Far more than the man needed him.

The reason was simple. Tyson hadn't copped a full night's sleep in nearly six months. This study was his last hope. He was desperate. As much as he hated the word, Tyson Barrett was desperate with a capital D.

Perhaps it was that desperation that was making him sweat so much—his navy blue shirt had dark patches at the armpits and a long, wide son of a bitch running down his back.

Stevens motioned to the chair on the other side of his desk and Tyson sat down, feeling a long winding creak of tension crawl up from the base of his spine.

"As you've no doubt gathered by now, I'm the coordinator here at the facility. We're conducting phase II clinical trials on Noxil for Sino-Meck."

That self-important look was back on Stevens' face and Tyson did everything he could to smile and nod.

"Phase II is where we take people like yourself, who are suffering symptoms of anxiety, and see what effect the drug—"

"Nightmares. I mean... this will get rid of my nightmares, right?"

"Noxil is designed to treat PTSD."

"PTSD?"

Stevens smirked the way a lord might smirk at a simple minded peasant. "Of course. I forgot. Post-traumatic Stress Disorder."

"But it'll cure my nightmares?"

A momentary look of annoyance crossed Stevens' face before vanishing. "That's what we're hoping for." Stevens paused and Tyson couldn't help but notice the doctor scanning his face, noting the heavy purple bags under his eyes.

"You did read the study requirements, I assume," Stevens said casually.

Tyson was pulling at the cuff of his shirt, trying to give his armpits a bit of breathing room. "Sure."

"Then I'm assuming you saw that we're looking for subjects between the ages of eighteen and thirty-seven. It says here that you just celebrated your thirty-eighth birthday."

"I can tell you it wasn't much of a celebration." Tyson was trying to smile but wasn't having much success.

Stevens stood. "I'm so sorry."

Tyson rose to his feet in a single stiff motion. "Sorry?"

"You no longer qualify."

"But my birthday was less than a week ago. Please."

Stevens began moving for the door and Tyson stood in his way. "Doctor, I'm begging you. I'm at the tail end here. My life's a wreck. If I don't get this study..." Tears welled up in Tyson's puffy eyes. He looked down and saw his hands clamped around Stevens' shoulders. He removed them one at a time and straightened the man's lab coat. "I haven't had a proper night's sleep in months." Tyson could see in the doctor's eyes how much he loved that sliver of power, but for Tyson things had transcended mere ego.

"This would be a major infraction," Stevens began.

Tyson wiped at his eyes with the palms of his hands. "I won't tell a soul, I swear."

Slowly, Stevens returned to his chair and eased back into it. "There is something I'm legally obliged to tell you."

Tyson raised his eyebrows. Oh no, he thought, feeling that glimmer of hope inching from his grasp again. They know I've lied on my application, and all that begging didn't accomplish anything more than making Stevens feel like some big shot.

"There is some red tape Sino-Meck is trying to overcome with the government. A formality at most, I assure you."

"I'm not sure I follow."

"Final approval from the FDA and our local IRB hasn't arrived yet. You see, most drugs have some pretty nasty side effects. I'm sure you've seen some of the commercials they're putting on television these days."

"Christ, who hasn't?" Tyson tried to laugh, but it

sounded stilted and forced.

Stevens was examining something on the nail of his index finger. "You tamper with the body's chemistry and side effects tend to occur. At the end of the day, what the IRB and our friends at the FDA have to consider is whether the benefits of a given drug outweigh its harmful effects. It's a pretty simple equation really."

"Yeah, I'm sure it is. I think I understand what you're saying. If I start taking Noxil, I may grow a pair of tits or my balls might swell to the size of grapefruits, right?"

Stevens smiled, this time genuinely and Tyson wondered whether his face was going to crack.

"No, our problem is quite different. You see, Noxil has no side effects."

Tyson's back straightened against the chair. "No side effects? Is that possible? Not even cotton mouth, profuse sweating, nausea… heart palpitations?"

"You seem to know your drugs, Mr. Barrett."

Tyson's eyes flickered with momentary guilt. He had let his guard down and he was angry at himself for doing it. One more missed step and he was out.

"It is hard to believe, I agree, and this is precisely why the FDA is dragging its feet. We've been given a conditional green light to proceed, but we've been instructed to inform all potential patients that the study's final approval is still pending."

Tyson nodded understanding.

"Now, there are a few things about your medical form we need to go over."

The knot of tension was creeping back into Tyson's neck.

"You say here," Stevens began, "that you're not on any other prescription medication."

"That's right," Tyson said, feeling the lie roll off his tongue with surprising ease.

"And no pre-existing medical conditions?"

9

"Clean as a whistle." Tyson could feel the asthma pump in his jeans pocket, pushing against his leg; for a panicked moment, he was sure Stevens could see it.

"Here's the problem: when we tell the FDA there are no side effects that we know of, it's implied the patients aren't on any other medication. If the patients are, it muddles our results and puts the patients... at risk. In some extreme cases it can cause the drug to have some... unintended and unexplainable side effects." Stevens did not meet his eyes as he cleared his throat and continued. "In others, mixing has been known to cause death. You understand, of course."

Tyson was doing his best not to think about how the medicine cabinet in his bathroom was filled to the brim with enough meds to keep an entire family in tip-top shape for a year.

"Have you ever participated in a clinical trial before, Mr. Barrett?"

"Never." This time he was telling the truth.

"You seem like a very honest person. It's not people like you we're trying to screen for really." Stevens leaned in. "It's the serial drug testers. They're a growing problem in the industry and something we've been battling for years."

Tyson's face registered confusion.

"Serial drug testers. Drug Cowboys. They join as many studies as they can, falsifying and tailoring their medical histories to fit whatever they feel the researcher is looking for. There's a lot of money to be made."

"I can see how that's a problem."

"An enormous problem, but enough about that. I need to understand a little more about your nightmares before we proceed."

Tyson swallowed and his throat made an audible clicking noise.

"Kinda hard to say. I mean, I don't remember all that

much. It's more sensations really."

"Oh, and how would you describe these sensations?"

Tyson looked at Stevens and the hazy sleepy feeling he'd carried around with him every day for the past six months was suddenly gone.

"Terror. I mean, whenever I let myself fall asleep, I wake up screaming. I'm not kidding. So loud my voice gets hoarse and I can't speak for days. Something's inside the room with me, that's all I really know for sure. I can smell it and hear it, shambling along the floor. I've never seen it, but every other sense tells me it's there." Tyson took a deep breath and looked away.

"Is that all?"

Tyson's hands were in his lap, clasped together so hard his fingers had gone bone white. "No, there's something else." Tyson shifted in the tiny plastic chair and it creaked loudly. "Flies. My dreams are filled with them. Thousands, maybe millions, and they're buzzing around me, trying to get into my mouth, crawling into my ears and up my nostrils. And then the flies are gone and there's something… someone in the room with me. It looks fuzzy, like when the projector guy at the movies falls asleep and everything goes out of whack. Somehow I know I shouldn't move. It's the movement he senses. Air displacement, thermal variations. CSI stuff. I'm not sure, but he can feel you. Even when every ounce of light's been sucked clean out of a room he knows where you are." Tyson's heart was hammering and he unsnapped the top button of his shirt. He wasn't getting enough air. He could feel his lungs contracting violently, trying to pull in precious oxygen. His hand started for the inhaler and he stopped himself. Physically stopped his hand. Thick threads of sweat streamed down his face.

"Mr. Barrett? Are you all right?" Stevens' voice was barren. Stephen Hawking and his robotic voice box might have sounded more compassionate.

Tyson's breathing slowed. He could feel his control inching back. A hint of color was returning to his otherwise opaque and tired complexion.

Stevens was looking at him intently now. "A mythological dream, interesting."

"I'm sorry?"

"What you're describing sounds like Ahriman."

Still reeling, Tyson didn't have the faintest idea what Stevens was going on about.

"A myth, sometimes used in psychological profiling. Ahriman was a demon the ancient Persians believed entered our world in the form of a fly."

"Oh great."

"Have you ever considered any of the several therapeutic avenues other than medication?"

"You name it, I've tried it: talk therapy, group therapy, meditation, biofeedback, hypnosis, acupuncture, cognitive behavioral therapy."

If Stevens could sense the lie he didn't show it. He stood up, straightened his white lab coat and thrust out that limp biscuit he called a hand. "I would like to congratulate you, Mr. Barrett. For now we'll overlook that little issue with your age. You've passed the screening. Welcome aboard."

Tyson stood and took Stevens' hand, a beaming smile on his face. He couldn't help feeling like a man in a long dark tunnel who has finally spotted a faint glimmer of light up ahead.

• • •

Tyson found the cot that would be his for the next hour. He was to take his introductory sample of Noxil and then record his initial reaction. Tyson had just sat down when he spotted the man in the bunk next to him.

The man had his back propped against the wall and a weathered cowboy hat slung over his face. One of the nurses was hunched over him, attempting to take a blood sample from his arm. She didn't appear to be having much luck.

He raised his hat with his free hand. "Watch my veins, honey," he mumbled. "They tend to roll."

Tyson caught the look of annoyance flash across her face.

"Looks like they found another guinea pig," the man said and burst into phlegmy laughter. His body gyrated wildly as though this were the funniest joke he'd ever heard and the nurse, now red faced and looking like she'd just about had enough, threw her hands into the air and stormed off.

His eyes followed the curve of her buttocks as she left. "Hell, we don't need her. The way she was poking and prodding you'd think she was takin' me to the prom."

The hand he held out was stubby and well manicured. The man hadn't worked a day in his life. "Vance Fowler. Call me Vance."

Tyson reciprocated. "Tyson."

"I feel like I've seen you before. Out on the circuit maybe? Were you at Flopoxia in Houston last month?"

"Flopox—"

"Hmm, or was it Xanadin back in January?" He seemed to be talking to himself now.

Tyson straightened. "This is my first clinical trial, if that's what you mean."

"Hell's bells, this is—" Vance said, counting his fingers now, "my thirty-fifth. No, thirty-sixth. So hard to keep track. I'm telling you, after the first dozen it's all a blur."

"So you're not here for nightmares?"

"Nightmares?" Vance let out a spastic burst of

laughter. "Only nightmare I have is about the check bouncing before I can cash it. Apparently they're paying 2k for this beaut. Most I've ever made on any clini is 10k, but that was a real whore down in Colorado. Had a tube stuck up my ass the size of a vacuum hose for nearly a week. Hose up the ass ain't pretty, but I'm sure ol' Dr. Stevens would disagree." Vance was winking wildly.

"He mentioned guys like you," Tyson said. "Called you serial testers."

"Yeah, well, Dr. Knowitall Stevens can hardly tell his arse from his elbow."

Vance glanced around and when he settled back on Tyson the expression on his face was dire. "I'm gonna tell you something. If you're thinking of making a go, this ain't no business for pussies. Two good buddies of mine got caught in that TGN1412 mess over in England. They'd done too much mixing, just gotten off more than a dozen studies between the two of them. Topped over fifty grand. Except one of them ended up a veggie burger and the other had his insides turned to mush." Vance paused, his eyes scrutinizing Tyson. "I gotta say, call me crazy, but with the way your eyes are all puffed out and that pale complexion of yours, I'd swear you were a pro."

Tyson felt the heat rise up his neck and into his face. He had to admit there was something he found downright fascinating about a guy who made his living whoring his body out to pharmaceutical companies. As far as looking like a bag of shit went, that was something he couldn't deny. The heavy sunken eyes, the pale, translucent skin. Running these last six months on a total of twelve hours of restless sleep would make anyone look like a Courtney Love stunt double. Tyson was midway through convincing himself that Vance had dropped one too many Noxil when he saw an image of himself at home in his bathroom, wrapped in a dirty housecoat, peeling open the medicine cabinet. Saw his hand, lined

14

with thick bulbous veins, searching frantically through a veritable cityscape of pill bottles. One of them careened off the thin glass ledge and tumbled end over end until it connected with the bathroom sink and exploded, spraying tiny yellow capsules in all directions. He had been looking for a remedy for whatever disease or obscure sickness had been ailing him at the time. The memory couldn't have been much more than a day old.

"Mr. Barrett?"

The voice was delicate and young and Tyson looked up, wondering for a moment if he was dreaming. The nurse was beautiful and she filled her uniform in all the right places. The hazy smile on Tyson's face probably made him look medicated.

The nurse placed a small plastic container on the table next to him, undid the two latches and lifted the lid. Inside was something that looked like a stun gun.

"What's that for?" Tyson asked. Her eyes were like two swimming pools filled with sapphires and he was having a hard time looking away.

"This is your auto injector. It's a spring-powered jet gun." The nurse removed a tiny vial of blue liquid from the pocket of her uniform and slid it into the back of the injector. "Sit back and relax, this won't hurt a bit."

Tyson did as he was told. The nurse placed the rounded tip against the flesh of his arm and pressed a button with her thumb. It made a whooshing that sounded a lot like his asthma pump. Something about that noise set him at ease.

His eyes focused on the shape next to him and found Vance looking on with an amused expression. Tyson thought of what Vance had just said about too much mixing and what it had done to those friends of his in England. The muscles in Tyson's gut started to slowly curl into a tight fist.

Maybe there was a bit of a pro in him after all.

Chapter 3

Sunnybrook Asylum, Upstate NY

"The facility houses over five hundred patients," Dr. Kenneth Bowes was saying as the elevator doors slid open onto the eighth floor. He stepped out, followed closely by Dr. Elias Hunter. Peering down at the top of Dr. Bowes' balding head, Hunter was struck for the first time by how truly short the man was.

And tanned.

He'd heard about doctors like Bowes in med school. The kind who left every lunch hour for a quick round of golf. He was beginning to wonder if he hadn't made a mistake accepting the job at Sunnybrook.

"The eighth floor is where we keep patients who've been convicted of violent crimes."

"You mean the ones who copped an insanity plea," Hunter added.

Dr. Bowes glanced back and his eyes were hard and gray. "I mean the ones with great lawyers."

Hunter laughed even though he suspected Bowes hadn't been joking.

"I'd say only somewhere around half of the patients on this floor truly deserve to be here."

They turned a corner and headed down a dimly lit hallway. On either side, thick metal doors with tiny glass porthole windows stretched on for as far as the eye could see.

A woman shrieked from a room somewhere behind them and Hunter nearly jumped. But he didn't. And that was the point. He caught himself because he knew very well that Dr. Bowes had his radar switched on, searching for just such a reaction. It was what this entire tour was really all about.

The goal wasn't to show Hunter around the shadowy maze that was Sunnybrook Asylum. It was about checking him at the door for any signs of fear. Hunter knew from experience that if any of the doctors or even a staffer could see it, you could bet the nuts—patients, he corrected himself, patients—could smell it coming a mile away, just as they could probably smell Dr. Bowes' cheap cologne the minute he pulled into the staff parking lot.

"In addition to taking care of Sunnybrook's daily operations, I'm also the resident MD," Bowes was saying. "So you can imagine how much I have on my plate. That was why we even gave your application a second look. We didn't even care that you graduated from Albany Medical College. Hey, not everyone can afford John Hopkins." Bowes paused and Hunter wondered if the old man was taking a second to let the burn sink in. "All that aside, it'll be nice to have another physician on staff."

The two men were padding down the hallway at a decent clip when something in room H-16 caught Hunter's attention. It looked like a woman surrounded by a battery of medical equipment. Perhaps that sort of thing might not look out of place in an ER, but here?

"Who's this?" Hunter asked, reaching for the door handle. Dr. Bowes rushed forward to stop him. Hunter could see the white lines on Bowes' face where the golf course sun hadn't quite been able to breach his wrinkled skin.

"We never just enter a patient's room without following the proper protocol, Dr. Hunter."

Bowes stepped up to the thick metal door and peered through the concave glass.

"Room H-16 belongs to Brenda Barrett," he said with a hint of derision.

"She's not doing very well, is she?"

"Brenda's been under constant medical supervision since she slipped into a coma last fall. No room in any of the proper big city facilities, so we've had to hang on to her."

"How bad is she?"

"Her coma's about as deep as they come. Level three on the Glasgow scale, which I'm sure you learned at Albany, means she doesn't do much more than just lie there. She wouldn't even be breathing if it weren't for all the hardware we have her hooked up to."

Hunter ignored the dig. "Any idea what caused it?"

"At the moment we have no idea. We suspect she may have been given the wrong medication. There is a woman at the end of the hall named Beverly Barretti, getting Paxilin, so it's not implausible that a mix-up might have happened."

"All that time and she's not brain-dead?" Even Hunter wasn't quite sure if he was asking a question or making a statement.

"Brain-dead? Far from it. Brenda's CT scans show that her brain activity is abnormally high."

"When you say abnormally high…"

"Off the charts."

"I'm not sure I follow. She's in a coma, but her brain is—"

"As active as someone playing Tchaikovsky's Third Symphony."

Hunter's eyes widened. "Impressive, the Third Symphony's a complicated piece. Which instrument are you referring to?"

Bowes looked up at him. "All of them."

Hunter couldn't hide his astonishment. "Any idea what's causing it?"

A strange mix of concern and fear washed over Dr. Bowes' face.

"We think she's dreaming."

Chapter 4

Tyson could see the cottage in the distance now, through a clearing of dense foliage; a brown, bungalow-style building with a single stone chimney, nestled along the edge of Lake Harmony. Although it couldn't have been much more than an hour west of New York City, the ride had been a near disaster.

His eyes had kept trying to close on him.

The sluggish feeling had started no more than thirty minutes after he had hit the 17 North and an hour after the sexy nurse had given him his first shot of Noxil.

Twice he had stopped to splash water on this face and check his messages. There were two. Both from his longtime friend and business partner Skip Williams. Skip was wondering if he had managed to find the cottage all right. This whole getaway had been Skip's brainchild and it had come wrapped in the form of a stinging ultimatum.

Deep down, Tyson couldn't really blame him. Even now, he was still lucid enough to recognize that trying to run your life, let alone your business, on zero sleep was next to impossible. When Ruma had packed up their five-year-old son Kavi and told him she was moving into an apartment, well, the shit had really hit the fan. Added to that was the brilliant news that she was doing her gynecologist.

Tyson's life had been in the process of slowly circling the toilet bowel when Skip had first suggested he join the clinical trial. Yes, it was still somewhat of an underground study, Skip had told him, but what have you got to lose?

It was then that his friend and business partner of over a decade had offered this little gem as an incentive: "Tyson, I love you, buddy, and that's why I'm giving you two choices. A: Take some time off and come back when you've got this thing under control, or B: Sign our company and all of its assets over to me right now." He had even brought the bloody documents and a pen—the same Mont Blanc fountain pen Tyson had given him last year for his birthday.

As much as Tyson didn't like to admit it, there had been something self-destructively appealing about option B. The prospect of watching your life go so effortlessly up in flames had become an almost daily fantasy. And the truth was that for a time, he hadn't been sure which one he would choose. In the end, Skip had made that decision for him in a way that only Skip could do.

"Wondering if you could do me a big favor during that hiatus of yours," Skip had asked sheepishly, as though the 'hiatus' was already a done deal. "Spring's in full swing and the local crank who normally opens my summer home, airs everything out and dusts away the cobwebs, had a stroke. I know I'm asking a lot, but I'm wondering if you'd be willing to take those few days to help an old friend out."

Old friend! You sly son of a bitch, you!

Tyson knew what his friend was up to and he certainly appreciated it but...

"Shouldn't really take you more than a day or two to get her in order. Turn the water back on, check the oil in the furnace—should still be full if it hasn't leaked all over the goddamn place—and remove the dust covers from the furniture. You run into any trouble you can always give Judy Stahl a call. She's just down the lake and would be happy to give you a hand—hell, Ty, you might even get lucky."

They laughed, each for different reasons. Tyson, because he couldn't imagine any woman wanting him in his current state. Even though it had been some time since the separation, Ruma's little indiscretion and subsequent disappearing act had left him wary of females. No, he wouldn't call Judy Stahl, he decided, even if the place looked like it might go sliding into the lake. What he needed was a little solo time, in a place where things moved at a pace where he could get a firm handle on where he was and where he wanted to go.

Skip had seen the tide turning in the internal debate raging in Tyson's head and a gap-toothed grin began to appear. "When you get back we'll be poised to get this dot-com of ours off the ground. The venture capitalists are circling, Tyson. Good things are in store. I can feel it!"

Yeah, well, 'good things' hadn't been spending much time with Tyson Barrett as of late. He wanted to believe Skip. Believe that this new drug and a few days off were going to make a difference. Wanted to believe it more than ever. "You're one hell of a salesman, Skip, you know that?"

Tyson pulled the Corolla up to the cottage and killed the engine. He sat for a moment listening to the engine tick down in the late afternoon sun.

His hand went to the ignition switch to remove the keys. He paused and then reached into his overnight bag and fished out the black Noxil case with its small jet injector and a dozen glass vials, filled with dark blue liquid.

The instructions said to take one shot three times a day. The car's digital clock read half past twelve. Tyson reached into the glove compartment, shuffled around for the granola bar he knew was in there somewhere, and when he finally found it, wolfed it down in three bites.

Tyson then removed the injector, opened the back and slid one of the blue vials inside. He held the device to his temple, in mock suicide, before lowering the nozzle to his shoulder.

"Here's to new beginnings," he said quietly and pulled the trigger. Tyson felt a tiny displacement of air, but otherwise, the process was painless.

Although Dr. Stevens had assured him it should take several minutes for the medication to flow into his blood stream, the very act of injecting himself with a device straight out of Star Trek made him feel better already. He slid the keys from the ignition into his pocket and popped the trunk.

The cottage's interior did nothing to break with the quiet unassuming character he had seen driving up the gravel path. A glass door hinged open into a sunroom, the legs of wicker chairs peeking out from under white sheets. Beyond that, a connected kitchen and living room with a stove fireplace, and then a narrow hallway with three bedrooms, two on the left, one on the right.

The master.

That was where Tyson would sleep, he decided with uncharacteristic certainty. He dumped his bag on the king-size bed and watched it bounce jovially.

It looked like so much fun he couldn't resist doing it himself. Down he went, falling onto the bed. When it settled, he turned on his side and peered into the hallway. The room opposite his had a large bay window which faced onto the lake. He could see a tiny orange and yellow sailboat cutting through the choppy spring water. Tyson drew in a deep breath and smiled. Noxil or not, for the first time in a long while he was happy.

In his pocket was a list of instructions for getting the place in order. He removed it and started reading.

Dear Tyson,

I wasn't able to get to the lake so thanks again for all your help.

The electricity and the water will be off when you arrive. Turning them on is easy enough. Simply follow the path that leads under the deck and make a right at the first door, the second is just storage and some old tools that don't see much action anymore. Inside, on the left wall, you'll find one switch for the power and one for the water.

Now for the boathouse. As you may already have seen, the boathouse is hardly lacking amenities—canoes, kayaks, even a motorboat, albeit aging and stubborn at anything over 20mph—but good enough for any half decent pleasure cruise. There's also some snorkeling gear and a speargun, but you might find it easier to get your food at the local market in town. Oh, and in case anything should go wrong, there's a list of emergency response numbers next to the phone, above where the life jackets and paddles are stored. Judy Stahl's number should be there.

As for sleeping arrangements, I'll leave that up to you. However, you might think about taking the master bedroom since it has the largest and bounciest bed.

Your friend, Skip

Way ahead of you Skip. Way ahead of you.

Tyson came awake some time later to the sound of a loon crying from the lake. He bolted up with a start. He had fallen into a blissful sleep, filled with the kind of happy dreams you hope will never end. He swung himself off the bed and headed for the bathroom on a pair of wobbly legs. The cottage was dim and unfamiliar and it took Tyson a moment to realize he wasn't at home. He was perhaps three-quarters of the way through the longest piss in history when the full weight of what had just happened came crashing down on him.

That momentary lapse in attention was enough to make him pelt the seat with a thick stream of urine. The first commandment in his married life had been "thou shalt lift the toilet seat before taking a piss" and when Ruma had so conscientiously packed up her things and left them in a neat bundle by the front door, that was the first rule to go flying out the window.

But it was after an especially long piss, as he stared into the mirror, that the loose threads finally pulled together in his mind.

Holy shit, he had slept.

For the first time in months he had shut his eyes and drifted off. And not just for an hour or two. That wasn't an enormous feat in and of itself, but judging by the gunky build up in his mouth and the tingling feeling in his legs, he must have been out for a while. Those dark circles under his eyes also seemed to be fading, even if it was only by a shade or two. He took a closer look at his chin covered with a thick carpet of coarse stubble and suddenly felt like a character out of a Washington Irving novel.

That was when the bomb in his head really went off. All that sleep and not a single nightmare. In fact, his dreams had been rather pleasant. One of them stood out above the rest. He was a child again and playing happily with his Han Solo and Chewbacca action figures. The dream had been incredibly vivid. As though all of his senses were turned on and a knob in his head set to full. It was coming back to him now, in glorious high definition, even down to Han's missing left arm, an unfortunate wound that he had forgotten about until now. Standing here awake, at least he thought he was awake, he was almost overcome by the smell of detergent from childhood T-shirts and hardwood floors lathered with buckets of industrial strength disinfectant. For a moment, he felt himself swimming between two competing worlds and it was only with a conscious act of willpower that he was able to pull himself back.

And then another smell. One he didn't like. Didn't like one bit. The smell of pine trees wafting in the air and his nose curled up and his insides twisted like a basket full of coiled, hissing snakes.

His overnight bag was on the bathroom counter. Nestled atop his Xanax and Valium and snuggled beside his asthma inhaler were the injector and the vials of Noxil. He plucked out one of the vials and studied it. A quiet smile made slow progress across his face.

"This shit really works."

For the first time in nearly six months, he had eked out an entire night's sleep and this blue concoction—no more than a thimbleful—had made that possible. It was all so hard to believe.

The sense of bewildered elation stayed with him all the way to the local Grand Union and back. He would need supplies if he was going to stay here for any length of time. A check-out girl named Candice gave him a smile and for the first time in a long while he had started to feel like himself again.

Tyson began putting his groceries away. Perishables in the fridge, canned goods and dried pastas in the pantry. Dish soap and sponges under the sink, and a drying towel—he hadn't been able to find one at the cottage for the life of him—in a drawer by the stove. He pulled that last drawer open and jumped back, his hand flying into the air as though he'd been holding the tail of a scorpion. Inside sat two objects that belonged to a young child. Objects he knew very well. Action figures. Two of them. Han Solo and Chewbacca. Han's left arm was missing.

Tyson slammed the drawer closed with a bang. The flesh on his arms had pricked up. His eyes were wide and disbelieving. He watched the drawer, somehow expecting it to pop open and spit its contents out at him. The room was suddenly tiny and claustrophobic, seeming to grow smaller every second. Tyson's breathing was ratcheting up again and he rushed to the bathroom for his asthma inhaler.

He was at the bathroom sink when it dawned on him, feeling dense for not seeing it before: a testament perhaps to how far down the can he had let himself fall. The whole thing had the nasty aftertaste of a Skip Williams special; a prank, crude and elaborate enough to belong to one man and one man alone. Tyson stormed into the bedroom and snatched up his phone. He would call Skip and tell him what an asshole he was. After all, hadn't he come all this way to try and get his shit back together? Not to have his mind played with. The message light on his phone was blinking. He removed the key lock and saw eight messages waiting for him.

Tyson stared at the screen in disbelief, convinced his phone must be acting up. The date was all wrong too. Hadn't he arrived on the nineteenth? So why was his phone now reading the twenty-first? Where the hell had the twentieth gone? Had he been stone-dead asleep for thirty-six hours? His annoyance was starting to turn to fear.

What in God's name is going on here?

With shaking fingers, he pulled up Skip's number. The line rang a handful of times before finally being picked up. The voice on the other end sounded annoyed and drunk.

"You're a real smart ass, you know that, Skip?"

"Who is this?"

"The butt of your piss poor sense of humor, that's who."

"Tyson?"

Tyson peeled open the drawer and peeked inside. "I found the two little presents you left me and I gotta say, I'm not sure how you got your hands on them, but I don't find it one bit funny. You're gonna have to try harder than that …"

"Presents? I have no idea what the fuck you're talking about."

Tyson swapped the phone to the other ear, suddenly not so sure of himself. A while back, Tyson had seen Skip whack his thumb with a hammer and the worst thing that came out was a damnit. The word fuck just wasn't in Skip's vocabulary. A slow sinking feeling began to grip him, the realization that maybe Skip had nothing to do with the Han and Chewy dolls he'd found. Right behind that was another question. A disturbing question he wasn't sure he wanted to ask. If Skip hadn't done this, then who had?

"You swear this wasn't you? Leaving something here for me to find wasn't your idea of a hilarious joke to play on old Ty?"

"Why would I do that when I need you back in one piece, not in a padded room in Sunnybrook with a view of the Hudson? I will, however, tell you what is definitely not a prank. Castleman called me today. Told me he and his associates decided to take a pass on Onesizefitsall.com. Says our business plan showed promise, but that he didn't have faith in our professionalism. He wouldn't say any more and I haven't the foggiest idea what he's talking about. I know I haven't spoken to him since we pitched the company." There was a pause on the other end of the line. A bad kind of pause and Tyson thought he knew what was going to come next. "You didn't call him at any point in one of your delirious sleep deprived states did you?"

"No, Skip, for Christ's sake, of course I didn't." But there seemed to be large stretches in the last six months that were either blurry or had been wiped from his memory completely. It was hard to get a firm handle on the world when you hadn't caught so much as ten consecutive winks in months. Was it possible he had called Castleman's office after their presentation to

28

supplement a few sales figures he might have left out when it was his turn to speak? Possibly. Or was it more probable that Castleman had seen the dark lines ringing Tyson's eyes and worried he was mentally unstable? He felt his throat tighten, found his hand reaching for the inhaler and stopped himself.

"Looks like we just lost our million dollar financing. Unless you can pull stacks of fifties and hundreds out of your butt, we're back to square one."

"What about O'Donnell and those two brothers of his? The ones that own the paving company."

"They've agreed to ten thousand each. But it's barely a drop in the ocean. Listen Ty, you just sort yourself out and get back here as soon as you can." Skip paused. His voice was softer now. "How are things going up there? I didn't even ask about the …"

"The Noxil?" Tyson said absently.

"Yeah, is it working?"

Tyson couldn't quite bring himself to say yes. He slid open the kitchen drawer again. Han and Chewy were still there, their eyes tiny pinpoints of ink, nothing more. The drug was doing something all right. Anyone could see that. Just what that was, he couldn't yet say.

"Let me get back to you on that," Tyson said and hung up.

Chapter 5

Hunter's third day at Sunnybrook started out uneventfully. His instructions were simple enough: he was to shadow Dr. Bowes as he made his rounds of the seventh and eighth floors. Clearly Dr. Bowes' job was, for all intents and purposes, more supervisory than medical. He conferred with nurses and orderlies, ensured patients received the proper dosage of medication and occasionally spoke with a patient or two. And if what Hunter had seen so far was anything to go by, occasionally was an overstatement. When Bowes would hear news that one of the patients had asked for him, he usually responded with the sigh of a lazy man who had grown accustomed to delegating the 'uninteresting bits' to his underlings.

The way things were going, Hunter was becoming more and more certain that once these practice rounds were done, the bulk of Bowes' daily grind and 'uninteresting bits' would fall to him. But shit always tended to roll downhill, didn't it?

Even some of the nurses weren't immune to this mental hazing. On his first day, a big boned young nurse with a pretty face named Cindi Jaworski had slid into the cafeteria seat next to him at lunch.

"So have you been to eight yet?" Her eyes were brimming with curiosity.

Hunter nodded. In fact, he had just returned from H-16; Brenda's room on the eighth floor.

"When Dr. Bowes was giving you the grand tour - that's what he likes to call it - did you ask him why eight has so few patients?"

"Should I have?"

"No, it's a good thing you didn't, 'cause he hates when newbies ask him that."

Hunter paused to consider what Cindi had just said. "I suppose I just assumed the criminally insane pop here was proportionate."

"Proportionate to what? There are thirty-four patients on eight. You thought all of New York State couldn't produce more than thirty-four class-one whack jobs?" She was teasing him, of course, but Hunter still thought he detected a touch of mockery in her tone. Perhaps more than a touch.

"Maybe I assumed Sunnybrook had taken the spill-over from the Kirby, in Manhattan."

"Despite what mister 'do it my way or don't do it at all' thinks, it's no secret around here that Bowes hates the eighth floor. Might be something you should ask him about, seeing as how you'll be working up there quite a bit. Might even be the reason you were hired. To take eight off his hands."

By the early afternoon, they had finished with seven and moved on to eight and Dr. Bowes' mood seemed to suddenly shift. The man's cocky swagger was gone. His steps were smaller and more cautious. Dare say, Hunter thought he was almost hesitant. A pattern that seemed to intensify as they approached room H-16.

Inside Brenda Barrett's dim and sparsely furnished cell, a single bed faced a small bookshelf, its contents neatly ordered. She was surrounded by machines and blinking lights and she looked like something out of a science fiction movie. An aging ventilator by her bed kept her breathing. Beside that, an EKG monitored her heart.

On the way up, Bowes had told Hunter about the rounds. That every day someone came in to reposition Brenda.

"Bedsores are always a problem," Bowes had said. "But the real problem is that most of my orderlies are superstitious Latinos, who routinely skip Brenda's room altogether, leaving her to stew in her own..." Bowes paused searching for the least offensive word, "filth... at times for days on end."

There was something about this room that the orderlies didn't like. Hunter wondered if it had more to do with the woman lying in it than the room itself. She was still and quiet, but then so was a Venus Fly Trap.

Clak-clak-clak-clak-clak-clak.

Bowes had started clicking his pen the minute they entered the room. His face was a mask of tension. Try as he might, Bowes couldn't hide the fact that he was scared of this woman. But what could she have done to shake even a hardened professional drone like Bowes?

Hunter watched her lying there with tubes snaking out of her mouth, a ninety-seven pound hunk of inanimate flesh. You don't get more powerless than this, he thought, and yet she seemed to have everyone at Sunnybrook running for the hills. Then a light went on in his head. This was a test. And Brenda was the big bad voodoo mamma who was meant to reveal him as a coward.

Dr. Bowes was over by the EKG, checking off boxes on a clipboard, when a thin, homely nurse burst into the room, panting. "Doctor, I need you in H-4, Hillinger just bit his tongue off."

"Oh Jesus, not again."

There was a white blur as Bowes and the nurse tore from the room. Hunter could hear their frantic footfalls receding down the impossibly long corridor until they were swallowed away by the room's gloomy stillness. But it wasn't entirely quiet of course. The respirator that was feeding oxygen into Brenda's lungs was making a fine racket and he could hear the heart monitor going blip blip blip at the steady pace of her beating heart. For all intents and purposes, Dr. Hunter was alone, but somehow he didn't feel that way.

He snatched the clipboard that Bowes had flung onto the bed when he'd rushed off to check on Hillinger.

Vital signs.

Responsiveness.

Looked like fairly standard stuff.

Bowes had said Brenda was a three on the Glasgow scale which really was a polite way of saying she was about as active and coherent as piece of vegetable lasagna. Hunter took the flashlight pen out of his breast pocket and slid one of her eyelids back. Her pupils were dilated. He swung the light back and forth but her eyes remained unresponsive.

The next part of the test required him to speak to her and wait for a response.

"Brenda," he said. "This is Dr. Hunter, can you hear me?"

Almost a full minute passed without a reply.

"Brenda?"

Blip blip blip

He was looking at her bookcase as he waited, marveling at how neatly it was stacked and organized. Spines out, large to small from left to right. One of them caught his attention.

Curious George Goes to the Hospital.

Nostalgia rushed through him and he approached the bookcase with all the wonder of a child. He scanned through the titles.

Cat in the Hat... Are You My Mother?... The Very Hungry Caterpillar...

She must have over a hundred books here and all of them for children. Hunter plucked *Curious George* from the stack and held it with reverence. The cardboard edges were frayed and several of the pages bent or scribbled on, which only seemed to strengthen the warm feeling he got from holding it. He flipped through crisp pages, smiling whenever he came to a picture or part he particularly cherished. When he arrived at the bit where George gets his X-ray, he noticed the slanted, open looped handwriting in the margin. Hunter began to read.

The human body is a cesspool of germs and bacteria. Slithering eating shitting fucking all over your skin and in your mouth and in your guts. I was a nurse for fifteen years I know I know I know I know. I've seen it. The miracle of life. Bullshit. The real miracle is that it manages to go on in spite of the filth and the contamination. No one is immune. No matter how careful. Drop your guard for a moment and you're a goner. One slip. One teensy-weensy slip. That's all it ...

The noise behind him clamored for his attention. Brenda's heart monitor was pinging like mad.

BLIP BLIP BLIP

He hurried to her side. Her heart rate was doing 190 beats per minute and Hunter could see the line zigzagging across the screen. He was still looking at the machine when he heard the other noise just below the racket of the chirping machines. A voice. One he didn't recognize. Not at first. A woman's voice.

"Die... son."

It sounded raspy and slurred like someone stirring from a long sleep. Or was it the hoarse, ragged voice of someone trying to talk with a tube crammed down their throat?

"Die... son."

Hunter's heart was slamming wildly inside his chest. He looked down at Brenda's face and saw her lips. They were chapped and raw and they were moving.

When she spoke again he realized it was a question she was asking.

"Die son?"

"Dr. Hunter!"

Hunter swung around so fast that *Curious George* fell from his hands and made a slapping sound as it smacked against the linoleum floor.

Bowes scanned the book at his feet. "I didn't leave you here to peruse Mrs. Barrett's library."

Hunter looked at Brenda's limp body, tubes running in and out. Her heart rate steady now. His hand went up, he was pointing at her, almost in accusation.

"She said something."

"What are you talking about?"

"She spoke."

Dr. Bowes nudged Hunter aside, lifted one of Brenda's eyelids and flashed a light in her face. "Dr. Hunter, this better not be some kind of joke."

"I'm telling you!"

"Her pupils are dilated and unresponsive." Bowes removed a safety pin from the pocket of his lab coat, opened it and slid the tip of it underneath the nail on Brenda's right index finger.

"Don't!" Hunter shouted.

Bowes inserted the pin and a thin trickle of blood spilled out. But Brenda didn't move.

"I'm not a big fan of pranks, Dr. Hunter. I should tell you that right now, so we don't have any more misunderstandings. Jokes and goofing off have their place, I won't deny that. I assure you I'm as good a sport as any. But I just had to sew a man's tongue back on for the third time this year. I hope you understand."

Hunter reached down and scooped up *Curious George*, his eyes never leaving Brenda. "Perfectly," he said and he replaced the book on the shelf where he'd found it. Maybe Brenda's deep coma and steady vitals meant she wasn't even capable of the most primitive grunts and groans. But imagined or not, Hunter knew for sure he had distinctly heard her say two words: *die* and *son*.

Hunter spun around. "I'm curious about something, Dr. Bowes, if you'll indulge a newbie. Why was Brenda admitted to Sunnybrook?"

Bowes stopped thumbing the push button on his pen. "The patients housed on the eighth floor have a rather disturbing past, Dr. Hunter. That should come as no surprise to you."

"Was she an abuser?"

"She had a son, but let's just say she wasn't up for the mother of the year award. Can we leave it at that?"

"She murdered him?" Hunter's guessing game was starting to annoy Bowes even more.

"The woman's in a coma, I don't see how any of this is relevant."

Hunter nodded. His line of questioning was making Bowes uncomfortable. The old man might not have come right out and said it, but the way his jaw muscles had tensed was all he needed.

And it was then that it hit him.

DIE SON.

But the tone of her garbled voice when she had said it made him all the more certain she was asking a question.

DIE SON?

Was it her dead son she was asking for? The rational part of his mind cried out in protest. No, no, no. Of course it wasn't. He had found *Curious George* and there, scribbled in the margin, were the disjointed thoughts of an insane woman. His mind had fabricated the rest. You were freaked out, Hunter, admit it. They got you. Dr.

Bowes, Cindi. They got you all wound up and then let you go spinning in circles.

Or maybe he was projecting. He had done an entire project on it for a psych elective he had taken in college. Hunter scanned her bookcase for a second time, his eyes running over the spines of the children's books, wondering how many others might contain cryptic passages. The woman's entire psychological profile might be laid out before him. These books could be the very window into Brenda's mental illness he needed. A portal through which he could observe and record the strange and curious shapes he found lurking in those dark places no one wanted to look. Dr. Bowes mustn't know about this. Hunter was sure a lazy bastard like Bowes would love nothing more than to steal his hard work and take all the glory for himself.

Yes, he thought, turning the idea over in his mind without finding a single crack. The prospect of working here at Sunnybrook might not be so bad after all. In fact, he felt like he may enjoy it a great deal.

Chapter 6

He wasn't sure exactly why he still wore his wedding ring. God knows Tyson had passed up more than half a dozen opportunities to hock the thing. The band itself was fairly simple, nothing flashy or pretentious. Probably not worth a whole hell of a lot, either. Three hundred tops. Nowhere near the million they had lost now Castleman had gotten cold feet. No, the ring meant nothing to him, which was maybe why he was so surprised at how upset he became when he thought he had lost it. He had placed the ring by the kitchen sink so he could wash his hands after pan frying a piece of Chilean Sea Bass. Grasping for a paper towel, he had sent the ring tumbling into the sink and dangerously close to the garbage disposal. With lightning speed, he had snatched it up, but not before cursing himself for his stupidity. He'd held the ring for a long time after that, thinking about his son, Kavi. Thinking about Ruma.

But she wasn't his anymore, was she? Lately he had been quick to remind himself of this new reality, but this time, the sting was particularly harsh.

During the darkest times, when his life had started spinning completely out of control, there was no doubt that his family had been the first casualty. That old saying was playing loudly in his head: You hurt the ones you love the most. It certainly wasn't an active transgression he was guilty of.

Of course, he had been cross and short tempered with both of them from time to time, maybe a touch more, but it wasn't exactly him that was doing it. It was the Tyson that hadn't had a proper night's sleep in six months. Surely they knew that? In a strange sort of way, sitting in Skip's cottage, in the middle of nowhere, sleeping again for the first time, his life was taking on a new clarity.

Tyson fished his cell phone out of his pocket and dialed.

The phone kept ringing. "Come on, Ruma, pick up."

The line clicked and a woman's voice answered. "Hello?"

For a moment Tyson wasn't sure he had done the right thing in calling.

"Tyson, is that you?" The voice sounded annoyed.

"Hi, Honey."

"Please don't call me that." A tinge of her Bengali accent came through, as it always did when she was pissed off at him.

"Technically we're still married," Tyson said.

"I'm assuming you called to talk to Kavi? He's been asking about you again."

"I was kinda hoping that we could talk first."

She laughed and the sound felt like hot knives sliding into his flesh.

"We haven't had a proper conversation in almost ten years. Why start now?"

"It's not too late to repair this. These last few months have been a doozy, I know, but we have too much history together to throw everything away so easily. I'm at the point now where I don't care anymore about what happened between you and your gynecologist, Dr. Peekaboo or whatever his name is. "

"First of all, you need to get your facts straight. His name is Packer, he's a GP, not a gynecologist and nothing happened between us. You really need to stop trying to hand the responsibility for this off onto me all the time. And for your information, our problems started long before this little sleeping crisis of yours transformed you into something out of a George Romero movie."

Tyson drew in a deep breath. "I'm sorry, Ruma. You're right. I was way out of line. It's just that Skip got me in touch with this doctor who's given me this new drug. Without a word of a lie, I haven't slept so soundly in all my life. I'm telling you, I've been reborn."

"More drugs?"

"No, this one's FDA approved, well, nearly."

"I'm not sure I believe you anymore."

Tyson felt his temper rising. He was laying his nuts out on a chopping block and she was winding up for a two-handed swing. "Come on, Ruma."

"You've spent your entire life failing, so why stop now?"

"Bullshit," he screamed, wondering whether Kavi was sitting nearby, listening to his dad shouting. "This website Skip and I are working on, Onesizefitsall.com. It's gonna be huge. That's not my opinion, that's a fact."

"Another pipe dream, Tyson. When are you gonna wake up and join the rest of us in the real world? For years I've supported you in every way I could, while you ran around from one dream to another. First that pyramid scheme that nearly wiped us out. Then that rental property. Why make money busting your hump when other people can make it for you? That's what you said. And Kavi's medical bills. Every time you find a new disease on the Internet you whisk him off to Doctor Cohen's office." He could hear her accent becoming thicker. "Those visits cost money. Lots of money. Money we don't have. You used to wake up in the middle of the night screaming and for a long time I held you and then you grew distant and abusive and I stopped holding you. You take the people you love for granted and you do that for long enough, you can kill the love, I don't care how strong the love is, you can kill it."

He didn't say anything.

She wasn't done.

"If I was a wiser person I'd have recognized it before, but it's only in this last home stretch that I've seen the truth. In all those pipe dreams of yours, you weren't chasing something. Something has been chasing you and you've been running ever since. For the life of me I don't know what it is. God knows in all the years we've been together you've never spoken to me about your childhood and what it must have been like to grow up with foster parents. But whatever happened in your life to make you this way, it started long before you and I and that's something you can't outrun, Tyson, no matter how far or how fast you go. I'll bet all those times you woke up screaming, that's exactly what you're doing. Running."

"I don't run in my dreams." Tyson's voice was flat.

The suddenness of his answer stunned Ruma into silence for a moment.

"I mean, I don't remember much of my dreams. Only snippets. But I know I'm not running. There's something horrible in my head. It's trapped in there and it's angry and it's pounding to get out. It's an ugly thing and it wants to destroy everything I love, including you and Kavi." More silence and Tyson wondered if he was scaring her. "I know this is the kinda thing a guy says before he buys a meat cleaver and chops his family into tiny bits, but I'm not crazy. And I don't have a violent bone in my body. You know that."

He could hear her breathing on the other end of the line—or was she crying? "So what is this drug you're taking? Nothing illegal, I hope."

"No, no. There's a trial Skip told me about in lower Manhattan. It's run by a snobby little man named Stevens, but it seems to be working. And that's my point, things may finally be turning around for me."

"So you joined a clinical trial. Why didn't you come to me? You don't spend ten years in the marketing department for a major Pharma company without knowing a thing or two about drugs."

"I wanted to, but I wanted to show you I could do this on my own. Besides, you probably would have signed me up for electro shock therapy instead."

"Don't think the thought hasn't crossed my mind." She laughed and this time there was none of the biting edge from before. This was the Ruma he had fallen in love with. "I'm glad to hear you're sleeping again."

"Maybe someday soon I'll be sleeping next to you, instead of here at Skip's summer house."

She didn't dignify the comment with a reply and Tyson wasn't sure whether that was a good or a bad thing.

"Someone wants to talk to you," she said.

The sound of rustling, as though the phone were being dragged across the floor and then silence.

"Hello?" Tyson said, wondering if Kavi had hung up by mistake. It wouldn't be the first time. After all, he was only five years old.

"Buzz, you there? Talk to Daddy for a minute."

Then Ruma again. "He's been asking to call you all night and now he's clamming up. I'm putting you on speakerphone."

"Kavi, your daddy loves you so much, you know that?"

On the other end, Tyson could hear Ruma giggling. "He's nodding. Daddy can't see you, honey. We're not on the computer."

"All right, well, give him a kiss for me."

"Will do."

The line went dead and Tyson set the cell phone on the counter. He could feel his stomach grumbling so he busied himself with finishing dinner. Before long he was seated before a thirteen-inch TV, wolfing down the sea bass, grilled potatoes and some wild rice. He chased that down with a glass of red wine and flipped between the only three channels that weren't completely fuzzy. One of those channels, he thanked God, was WNBC 4 from New York, where he could get his Mets scores and news highlights. Maybe tomorrow he would climb up on the roof and see if he couldn't do something about fixing that antenna.

From where he was sitting, Tyson could see the injector sitting on the kitchen counter and beside that, the dark blue vials of Noxil. The sight of them reminded him of the journal he was supposed to be keeping. That was the agreement, right? He got to be the guinea pig and they got their diary outlining all the ghoulish side effects he experienced. He could just imagine Skip coming to close the place up in the fall, wondering why he hadn't heard from his friend in so long. Wasn't hard to visualize the horror on Skip's face when he found Tyson lying on the floor with the injector in his hand, dead and bloated. A diary lying next to his ghastly corpse and on its pages the unspeakable details of how a little vial of blue liquid had slowly killed him.

He let out a dry, humorless laugh and tried to shake off the thought as one might try to shake off a cold sweat. Man dies taking experimental drug. Wouldn't Sino-Meck just love that kind of publicity? But truth be told, he wasn't sure yet what he should put in that diary. He'd slept for a thirty-six-hour stretch without a single nightmare and that had definitely been a good thing.

Tyson went to the kitchen drawer and pulled it open, not completely aware that he was cringing. The Han and Chewy action figures were still there. He plucked them out of the drawer, gripping their tiny plastic bodies until he could feel the sharp edges biting into his palms. No, the pain was proof enough they were real. No doubt about that. Which was good, because it meant he wasn't going crazy. He also knew he wasn't at home in his bed right now dreaming all of this up. So what the hell was going on?

He decided to go over the facts one by one until he could make sense of what had happened. He arrived on the nineteenth, took a second dose and proceeded to sleep and presumably dream peacefully for thirty-six hours, give or take. One of those dreams, he remembered, had been about the very toys he was now clutching tightly in his hands.

Upon awakening, he left briefly to do some shopping and when he returned he found those same toys in a kitchen drawer. So the question was simple: how did they get there?

Tucked away in his storage locker in the basement of his apartment, behind an old water damaged reproduction Renoir and crammed beneath an unused Ab Roller, was a fairly nondescript little Star Wars lunchbox. The metal kind kids used to go crazy over. Resting inside were the sole surviving relics from Tyson's early childhood; it was there that he kept Han and Chewy. Granted, it had been years, perhaps even decades, since he'd peeked inside the box, but nevertheless he couldn't help but wonder: what if he were to look inside that box and find them sitting there? What would that mean?

Then another thought popped into his head and Tyson felt foolish for even allowing himself to entertain the idea. A foolish idea. An idea so preposterous he knew that when he looked back on all of this, it would give him the greatest laugh he'd had in a long time.

Could Han and Chewy have followed him back from his dream? The same way that stray dog had followed Tyson home late one night as he cut through an alley by Broadway and Thirty-Seventh?

But how had they teleported from that old lunchbox he kept in the storage locker of his condo to Skip's cottage?

Tyson glanced down at Chewy and had the unsettling impression those beady little eyes were looking back at him. He shoved the toys deep inside his pocket and headed for the little vial of blue heaven that was supposed to follow every meal.

Without a doubt, a strange thing had happened, but he was certain there was a perfectly rational, scientific reason for it. Until he found that reason and got a better handle on what was happening, he would hold off on the drug trial diary. He certainly didn't want that asshole Stevens cutting him off over concerns for his mental health.

Not long after, Tyson was sliding under the covers in a pantomime he had enacted on many previous nights. Only now he was beginning to feel more confident that it would end with him sound asleep instead of awake and screaming within a matter of minutes. Han and Chewy stood poised on the night table beside him. Tyson would keep them well within sight and when he got home, he would check the dusty old lunchbox, stuffed somewhere deep inside his storage locker and would probably find them missing. Someone was messing with his head. He was sure of it.

Tyson switched off the light and couldn't help but think about Ruma as he dozed. There had been so much he had wanted to tell her. Castleman jumping ship and the massive pile of shit he and Skip were knee deep in.

God knew if ever there was a time he needed a shoulder to lean on, it was now. But Tyson also knew news like that would only add fuel to Ruma's already volatile conviction that he was a go-nowhere dreamer in desperate need of a reality check. Without that million dollars, Onesizefitsall.com would be stillborn. And that was exactly how Tyson Barrett came to fall asleep thinking about money.

Chapter 7

At four thirty in the morning, Tyson's bladder started tingling. By five thirty, that tingle had become a stabbing pain that couldn't be ignored any longer. He stumbled out of bed and was hobbling through the living room toward the bathroom when his foot connected with something hard. Tyson yelped and hit the ground with all the grace of a drunken Ice Capade. For a few agonizing moments, he lay on his back, inventing new swear words. bluish predawn light floated in from outside through the large windows that overlooked the lake.

He'd had too much wine last night. Not nearly enough to make him drunk, or even tipsy, but enough to stretch his bladder to the size of a cantaloupe. Tyson finished in the washroom and came back to see what had assaulted his foot. He switched on the light and rubbed his eyes, growing more and more convinced he was still asleep. The object before him hadn't been there when he'd gone to bed. The old steamer trunk was pushed against the side of the couch, as if someone had thrust it there in a great hurry. It was the same kind of trunk he'd seen so often in old black and white movies. On either side were thick leather handles and he grabbed one and tried to lift it, but the trunk refused to budge.

"You've got to be shitting me. This thing must weigh over two hundred pounds. The hell is in there?"

A dead body

He was about to take a step back when he noticed the trunk had a three digit combination lock. Tyson bent down and started flipping the small rotary dial until they each read 999. He wasn't sure just how he knew the right combination, but tiny snippets from his dream were coming back to him. He pulled at the heavy latch and when it gave way, he lifted the lid. Tyson's eyebrows shot up and his eyes grew to three times their normal size. He was suddenly glad he'd gone to the washroom, because otherwise he probably would have pissed all over himself. Inside the chest, stacked in what looked like piles of fives, tens and twenties, was more money than Tyson had ever seen in his life.

Chapter 8

It was approaching noon when he finished counting and stacking the money. The sun was high overhead, pushing the temperature inside the small cottage up into the high seventies. The smell of spring in the country was strong; wood shavings, birch trees and the vague odor of cow shit. Outside, motorboats roared across the lake at high speed. Something about that pine smell made Tyson's stomach tie into knots and he got up—bolts of fire shooting through his numb legs—and went to slam the kitchen window shut. He needed to eat, not so much because he was hungry or because he felt his stomach grumbling, but more out of habit and conditioning. It was noon, after all.

As to what he would have, that really wasn't an issue. Right about now, he could eat roasted goat ass and swear it tasted like filet mignon. The bagels and cream cheese he bought yesterday were at the bottom of the fridge and he figured they would do the job just fine. As he cut a bagel and plopped it into the toaster, his fingertips screamed back at him. They were red and tender from the morning he had spent leafing through a mountain of bills that now rose past his belly button.

By the final count, and Tyson hoped he wouldn't have to count it again, it had come to nine hundred sixty-six thousand six hundred eighty-one dollars. All in three old, weathered-looking denominations: twenties, tens and fives, though he had found a single one dollar bill floating around at the bottom of the trunk. A crumpled bill from 1974. Funny enough, that was the year he was born.

He sat at the kitchen table, eating bagels and watching the pyramid of money as though it might sprout a pair of legs and take off running.

Tyson reached into the side pocket of the khaki pants and pulled out the jet injector. It was already loaded with his morning dose. He rested the nozzle against the flesh on his shoulder and fired, loving the sound of the compressed air as it blasted the Noxil through his skin and into his bloodstream.

Looking at the cash again, one thing became certain. This trunk full of money—the very amount he and Skip were short, a striking coincidence which was by no means lost on Tyson—hadn't been there when he'd gone to bed. He stormed off to his bedroom and snatched Han and Chewy off the night table. He set them both down on the table, the money looming behind them in the background.

"What the hell is going on here?" he asked the figures out loud. "Am I going nuts or are things appearing out of thin air?"

Could he still be dreaming? Tyson slapped himself across the face and felt the stinging pain in his cheek.

Don't remember ever feeling that in a dream.

Was it possible the money belonged to Skip? After all, this was Skip's cottage. But of course that begged two questions. A) Why on earth would someone who had a million dollars leave it in a trunk at their summer home? and B) Why would they have needed Castleman if they had their own dough all along?

There only was one way to find out the answer. Tyson picked up the phone and called Skip. His friend answered on the first ring.

"Hey Ty, how you feeling?"

"Amazing!" he said. He swore he could almost feel the Noxil working its way through his system. "Can't remember ever being better."

"Well that's great news. When are you coming back?"

"Skip, there's something I need to ask you and I need you to be as honest with me as you can. Can you do that?"

"I don't like the sound of this, Ty, but go on, ask away."

"Is there anything you haven't told me?"

"Anything I haven't… that's kinda vague, Ty, can you be more specific? What's this all about?"

"I'm sitting here in your summer home, it's a beautiful sunny spring day and I'm looking at an old trunk."

"Okay, an old trunk. I give up. What am I supposed to get from that?"

"It's one of those steamer trunks."

"Great," Skip said and the drawn out way he said it, made it sound like greaaaaat.

"Well, it's not so much the trunk itself, but what I found inside it and I need to know if you're keeping anything from me."

Skip was starting to get annoyed, Tyson could tell by the heavy way he was breathing. "I have no clue what you're talking about. In fact, I don't even own a steamer trunk. Listen, Tyson, these phone calls you keep making. You're starting to really worry me."

"Trust me, Skippy old boy, there's nothing to be worried about, not anymore. Those money problems of ours. Gone. And screw Castleman and his associates. You know why? 'Cause we don't need them. Not anymore. I'm looking at a pile of money here, Skip. A million answers to all our problems."

There was a pause before Skip spoke. "I think I know what this is about and I'm sorry. I'm truly, truly sorry. You won't hear an apology from Skip Williams often, but I think I know what's been eating away at you, Ty, and it's my fault."

"What are you talking about?"

"Last night I accused you of sabotaging things with Castleman. I implied you'd said something to him. Listen to me. I was frustrated. You haven't been yourself lately with the insomnia and all that and I hit you below the be—"

"No, Skip, you don't understand... well, maybe I did say something to Castleman, I don't remember exactly, but that's not the point. I'm sitting here looking at a mountain of money. I'm sitting here with my legs up on a table that's filled with nearly a million dollars."

"Ty, old buddy, you know me well enough by now. You got my apology, please don't rub my face in it."

Tyson felt his blood pressure begin to rise. There was nothing that got to him faster than being called a liar. If a lifeguard yells shark, no one asks questions, they get the hell out of the water. But Tyson still had enough sense to know when to stop pushing. Skip was beginning to think he was losing his marbles. And could he blame him? Their last two conversations had gone from bad to worse in less than thirty seconds. No, Skip wouldn't believe him until he drove up to his house and dumped this trunk filled with cash over his head.

"All right, Skip, I accept your apology."

Their conversation went on for a while after that, but Tyson wasn't really there. He was thinking about the money. At last he hung up the phone, he grabbed a stack of twenties and flung it on the table, his heart skipping wildly in his chest as the money thudded heavily and slid across the oak finish with a faint whisper. There was something incredibly satisfying about that sound. It sounded like... freedom.

As frustrating as it was, Tyson's conversation with Skip had certainly been definitive. He reached into his pocket and came out with the small plastic case which held the vials. He wasn't sure how this stuff was doing it, but somehow when he drifted off to sleep, a hidden door in his mind creaked open.

A secret passage.

He thought of slapping himself awake again. Surely he was stuck in a dream. Things like this didn't happen in real life, not to guys like him at least. It's time to stop clinging to your cactus, he reminded himself. Good things come to those who are open to receiving them. Isn't that the kind of thing people pay those self-help gurus to tell them? That anyone can conquer the world with nothing more than positive thinking? This was the happiest he'd been in a long time and he was doing his best to dispel his many nagging concerns about how any of this was possible. But his anxiety wasn't so easy to dismiss. What if he was right about the drug opening some kind of hidden door inside his mind? A doorway between his dreams and reality. And what would happen if he stopped taking the drug? Would that door suddenly swing shut? What if it couldn't be closed anymore? Maybe at this stage, the Noxil was only keeping the bad dreams away?

Then a final terrifying thought crept into his mind and Tyson tried in vain to bat it away. If that door wouldn't close, and his nightmares started to return in earnest, it would no longer be piles of money coming through. It'd be other things. Ugly, unimaginable things.

Tyson shoved a frantic hand into his pocket and pulled out the black case with the Noxil. There were still nine vials left. Enough for three more days and then he'd have to head back to Dr. Stevens for more.

Back to your dealer, a tiny voice whispered.

"Shut up," he shouted at the empty room.

Then another voice chimed in. One he liked much better.

You have a million dollars sitting in front of you. Stop being such a doubting Thomas and go with it for once in your goddamn life.

If there was anything Tyson had learned from his ex-wife, it was this: There was no better therapy than retail therapy. And that was exactly what he intended to prove.

Chapter 9

Dr. Hunter closed the door to his new office and turned the lock until he heard the bolt slide into place. Normally there wasn't any reason to hide himself away in the cramped confines of his office. The stack of books cradled in the crook of his arm, however, said otherwise. They were children's books and he had taken them from Brenda's room. An odd rush of exhilaration had struck him as he snatched them. A guilty sort of pleasure—the same one he had felt at fourteen, sneaking copies of Penthouse magazine into the bathroom. Of course, this time it wasn't about satisfying any perverted fantasies. His interest was purely professional and he reminded himself of that as he laid the books on his desk and sat down. *Who knows*, he thought with a tinge of hope, *locked inside might be the raw data for the kind of research paper that could really skyrocket a man's career.* Hunter spread the books out and surveyed the titles before him. *The Little Engine That Could, Clifford the Big Red Dog, Are You My Mother? 100 of the Greatest Fairytales.*

He let his hand pass over the worn covers until his fingers came to rest on *Are You My Mother?* He opened the book somewhere in the middle and saw a gawky-looking bird talking to a cow. "Are you my mother?" the bird asked hopefully. "No," the cow said with indifference.

But it was what Hunter saw next that really got him excited. Lining the margins of the children's book was Brenda's malformed juvenile penmanship. There were no dates or headings. The words just started and Hunter read them as they came.

He'll never leave me. My little spider friend. I was afraid that I would open my eyes this morning and find him gone. He spent most of yesterday building his web. Shameful, all that work to catch one nasty little shit fly. Swiped my hand through his web to see what he would do. He scurried behind the bookshelf to safety. Ten minutes later he was out and right back at it like nothing had happened. The lamp is less than six inches away. I can already see his plan and it's brilliant. In the evening when the light is on, the insects will be drawn straight into his trap.

I'll name him Alexander. It's such a beautiful name, isn't it? I've been telling Dr. Bowes that I'd like to have another child. He gets funny when I say that. Told me I was too old to have kids anymore and then asked me if I remembered why I was here at Sunnybrook. I told him yes. I was here because I loved my children and tried to protect them. He still doesn't seem to get the point, no matter how many times I tell him. Death lurks around every corner. The devil doesn't have horns. No, no, no, he's much smaller. As small as a microbe. Most people don't know that, but if you're careful, the way I'm careful, you can protect them. Safety doesn't come cheap, no siree Bob. There are rules and procedures to follow and when those rules are broken, everyone's at risk. So of course you stupid Doctor Bowes I know what happened to my sons. Tyson loved his mother the most, but even that wasn't enough.

I want him back.

There was a knock on the door and Dr. Hunter looked up with a start. He could see a pair of feet under the crack, shuffling impatiently. Hunter's heart was pounding as he shoved the books under his desk. He unlocked his office door, pulled it open and saw the frown on Dr. Bowes' face.

"Why is your office door locked?"

Hunter suddenly felt the flesh under his arms moisten with perspiration. There really was no good reason to lock the door, was there? "I'm sorry, Dr. Bowes, it won't happen again."

Hunter could see Bowes' nose twitch and wondered if he was searching for the distinct scent of alcohol on his breath.

He remembered Brenda's diary and how she described the way Bowes had gone stiff when she told him about wanting another child. She got to him, in a way Hunter didn't quite understand. Unnerved him. Even now, lying in her room, defenseless and vulnerable, he was still scared. Hunter wanted that kind of power over the old man.

"Listen," Bowes was saying, "you've been working long hours lately and I appreciate that, but our meeting today with the government review board—you should have been there. No excuses."

Hunter's expression didn't change.

"Next time you take a cat nap, do it on your own time."

Bowes turned to leave.

"Oh, Doctor, before I forget. I was looking through our patient records and I couldn't find a file for Brenda Barrett."

Bowes stopped. "Records for patients on the eighth floor aren't kept there."

"Where can I find them then?"

"They're locked away in a safe place," Bowes said, clicking his heels impatiently. "Listen, Elias. I'm not sure I made this clear enough when you first started, but contrary to what you may have learned at Albany Medical College, we're not running a counseling service here at Sunnybrook. These people, especially the exceptional group up on eight, are not going to get better. They're never going to live normal lives like you and I. Own houses, white fences, golden labs, two point five children. I'd even go so far as to say they're probably the neediest people in the world, and you know what the biggest irony is? Most of their families want nothing to do with them. Like it or not, our job is to medicate and subjugate, not to reform. If you've come to cure people, Dr. Hunter, you've come to the wrong place."

Dr. Bowes was trying to make him feel like a naïve child. And in some ways it was working, but Hunter also knew that trying to shoo him away with ridicule was one battle the old man would lose.

"I have one more question," Hunter said, following Bowes as he walked away. "What happened to Brenda's kids?"

This time Bowes didn't even turn around. "Leave it alone, Dr. Hunter, and if I were you I'd start focusing on my real responsibilities."

Hunter watched Bowes march down the long corridor until he faded into the shadows. The good doctor didn't like being questioned, that much was clear. He had a cozy operation here and he didn't want anything to threaten the delicate little balance he had established. Only problem was that Bowes didn't know who he was dealing with. Bureaucratic stonewalling wasn't going to deter Elias Hunter.

Still, Hunter couldn't escape the raw and undeniable truth that he had let things slip a little lately. He was still new here and he would have to show some level of caution. Of course, he wouldn't stop reading up on Brenda Barrett. That much he'd decided the moment he'd found her words written on the inside of that children's book. This latest glitch only meant he would have to shift that side of his life to after hours.

By nine o'clock that evening, Hunter had decided to

stop off briefly at a local greasy spoon for a bite to eat. With some time and space between him and his altercation with Bowes that afternoon, he could understand the old man's position a little more. Delving into the life of a patient with a violent past was akin to voyeurism. And wasn't Bowes also right when he said that patients would never go on to lead normal lives? In a sense, they fell through the cracks of society. He'd heard the expression more than once before and hearing it again, in his own mind, made him realize how untrue it was. People like Brenda didn't just fall through the cracks of society. They were the cracks. But, by all means, she was a crack that needed to be studied and understood. Not for her sake. Clearly Brenda was too far gone to be helped, but what about the countless others in the early stages? Surely there was some way to help them.

Either way, he knew that Sunnybrook was the key.

Hidden somewhere within its walls lay a treasure trove of information on this woman. Bowes had said himself that the files on Brenda and the others on the eighth floor were kept separate from the other patients' histories. He also knew that pushing Bowes any more would be foolish, even career ending. The man clearly wasn't Brenda's biggest fan. At times he'd even seemed downright scared of her. Hunter took a bite of his burger, grease oozing between his fingers. He was running through the last conversation he'd had with Bowes outside his office in his mind.

How had the old man put it?

The files were locked away someplace safe.

Was he talking about some secret vault buried deep in the bowels of the asylum? Hunter doubted it. That was far too out of sight for a man like Bowes. He wanted those files all for himself, didn't he?

They're in his office.

The thought hit him with such vicious, blinding force

59

that he wondered if it belonged to him at all.

He was on his feet almost at once, slapping a ten dollar bill on the counter and heading for the door.

● ● ●

"Back already, Dr. Hunter?" Terrance, the night security guard, asked him. He had a mouthful of the whitest teeth Hunter had ever seen and a set of the sharpest eyes to match. "You ain't one of those workaholics, I hope."

Hunter smiled and felt the muscles in his face stiffen. "Not yet, but don't think Dr. Bowes isn't trying his hardest to turn me. I forgot something, is all. Mind if I go up?"

"I'm just teasing you, doc," Terrance said jovially and Hunter swiped his card and passed through the heavy security doors. Terrance watched him closely and Hunter was sure he saw a touch of doubt cross the night guard's face. Hunter pressed the elevator button and waited. Terrance was still looking his way. The guard stood up just as the elevator doors opened.

Hunter rushed inside, mashed the number seven and didn't let his breath out until the doors closed. He got out and made a left. Bowes' office was just down the hall. He stood before the door and jiggled the handle. Unlocked. Of course it was. All the offices were supposed to be left open until the cleaning staff had finished their rounds. Hunter swung open the door to Bowes' office and hesitated. It was one thing to pepper your boss with questions he clearly wasn't fond of answering and another thing entirely to root through his things. This next step was a big one. Getting caught didn't just mean losing his job, it meant going to jail.

Hunter took a deep breath and leaned forward until

he felt the ball of his shoe connect with the floor inside Bowes' office. He pulled the door closed behind him and turned the bolt until he heard it click.

Bowes' office was dimly lit and smelled of English Leather. It also looked like someone had redecorated it with a bulldozer. Books were stacked so high on his desk that it resembled a scale model of Manhattan. Hunter started with the filing cabinets. They too were overflowing with loose papers—what a stark contrast, he noted, to the bookshelf he had seen in Brenda's room.

He searched through them for fifteen minutes without finding much more than a list of highly-functioning patients who had never set foot on the eighth floor. Against the far wall was a metal cabinet. Inside were a series of pamphlets on every disorder from autism to Zivert's Syndrome. When he tried to nudge them gently to one side, the pile of pamphlets spilled onto the floor.

"Shit cakes," Hunter swore. For a moment, part of him wondered whether Bowes would really notice a few extra things strewn about. He decided he probably would and bent down to pick them up. He had already scooped up the vast majority of them when he spotted something odd on the bottom shelf of the cabinet. It looked like a leather bound scrapbook and Hunter was struck by how out of place it seemed. He removed and laid it in his lap and peeled back the cover. Inside were old newspaper articles. Papers from all over New York State. Watertown Daily Times; Times Herald; Newsday. The scrapbook was filled with articles about old court cases where the defendants had used an insanity plea. Most of them were household names too, John Hinkley, Ezra Pound. Hunter's personal favorite, the Civil War hero, Daniel Sickles.

Hunter flipped through the pages and felt his breath catch in his throat.

School Board Fires Young Nurse
After Allegations of Abuse
By Joseph Banks

Collingwood Elementary school nurse Brenda Barrett was fired today by the Columbia County School Board after pressure from parents who said her use of discipline was often extreme and at times inappropriate. According to allegations, students were often made to wash their hands and faces repeatedly. When one student failed to comply, Mrs. Barrett is said to have held his hand against the radiator. The board wouldn't comment on whether any legal action would be taken, but assured parents everything was being done to protect the children's welfare.

Hunter turned the page and gasped.

Five Children Dead in Mysterious Fire at
Collingwood Elementary.
By Joseph Banks

The sound of the door handle being turned nearly made Hunter jump with fright. Someone was outside and trying to get in. He scrambled to his feet and stashed the scrapbook back where he'd found it. Outside he could hear a man speaking into a walkie talkie.

"Terrance. It's Al. I'm here on seven and Dr. Bowes' office is locked."

Hunter padded up to the door. Al Quinlan was the overnight janitor.

"Gotcha." He heard Terrance say. "Be right there."

Hunter's pulse was racing. He scanned the room frantically, feeling like a rat caught in a trap. There was a phone on Dr. Bowes' desk. He went over to it and picked up the handle and dialed the security desk.

The phone rang three times before it picked up.

"Terrance?"

Terrance sounded out of breath, as though he'd run back from the elevators.

"Yes?"

"Listen, it's Dr. Hunter on the sixth floor. I have a terrible leak in my office, can you send Al over ASAP? I've got water everywhere."

"Will do."

Hunter laid the phone down quietly and went back to the door. Al's radio began to chirp. "Al, head to six first. The new guy says he's got a leak in his office."

Al sighed. The kinda sigh which spoke volumes about the way he felt about new guys.

"On my way."

Hunter could hear Al mumbling to himself as he lumbered down the hallway.

"If I had a nickel for every time one of these hot shot doctors needed old Aly to bail their asses out," he was saying, "I'd have a house in the Hamptons, I would."

Hunter nudged open the door and peered out. Al was heading for the elevators with his cleaning cart. In the other direction were the stairs. Hunter exited Bowes' office, closed the door behind him and raced in that direction. He took the stairs three and sometimes four at a time, certain he would make a critical miss and snap his ankle. He didn't and he burst through the door and onto six, dashing madly for his office. Down the hall he could hear the elevator ping and the doors pull open. Al was coming out still bitching to himself. Hunter found his office and threw himself inside just a second before Al came within visual range.

That was when he realized the full extent of his problem—the leak he'd called in about. His floor was bone dry. He could hear Al's uneven steps drawing closer. Hunter scanned his office. Beside his desk was a

63

water cooler. He lifted the heavy jug off its mount and tilted it at an angle. Water gurgled out and splashed against the floor. Hunter struggled to replace it. Sure enough, he had his leak, but when he looked down, Hunter realized the front of his pants were all wet.

The knock came just as Hunter was sliding into the chair behind his desk.

"Come in."

Some of the water had run into the hallway.

"Sweet Mary," Al said, his black shoes making slapping noises as he entered. "This is one hell of a leak you have here, Dr. Hunter." Mop in hand, he was scanning the ceiling, looking for the source.

"I'm not sure how this happened," Hunter said. He was still out of breath from his hundred meter dash and was fighting the almost overpowering urge to swallow huge gulps of air. "Just came in and found a lake in my office."

"Uh huh," Al said. He had stopped looking at the ceiling. His gaze had fallen to the half empty water cooler beside Hunter's desk, the liquid inside was swaying lazily back and forth. A water cooler, Hunter knew, that Al had filled up just yesterday.

Chapter 10

"And how may I help you sir?"

"I need a suit," Tyson said. He was holding a briefcase containing forty thousand dollars in cash.

The salesman had been eyeing Tyson suspiciously but when he saw the briefcase his expression changed all at once. He rubbed his hands together and let out a tiny giggle, as though Tyson had told him some dirty little joke. The money in the briefcase. The little bastard could smell it.

A pink scarf was wrapped around his thin little neck and each step he took was delicate and precise.

"Let me welcome you to Ralph Lauren's flag store."

Looking around, Tyson was beginning to wonder if he was really in New York City at all, or instead at some quaint chateaux in France. The place was a sea of dark mahogany. A hand carved wooden staircase spiraled up to the second floor, flanked on either side by paintings of people who had been dead for a better part of one hundred years.

Overhead was a Baccarat chandelier and under his feet an antique Persian rug. The warm smell of wealth was making him light-headed.

"Quite a place you have here."

"Indeed it is. Its turn of the century designers were inspired by the royal residences of the Loire. But when Mrs Waldo's husband died she abandoned construction and the place fell to pieces. Too many bad memories I suppose."

Tyson smiled wryly. "Been there."

"Haven't we all. Now, did you have anything particular in mind?"

Tyson thought at once back to Castleman and his assumption that he and Skip were somehow unprofessional.

"I wanna walk into a room and hear people gasp."

"Ah yes, then you're looking for our purple label collection. Come right this way, sir."

"I didn't catch your name."

"Henrique. My name is Henrique." Sounded French.

"Nice to meet you, Henrique." But when Tyson said the name it came out sounding more like Hen-rick instead of Hen-reek.

Tyson tightened his grip on the money. The trunk with the rest of it was sitting by the coffee table in his apartment on 153rd Street. He was supposed to meet Skip for lunch later and he couldn't wait to see the look on his friend's face when he took him to see that trunk.

● ● ●

Tyson tried on four fantastic-looking suits before he settled on the charcoal gray. Henrique, or whatever his real name was, assured him he'd made the right choice, but Tyson knew the little man was ready to tell him he looked like Brad Pitt if it meant making the sale.

When the price tag rang in at over ten thousand dollars, Tyson didn't even bat an eye. He unlocked his briefcase, removed two five thousand dollar bundles and set them neatly on the counter. The light in Henrique's eyes seemed to dim a little when he saw the stack was made up of twenties. Counting it was going to be a pain, Tyson knew, but money was money after all. He took a deep breath when he realized the ease with which he'd just dropped a significant percentage of his former annual income. Things were beginning to move for Tyson Barrett. After a lifetime of falling short by inches, he could finally say that the bad times were behind him. And that was exactly where they would stay.

An hour later, Skip came strolling into Le Bernardin dressed in jeans and a ball cap, looking like he'd just come back from a Mets game.

He pulled his chair out, but didn't sit.

"That's a three thousand dollar suit you're wearing," Skip said before even saying hello.

"Actually it was more like ten."

Skip took a seat and pulled his chair in. He gave the room a quick appraisal and noticed they were sitting in a sea of white-haired old men. "Really, Tyson, Le Bernardin? Have you lost your mind? This is one of the most expensive restaurants in the city." Skip removed his cap and slid it self-consciously into his back pocket.

"Isn't it normal to choose a nice restaurant when you have something to celebrate?"

"What are we celebrating? The fact that Castleman just pulled the rug out from under us?"

"We don't need Castleman, not anymore."

"What are you saying?"

"What I'm saying, Skip, captain my captain, brother of brothers, is that our money troubles are over. Finished. Finito."

"Please tell me you're not still going on about this trunk business."

"That's exactly what I'm going on about." Under the table, Tyson nudged the briefcase over to Skip with the tip of his new Bertuli.

Skip scooped it up and placed it on his lap. He undid the safety lever and got the lid about a quarter of the way open before he snapped it shut with a loud bang.

"This is filled with money," Skip whispered, glancing around nervously.

"Well, I wouldn't say full. There's a little under thirty thousand in there, give or take."

The worried look on Skip's face began to spread. "Tyson, old buddy. Please tell me you didn't cash out your 401k or hit up a loan shark so you could show me a briefcase full of money."

"I've got a steamer trunk sitting at home beside my shitty imitation Magnavox twenty-inch television and it's filled with the stuff. Almost a million bucks worth."

Skip's face blanched. "You robbed a bank, didn't you? You know what the minimum sentence is for robbery? Like ten years. You didn't use a gun, did you? Then it's armed robbery and you could get... well, a lot more than ten. I love you, Ty, we go way back, but I'm not getting involved with dirty money."

"Skip, relax. Take a deep breath. Order yourself a glass of wine. The Chateau Lafite is excellent." Tyson undid the button to his suit jacket and leaned in. "Now I can't go into how I got the money right now, because I'm still working that part out myself, but I can promise you I didn't steal a red cent of it. It just sort of fell into my lap."

The waiter appeared just then with two plates of grilled venison and the men stopped talking.

"I ordered for you. I hope you don't mind."

Skip looked down at the food before him and nudged it away with the palm of his hand. "Can't say I'm all that hungry right now."

Tyson was. He hadn't eaten a thing since that bagel this morning and he tore into the venison like a castaway.

"When we're done, we'll go to my place and I'll show you the money," Tyson said with his mouth full. "Maybe then you'll change your tune."

"I can't say that I will, Ty. Free money makes me nervous. Probably because there is no such thing as free money."

Tyson looked up briefly between mouthfuls, but the comment didn't register.

When the waiter came again, he removed one plate that looked like it had hardly been touched and another that might never have had food on it.

Tyson reached into the pants pocket of his new ten thousand dollar suit for his injector and the container with the vials, but instead came out with a set of car keys. In the other was his cell phone. A swell of panic began rising within him.

His look of dread wasn't lost on Skip.

Tyson was standing now, patting himself all over. Those little blue bastards had to be somewhere, he thought desperately.

"You look like a man who just realized his wallet's not where it should be."

"The Noxil. I'm supposed to take a shot after every meal and I haven't the foggiest idea where I put those little blue—"

"Maybe you left them back at the cottage?"

Tyson froze. "I might have. I'm telling you, these last couple of days have been something else. Come to think of it, I can't seem to find my inhaler either."

"Okay, no biggie. Just call that drug coordinator guy. What'd you say his name was? Stevens?"

"Yeah."

"Call Stevens in the morning and get some more."

"Morning?" Tyson shouted. "Are you crazy? I can't wait that long. I need them now." He plucked his phone from his pocket as well as the wallet from his hip. Inside was Stevens' card. He dialed the number. Tyson let the phone ring ten times before hanging up.

"Asshole's not answering!"

Tyson was pacing now.

"Easy, Ty. I think you're blowing this way out of proportion."

"I need that dose."

People were beginning to stare.

Skip straightened. "At least that tells me the stuff's working. You've been sleeping, I take it?"

Tyson didn't answer. He was busy wrestling with the lock on his briefcase. It finally opened. He grabbed a thick stack of twenties and slid it across the table. "This should cover lunch. Sorry, Skip, I gotta run."

Tyson took off, briefcase in hand, bounding for the door at nearly a full run, leaving Skip Williams just a little more certain that his longtime friend was losing his mind.

Chapter 11

Tyson's first stop was the Ralph Lauren store on Madison Avenue where he had earlier spent two hours getting pampered like the cowardly lion on his arrival in Oz.

"Oh, Mr. Barrett, I hope everything is all right with the suit. Oh shoot, there's a stain on our shirt."

"Did you find anything in my change room after I left?"

Henrique was still fiddling with the mark on Tyson's Keaton Twill dress shirt. "I'm not at all sure this will come out."

"I don't care about the shirt," Tyson snapped. "I'm looking for a small case with blue-colored vials inside. I may have left them here."

Henrique's expression turned serious. This was old hat for a salesman who mingled in the circles that Henrique did. Aren't rock stars, celebrities and royalty always losing their high class prescription dope?

"Give me a moment, Mr. Barrett," he said in a low calm voice, "and I'll see what I can do. Little blue vials, you said?"

"That's right."

Tyson was sure they were here. He must have dropped them when he was changing and hadn't heard them fall. He noticed he was pacing back and forth like a caged animal.

You're gonna give yourself an asthma attack and then where will you be? Flat on your back in the hospital or maybe even dead!

He looked in one of the full-length mirrors on the wall, admiring his new suit.

Then he caught the brown stain, not more than a few inches below his collar. The one Henrique's prissy little hands had been dabbing at. This was turning into a day full of new personal records. Biggest single windfall. Most expensive suit he'd ever purchased and now two grand flushed down the tubes on a shirt he had owned for less than an hour. And wasn't Henrique just heartbroken that Tyson had to shell out another huge wad of dough on more clothes. *I'll say this though, if he comes back with the Noxil, I'll buy ten shirts. Hell, I've got the bread, why not make it a hundred.*

Henrique did return but the solemn expression on his face made Tyson's stomach roll.

"Nowhere?"

"I've turned the place upside down, I'm afraid. Even spoke to each of the salespeople. I'm sorry, Mr. Barrett. Now about that stain. We have a new collection of—"

Tyson didn't catch the rest of Henrique's pitch, mostly because of the noise the revolving door made as it swung closed behind him. On his way to his car he dialed Stevens again. Twenty infuriating rings later and still no answer, he hung up. "Stevens better be there," he muttered. "For his sake, Stevens better be there."

Tyson got to the old commercial space that housed Sino-Meck's clinical trial to find that Dr. Charles Stevens, the arrogant prick of a head coordinator, wasn't there. Driving there as fast as he could through busy New York traffic, Tyson had prepared himself for that very eventuality. Stevens or not, he felt confident that if he simply gave someone his name, they could get him a fresh new case brimming with vials of Noxil. There had to be a list. If they wanted their 'oh so precious' test results, they had better keep feeding him his dope, right? But this time would be different, wouldn't it? This time he would empty out a two-gallon water jug and make sure they filled it right to the fucking rim with that dark blue hooch. When he arrived, however, what he found was far worse that he could ever have imagined.

Strung along the glass door was a wide yellow sticker. On it in bold black letters was the following:

By order of the Food and Drug Administration and the Greater New York Ethical Review Board all and any biomedical research conducted on these premises have henceforth been suspended.

Tyson felt the strength go out of his legs all at once. His knees buckled and before he knew what hit him, he'd taken a rather awkward seat on a dirty New York sidewalk in a suit that probably cost more than some families earned in a year. Foremost on his mind wasn't the very real fear that he might have just lost his meal ticket to endless riches. That one would hurt, sure, but his primary concern was something else entirely.

Stevens had flaunted Noxil's lack of side effects. Ha! But Tyson knew better. How about real solid things coming back with you from your dreams? Is that side effects enough for you, Dr. Stevens? He almost couldn't wait to fill out his journal.

Why bother? that annoying little voice began to ask. *Certainly not for your precious drug trial. Didn't you hear, that's been shut down for good.*

Somehow, the Noxil had managed to scatter away nightmares once filled with unspeakable horrors desperate to rip him apart on a nightly basis. For once, sleep had become a pleasant experience again and not something to be feared. And when objects began to follow him home from that other reality, wherever the hell that was, he had allowed that too because hey, who couldn't use a million dollars, right? Tyson was starting to feel as though he had signed a deal with a man who appeared to have a pair of rather large horns stuffed under an unbelievably small hat. Deal or not, there was one more place those vials could be. And if they weren't there? If he was bone dry, as the junkies liked to say, then he would at last discover the answer to that terrifying question bouncing around in his head all day long: What happens when the nightmares return?

Chapter 12

The cottage was dark and silent when Tyson arrived. He pulled into the gravel driveway, his headlights washing over the tiny country house. The outside looked different somehow. Sagging and tired. He got out of the car, every inch of his body aching, growing all the more certain he was projecting his own exhaustion onto a house that couldn't be more than a decade old.

The crickets were out in full deafening force. So much so that he could barely hear the water lapping against the side of the boathouse, down by the lake. But lapping water and crickets weren't why he had driven the hour and a half trip from New York City.

The inside of the cottage was exactly as he had left it. He had cleaned up as much as he could before he left, considering he'd been about to blow a chunk of the money he nearly broken his big toe on.

Tyson's first act was to scour the bathroom for any sign of the vials. He must have opened every drawer ten times, praying with each pull that they might magically appear. Of course they didn't, but that didn't stop him from trying. There was something comforting in the ritual. The thought that if he did things a certain way or enough times, everything would turn out okay. A shrink might have called it OCD. To Tyson, it was wishful thinking.

That his tendency to ritualize had anything to do with his biological mother and the disturbing environment in which he had spent the most formative years of his young life was little more than a vague and distant notion to him. His wife - ex-wife, he amended - had consistently accused him of being a hypochondriac. She had done so over the phone as recently as the other night, when he had spoken to her from this very cottage. She had once even gone so far as to suggest that the asthma pump he carried in his pocket was nothing more than a prop. That he was a healthy man playing sick.

"I've seen the way you try and pump Kavi full of meds every chance you get. There are enough real sick people in the world, Tyson, we don't need fakers."

In his shaving kit, Tyson kept a spare Asthma pump and he slid it into his pocket. Just the feeling of having it with him was reassuring enough. Hell, there'd been a few times today when he could probably have used it.

Ruma called it his security blanket, but his symptoms felt as real as they came. Did it really matter that he had seen eight doctors before he found one that would finally agree with his diagnosis?

"I love you, Tyson," she had said to him then, which right then seemed like a lifetime ago. "You can't lock away all the horrible things that were done to you as a child. That will only make them so much worse. I can't imagine what it must have been like, living with that crazy woman. But you need to understand something. She can't hurt you. Not anymore. Not when she's locked up a hundred miles away."

Tyson had paused when Ruma had said that, staring at her with a look bordering on rage. The event was less than a month old, but the rawness of it hadn't quite faded yet. "What do you mean locked up hundreds of miles away?"

The expression on Ruma's face had also changed and Tyson knew she had just revealed something he wasn't supposed to know.

"She's alive? Is that what you're saying?"

Ruma sighed.

"And how long have you known about this?"

"I don't know. Not long. Around the time you started acting strangely."

Tyson had gone to the cabinet, taken out a glass and poured himself more vodka than he could probably drink.

"Numbing yourself isn't going to solve anything."

"No, but it's a hell of a start."

"Darling, I've been so worried about you lately. The nightmares. Shrieking in the middle of the night. I needed to know you weren't going through some …" She paused, searching for the right word and finding none. "I needed to know you hadn't inherited a condition."

"Condition." His tone was flat. "You mean insanity."

"This is not easy for either of us. It feels like I'm the only one trying to keep our family together and I needed to know what I was up against. I tracked your mother down and spoke with one of her doctors at the asylum over the phone."

"Asylum. Great! Is there anything else about my life you're withholding?"

"Tyson, I wasn't trying to betray you. I was preparing myself for a worst case scenario."

"Worst case scenario. You sound like a fucking robot."

He had seen then that Ruma was crying and he had fallen back onto the sofa. He sat there for a while, vodka in hand, watching her wipe away the tears, mindful of her mascara.

When the initial blinding fury passed, he regained his ability to speak. "So what did he say, this doctor?"

"His name is Dr. Bowes and he wouldn't speak with me over the phone other than to say that yes your mother was under his care, but that she had fallen into a coma. I couldn't get any more out of him. But Tyson, all this isn't the point. Yes, she's alive, but she's old and locked away in a place where she will never hurt anyone ever again."

"Where is she?"

"Oh, Tyson, please. Please don't do this."

"I have a right to know," he shouted. "Where is she?"

"Sunnybrook," Ruma said, looking utterly deflated.

"That's upstate."

Tyson came and sat down beside her. He curled an arm around her shoulder and pulled her close to him.

"Deal with your past or it'll deal with you," he said, his mouth resting on the top of her dark hair. "You've always said that."

"It's the truth," she said. He could tell her bottom lip was quivering. "You haven't slept in weeks now and there's a chance it may trace back to what happened to you as a child. Those nightmares. A child's mind is a delicate thing. You suffered damage at the hands of that woman, Tyson. She isn't right in the head. She's disturbed and I can't even fathom what that life was like. I can only imagine it must have been…"

Sick. Little Tyson was suddenly pushing open that big peeling door and he was sure he was going to be sick. The smell from inside the room was so strong his eyes were tearing up. It was like old garbage mixed with the earthy scent of pine needles. The boiled ham Tyson had eaten for breakfast began to lurch up from his stomach and into his mouth. But he caught and held it there before it could spill out. The taste of bile was making his eyes water. He forced himself to swallow it down. There was no way he would make it to the toilet in time and he didn't even want to imagine what Mommy would do if

78

she came home to find throw up on the carpet. When he wiped the water out of his eyes, he could see tiny objects dangling from the ceiling. They were in the shape of Christmas trees. He had seen Mommy hanging those same shapes around the house and she had called them air fresheners.

Tyson peered through the gloom and was astonished to see what looked like the bedroom of a young boy. A boy who might have been five years old, just like he was. Toys were stacked neatly in one corner. A Buck Rogers rocket ship, a carrying case filled with toy cars and a Light Bright set still wrapped tightly in plastic.

Beyond that was a comfy looking bed with more dolls and stuffed animals than Tyson had ever seen. They watched him rather indifferently with their saucer shaped eyes. But from here, looking into this new room filled with shadow, well, it almost looked like one of those dolls wasn't looking back at him in quite the same way. One of those dolls didn't seem to have eyes at all, but two cavernous sockets. Tyson took a steady step closer, his heart beginning to hammer a rising beat in his tiny chest.

And it was then that a single fly, buzzing lazily about his head, crashed right into his eye. He swatted it away and was suddenly aware of a deeper sound. A drone that had perhaps been there from the beginning, but one he hadn't been attuned to. Just then a second fly bounced off his forehead. A third off his nose. Then the room was full of them, all buzzing madly about as if they had somehow smelled him entering the room and now they were coming for him. Tyson's eyes were slowly adjusting to the light and he was beginning to get a better idea of where he was and why that doll buried in with the others didn't seem to have any eyes. He was close enough now where he could see it rather clearly and he knew at once that what he was seeing was no toy at all. He screamed. It must have been a loud scream too, louder than he'd ever screamed before, because he didn't hear the front door open and close. Didn't hear his name being called. Didn't hear a thing until he looked back and saw the long shadowy silhouette running toward him, a grinning face all twisted out of shape.

Mommy was home.

Chapter 13

Sunnybrook Asylum

A diseased shit fly lands on my toast and jam and looks up at me. His eyes glisten like jewels. He's staring at me and rubbing his legs together like he wants to play some sort of nasty little trick. The latrine. That's where he's from. Everyone knows our communal washroom next door is a cesspool. I've told Dr. Bowes a million times to move me somewhere else, but he never does. They want me dead and they've decided to kill me by sending diseased flies into my room. They think they can play God.

But we'll have the last laugh on them and their little shit fly, won't we, Alexander? I snatch that fly right out of the air. Feel it buzzing around inside my hand and I toss him into Alexander's web. Squirming to break free. The panic. That's what brings him. I'm so proud of my Alexander. He comes shuffling out from behind the book case and is on that fat shit fly before it even knows what hit him. He's still wiggling as Alexander wraps him up. Then Alexander turns to me and says, "Thank you, Mommy, for this meal I am about to eat." And I say: "I love you, Alexander."

"I love you too, Mommy, more than life itself."

"I know you do, son. Eat well."

"Elias, have you heard a word I've been saying?"

"Huh? Yeah, sure I have," Hunter lied, stumbling into the present. "You were saying how Denise Crosby on five is sleeping with Dr. Cruz on two."

"I said I think they're sleeping together, I didn't state it as a fact, silly. You've been so flaky lately, everything all right?"

Hunter found himself nodding before his brain had even understood the question. Cindi Jaworski was staring back at him with those big nurse's eyes of hers, looking concerned. She wanted to sleep with him. On some primitive level where animals communicate with one another, Hunter knew that. And at one time, he might even have been interested, but lately, something inside him had shifted a little. Nothing earth shattering, but a subtle movement that had rendered past pleasures stale and suddenly unsatisfying. She was still looking at him with those bug eyes of hers and he realized they were probably what had made him think of Brenda's diary. He had been reading another entry he'd found scrawled inside one of her children's books. It was amazing really that no one had ever looked inside them before. In a way, Hunter felt as though he had stumbled upon a treasure of vast importance, sitting right under everyone's noses, ignored for years.

Cindi was still talking.

"Have you been sleeping at all, because your eyes are really dark... I hope that Dr. Bowes hasn't been working you ragged just because you're new here. Done it before to a new guy a few years ago. Had to go on disability and he never came back. Rumor going around said he got mono and Bowes had his disability wages withheld."

She barely gave herself time to breathe.

Hunter shook his head. He wasn't getting much sleep that was true, but mostly because he had been burning the midnight oil in Bowes' office searching for everything he could find on Brenda.

"I know a great place over on Hinley Street," Cindi said. Hunter found himself counting her chins. She had three and a half. "I thought maybe you and I could grab a drink after you're done today, since I live around the corner from there and I don't work early tomorrow, so if you wanted to stay—"

That great place she was talking about on Hinley was a TGIF and the very thought of it suddenly made him want to barf all over her.

"I'm gonna be stuck here late again, Cindi," he said apologetically. "But maybe some other time. I hear their Strawberry Daiquiris are to die for."

Suddenly the glum expression on Cindi's face evaporated. "Oh yeah! They are great, aren't they?" She was smiling now. A real beamer if ever Hunter had seen one. "Oklie-doklie, I'm gonna hold you to that promise, mister."

Hunter summoned a smile that almost looked genuine. "I hope you do."

Chapter 14

"GET THE FUCK OUT!"

Tyson sprang out of bed, slamming the small of his back against the wall behind him. The sound of cracking wood followed a microsecond later by a hollow thud rang through the cottage. For a moment, the whole place seemed to rock back and forth. His eyes sprang open and he became aware that he had been dreaming. He shook his head, trying to clear away the fog. He was still groggy when he clawed his way back into bed, his chest heaving violently. His sheets and his boxer briefs were soaked with perspiration. The face from his dream was still so fresh in his mind he didn't dare close his eyes.

In his dream, he had been lying in bed, trying to fall asleep. Outside it was dark and windy. He remembered the wind. The way it shook the pine trees outside. The needles scrapping against the windows like long fingernails. He remembered being afraid. Afraid of the trees. Growing more and more certain they were trying to get inside the room. He was watching the branches sway back and forth when he saw the old woman staring back at him from outside. His mother. He wasn't sure how he knew. Didn't have the foggiest notion what she looked like. He was five years old, after all, but somehow, in a dream-logic sort of way, it all made perfect sense.

She was outside, and she had to be standing up to her ankles in mud and pine needles because it had rained earlier and when it rained here, the ground turned to mush. She was wearing a blood soaked Johnny gown and he could see the heavy wet fabric rippling slowly as she stood glaring in at him. She was saying something, her lips, cracked and bleeding, mouthing the words, but he couldn't quite make them out.

He blinked and she was gone.

That's when his dream got really weird, because that's when the front door started sliding open and he jumped because he knew she was inside the cottage. Somewhere in the dark. Coming for him. He could hear her wet, soggy feet as she drew nearer. Could hear her breathing from the other room. Heavy and labored as though she had tubes stuck down her throat. Tyson's eyes had darted around the room. There was nowhere to run and he felt the cold hand of panic begin to seize him. Heart hammering, Tyson's hands gripped the covers and pulled them up under his chin like a child trying to shield himself from a bogeyman that was, at that very moment, shambling through the living room.

Through the dim light he watched as she shambled into the room, her movements strange and unnatural. She stopped at his bedside, her bare feet still wet and he could hear them sticking to the hardwood floor.

"You were a naughty boy to leave Mommy like that," she said. Her voice sounded hollow and distorted, as though she was speaking through the business end of a vacuum cleaner. "Mommy loves you so much, Tyson. I want you to know that Mommy loved you most of all. Come home with me. Come home and I'll see that you never leave again. Come home to Mommy."

She had reached out a scaly hand to touch him and he had started to scream.

GET THE FUCK OUT OF HERE! GET THE FUCK OUT! GET THE...

Tyson lay in his damp bed, still reeling from the dream. His heartbeat drummed wildly in his neck.

Oh my God, how real it felt. That was what struck him more than anything else. The level of recall was also unusual. It wasn't often that he remembered all that much of his dreams. Perhaps because this one had been different. He couldn't think of the last time he had dreamed of his mother, at least not in this much detail.

He closed his eyes, thinking about the Noxil again. Thinking about how desperate he was to get his hands on those vials. How he would even crunch the used ones between his teeth if he thought it would do any good.

A fly landed on his ear in the darkness and Tyson whacked the side of his head.

Damnit!

It was a stupid move and right away, he could feel his ear beginning to throb. He was on edge. His body was craving sleep, while his mind begged him to stay awake.

You know what will happen if you sleep. What might come through.

Something else touched his forehead and that's when he heard it. A low hum. The same noise he'd heard as a child, in the room with the toys and the thing he dared not mention.

Every second it was growing louder. A fly brushed against his hand. Another tried to crawl into his nostril. He could hear them bouncing off the screen. Up against the window, their wings vibrating together, making a horrible sound.

Tyson switched on the light and gasped.

The ceiling was a black undulating mass. He had never seen so many flies in his whole life. Some of them started to descend and Tyson yanked off the pillowcase and wrapped it around his head. They were everywhere. He could barely keep his eyes open. He waded through the mass, gasping for air. Jabbing his hand out in front of him, he found the screen and yanked it open. A second later he was in the living room. The door to the master bedroom slammed tight. Behind him, the low drone of thousands of flies swirling in a black mass. Tyson looked around the living room in disbelief. There wasn't a single fly in there.

Inside the master bedroom, he could hear thousands of tiny insect wings scraping against the door.

He would sleep in the car, he decided. He was halfway to the kitchen when he stopped. The problem wasn't finding a safer place to sleep, was it? His mind was still a foggy mess, but things were still clear enough for him to recognize it didn't matter where he went. Cottage, car, or even Skip's goddamned boathouse. The problem wasn't where to sleep, it was how to stay awake.

Already the noise of flies buzzing around his bedroom wasn't nearly as loud as it had been a moment ago. He would let them stay in there until they all died. In the morning, he'd look to see if Skip had one of those Shop Vacs to scoop them up with.

In the meantime, thankfully, Skip's cottage had more than one bedroom and Tyson headed to one of the remaining two.

This room he chose smelled musty, and the sheets were damp, but it was a bed and it was a hell of a lot better than being propped up in a chair all night long. He wondered for a moment if his trip to the clinical trial hadn't really been a trip into hell. The more his mind worked, the tighter the knot in his belly grew. Not because he feared the unknown; no, it was the opposite that terrified him. On some level, perhaps one he wasn't ready to admit to himself just yet, he knew exactly what was coming. The only unknown was what it would do once it found him. Tyson spent the rest of the night tossing and turning in his damp bed, listening for flies.

● ● ●

A knocking the next morning startled him.

"Hello? Anyone home? Hello?"

Sounded like someone was already in the kitchen.

Tyson scrambled out of bed and shrugged on a pair of jeans. Memories from last night were trickling back. He went to the master bedroom and cautiously peeled the door open.

Hello?

That voice again.

He drew in a sharp breath. The room was mostly empty, apart from something behind the bed. It looked like snake skin, but it was too thick to be snake skin.

Anyone home?

Tyson looked up and saw a stunning woman standing in the kitchen. Her eyes immediately darted away with embarrassment. "Oh, forgive me."

He saw the reason for her discomfort. He wasn't wearing a shirt and his pants were unbuttoned.

"I just saw Skip's door open and wasn't sure. I mean, it's not like Skip to leave the door wide open." She stepped forward. "I'm Judy, I have a cottage down the road."

Judy looked down and both of them seemed to notice the muddy footprints at the same time. Footprints that led from the door, right through to the bedroom.

Tyson's jaw fell open.

You've got to be shitting me.

"Do you have a name?" the woman asked.

He was still thinking about the footprints. "Tyson."

"Oh yes," she said and smiled, revealing perhaps the most perfect set of teeth Tyson had ever seen. "He mentioned you."

Tyson was rubbing his eyes. "Did he?"

"Skip said he was sending a friend up to prep the place for summer."

Then it hit him like a sharp left hook. Yes, of course. Judy Stahl from Skip's letter. The one he had jokingly suggested Tyson make a pass at.

Skip, you dog you, she's hot as hell.

For a moment, all thought of footprints receded to the back of his mind. He had pictured an older woman, in her mid to late fifties, not a twenty-something model from Maxim magazine. Not that he was complaining. No, not at all. Dark wavy hair, soft olive skin. He could see a pair of deceivingly large breasts moving freely under her loose shirt and was suddenly overcome by a powerful desire to see what her body looked like unhampered by all those clothes.

Judy's eyes dropped again to the trail of mud on the floor and Tyson was suddenly yanked back from a rather savage bout of lust.

He dropped down and scooped up a piece of the hardened dirt and crushed it between his fingers.

"Got a broom?" Judy offered. "I can help you take care of this."

"Oh no, no," Tyson stammered. "A branch kept smacking the bedroom window last night and I cut it down."

"In your bare feet?"

Tyson paused. He could feel a layer of perspiration building on his forehead and he was certain she could see it too. "Yeah, couldn't find my shoes," he said without much conviction.

"Well, if you need anything I'm two houses down."

"Roger that," Tyson said smiling and holding onto the door. He watched her walk away, trying not to stare at the tight, athletic curve of her behind.

He was still holding the door when he noticed that the muddy trail led outside and around the side of the house. He followed it. The shallow indentations in the mud ended at an open window and when he looked through it he saw his bed and the wall next to it, damaged from where he had jumped with fright. Tyson crouched and studied the muddy tracks.

This isn't happening. I'm imagining all of this. I'm in my apartment back in New York City and my alarm's going off, but I just can't hear it.

In the last forty-eight hours, he had seen toys appearing out of nowhere, trunks filled with money popping out of thin air, and part of him knew that what made those footprints was the same thing that had come into his room last night. But that was just downright crazy.

Crazy like a trunk filled with a million dollars?

Tyson went back to the kitchen, picked up his cell phone and dialed Dr. Stevens.

"Come on, you son of a bitch, pick up!"

Tyson was about to hang the phone up by hurling it across the room, when he heard a voice on the other end.

"Yes?"

"Dr. Stevens?"

"Who is this?"

"Tyson. Tyson Barrett."

"Tyson Barrett?" Stevens seemed to be drawing a blank.

"From the Noxil drug trial." Tyson wanted to reach through the phone and throttle him.

"I'm sorry, but that study's been shut down. There's nothing more I can do for you."

"Hold on a second, don't hang up. Why was the study shut down? You said final acceptance from the FDA was just a formality."

"I know what I said."

"So what happened?"

"I'm not permitted to discuss it over the phone."

"Please, you can't possibly imagine how desperate I am right now."

The pause on the other end of the line was excruciating. "There's been a fatality."

"A fatality? One of the patients? Please, Dr. Stevens."

"Vance Fowler."

Tyson felt his throat constrict and for a second it was hard to breathe. The cowboy? "Was it from the Noxil?"

"There may have been complications. Mr. Fowler apparently died of an embolism. I'm sure I explained how mixing these kinds of powerful drugs can lead to unimaginable consequences."

"No shit. Listen, I need to meet with you."

"Mr. Barrett, I'm sorry, that's impossible. I've told you, the FDA and the IRB have shut us down. They aren't taking any chances."

"But you have to. It's a matter of life or death."

Silence.

"I joined your study under good faith and now I'm in trouble and I need your help."

"If you're suffering any adverse reactions, you need an emergency room doctor, not a researcher. What help can I possibly give you?"

"I need more Noxil."

Stevens let out what almost sounded like a cackle.

"Oh, Mr. Barrett."

"I have money, I can pay you."

"You realize I could lose my license."

"A thousand dollars."

"I'm sorry?"

"Bring me as many as of those vials as you can lay your hands on and I'll give you a thousand dollars."

This time the silence was so long Tyson was sure Dr. Stevens had hung up. "I'll do it for a thousand... per vial."

Tyson gritted his teeth. His eye caught the mud trail running through the length of the cottage. "Fine."

"I'll see what I can do," Stevens said. "Stay by your phone. I'll call you in about an hour." And this time Stevens did hang up.

Tyson grabbed his things and raced for the car. Barreling out of the driveway, a ghostly vision of his mother's face rose up before his mind's eye. Old and decrepit, she was reaching out to grab him and he pressed down on the gas, hoping to outrun the ghastly image.

Chapter 15

Hunter tapped the arm, found what looked like a vein and buried the needle in as far as it would go. The shaft was long. The longest he could find. The arm, however, wasn't his own. He was on seven, in a room that belonged to a former drug addict named Dan Sikes. Sikes had apparently wanted to see God so badly he'd mixed copious amounts of Methamphetamines with a similar amount of LSD. Whether Sikes saw God or not, Hunter didn't know. What he did know was that Sikes' brain now looked like a tuna casserole.

According to Sikes' file, six months after he had tried to play Icarus, something curious had happened. Although his brain's ability to distinguish between reality and fantasy had been destroyed, somehow his tolerance for pain had fallen to near zero. Another way to put it was that a tap on the shoulder felt to Dan Sikes like a hammer blow and a hammer blow like a cannon ball had torn a searing hole through his body.

Sikes' arms and legs were restrained—a standard precaution whenever a doctor needed to enter any patient's room with a sharp object. The solution in the needle was straight up IV fluid. But it was the needle itself that was the star of the show, not the liquid inside it.

Hunter's world suddenly seemed to take on a slow, detached sort of quality. As though he were viewing all of this from the comfort of his couch, back home.

He watched his own hand jiggle the needle and stared in amazement as Sikes' eyes began to tear. Hunter's body tensed.

Sikes should have screamed from the pain. He probably would have, the minute he felt the bevel pierce his skin, but he didn't. He didn't because Hunter had his other hand clamped over the patient's mouth.

He had been reading one of Brenda's journals again that morning. One where she had written that pain and pleasure shared a unique symbiotic relationship. One unlike any of the other dualities most of us encountered on a daily basis. High and low. Big and small. Those were observational qualities. But pain on the other hand, personal pain was experience and the clearest form of it. Almost all other stimuli paled in comparison. Except for one, she had written. And that was inflicting pain on another. There was an almost mystical quality to the sexual high you got from breaking someone's arm or holding their hand in a boiling pot of water. Somewhere deep inside that pain, down at its glowing hot center, was where God lived. The Medieval Inquisitors knew it. So did serial killers. Like it or not, when you stripped away all of the window dressing, wasn't that what serial killers were really after? Communion with God.

Hunter watched the man writhing beneath him, his face the color of squashed tomatoes. If only Sikes could grasp the concept. He might have turned away from abusing himself and refocused that energy onto someone else. Of course, Brenda's way of explaining it had been rather crass, but the gist of it was there.

He had read the passage half a dozen times, intrigued that something so deranged could make so much sense. Were these simply the mad ramblings of a psychotic woman? Or was there more?

He also knew that the research paper he would write on Brenda couldn't be anything more than a cursory investigation into child abuse and psychosis unless he opened his mind and explored all the possibilities.

You took an oath never to do harm, a disembodied voice shouted at him from far away.

Go ahead, Dr. Hunter. This time it was Brenda's voice he was hearing and for a moment he could feel her swimming around inside his head.

But at its heart, wasn't that oath about saving those who weren't even sick yet? How many might be saved from Brenda's fate if he could only understand how she had arrived there? There was an undiscovered clinical name for it, that dark corner of her mind she now inhabited. He was certain of that, and when all the research was done, they would let him coin it.

The questions were endless, almost daunting.

What factors shaped the private and twisted world of Brenda Barrett? Was it predominantly nature or nurture? Or was it simply the product of brain chemistry and faulty wiring? After that he would tackle the more disturbing implications. Like what if her condition wasn't an aberration at all, but something that existed in all of us? Something we denied only by the thinnest of margins. Maybe this was what Hunter was testing. That thin membrane that separated a Brenda Barrett from an Elias Hunter.

Hunter's attention fell to Sikes. It sounded like Sikes was pleading. The words were muffled and hard to make out, but Hunter thought he heard him say *please stop*.

Hunter jerked his hand away with the speed of a man holding hot plate.

What on earth am I doing?

Sikes' own eyes were wide and brimming with fear. Hunter removed the needle and undid the shackles and hurried away. That tingling feeling, like butterflies fluttering around in his stomach, was growing stronger. His head felt light and dreamy, as though it were trailing behind him, attached by a light silver cord.

Back in the relative safety of his office, Hunter became aware of the patch of moisture at his crotch. He fell back into his chair, overcome by what felt like the last great spasm of post coital euphoria. He may not have seen God, but he had come close.

Chapter 16

Stevens' call came as Tyson was cutting through the shadow cast by the Washington Bridge's second massive steel tower.

"Mr. Barrett," he said, sounding about as jovial as a man who's just been diagnosed with stage four cancer. "There's a statue in Central Park called the Three Dancing Maidens. Do you know it?"

"The one by 106th Street?"

"That's the one. Can you be there by three?"

"Do you have the Noxil?" Tyson stammered.

"I may be able to get two boxes for you. That's twenty-four vials."

"That's it?" Tyson could feel the air being sucked out of his lungs. His hand found the asthma pump, put it to his lips and fired off a round. "I was hoping for a case of the stuff."

"I'm breaking every ethical and legal rule in the book. Risking my entire career for two boxes of Noxil and thirty thousand dollars is hardly worth it, wouldn't you agree?"

"I thought it was a thousand a vial. That's twenty-four thousand."

"Yes, well the price just went up."

"If you knew how much I needed it..."

"I'm perfectly aware. And there may be more like you, Mr. Barrett. The death of that one serial drug tester alone will cost us tens of millions in delays and lobbying. Could be five years before we can clear away enough red tape to start testing Noxil again. I told you before that these cowboys were a nuisance and now I hope you see I wasn't kidding. No one really knows what chemicals they have lurking in their systems when they lie and cheat their way into a study."

Tyson was suddenly struck by a thought that seemed too horrible to face. What if the pills and the meds he had been cramming down his throat all these years had somehow mixed with the Noxil to create what Stevens called an 'unimaginable side effects'? Except, in his case, it wasn't an embolism that would get him, the way it had gotten Vance Fowler, but something else altogether. A side effect of monumental proportions.

Maybe the longer he stayed on the Noxil, the worse the reaction would become if he stopped? To call it a vicious circle seemed like the biggest understatement of the year. But what other choice did he have? He could either sit back and watch his life be torn to shreds before his very eyes, or he could hang on a little longer and hope and pray for a way out of this mess.

"Three o'clock then," Stevens said. It was more of a statement than a question and before Tyson could respond the line went dead.

● ● ●

Ten minutes later Tyson was standing before the door to his apartment, struggling with the three dead bolts he had installed the same day he moved in. Not that there was much here for the crooks and the addicts to take—apart from a trunk stuffed with money sitting in his living room.

When Ruma had told him it was time he started looking for another place to live, he hadn't taken all that much with him. The bed and dresser from the guest room. A lamp and TV from the office. The rest he had scraped together from donations by Skip and more than a few trips to the Salvation Army. Most of what he now owned were items of sentimental value. At the time, he suspected Ruma wouldn't have given a second thought to tossing all of it on the trash heap. No doubt, next to the Spartan conditions of his apartment, his storage locker downstairs looked positively bursting. Somewhere in there, he reminded himself, was an old lunchbox with some pictures, an adoption certificate and Han and Chewy. Although with the way things had been going, his theory that someone had snatched them so they could be found at Skip's summer house was looking more and more remote. Tyson wasn't even sure he'd be able to find them himself.

He checked the time on his phone. Twenty after two. In forty minutes he would meet Stevens.

On the kitchen table was the briefcase he had brought to Le Bernardin. The leather one filled with cash that had made Skip's eyes nearly bug out of his skull. It was lying there askew, just as he left it when he'd made the mad dash up to the cottage yesterday looking for his fix.

You're a junkie, admit it. Not much more than a single shaky step away from joining those crack addicts you see wandering the streets.

But he was hardly a junkie for wanting his life back. Clearly, something inexplicable had started happening to him. Tyson's own thin curtain that separated dreams from reality had been pulled aside. The light back there wasn't so good, just enough for him to see the dark shapes moving about. They were starting to cross over into this world and the thought of what might happen when they made it all the way through was almost too frightening to contemplate.

His stomach was grumbling again. He would get the money together, he decided, and then he would worry about the uncomfortable feeling in his belly. Tyson rubbed at his eyes. They felt red and puffy. He had caught a glimpse of himself in the rearview mirror on his way into town. But right now sleep wasn't an option for him. Not yet, at least.

Thirty more minutes, he told himself. *Thirty more minutes and we can start putting humpty dumpty back together again.*

He grabbed the briefcase. As far as anyone would be able to tell, he was a business man, enjoying the late afternoon sun and not some guy waiting to buy thirty thousand dollars' worth of pharmaceuticals.

Tyson had taken no more than a few cursory steps toward the living room when he stopped. The case felt particularly light. Fact, now that he thought of it, he couldn't remember hearing the sound stacks of money make as they go sloshing around inside an empty briefcase. He opened it and nearly screamed. All the blood ran out of his face.

The money in the briefcase was gone.

Maybe he had put it back in the trunk. He didn't think so. Not that he could be completely sure, given his frantic state of mind after his lunch with Skip.

Then a horrible, almost unthinkable possibility popped into his head and he chased it directly into his sparsely furnished living room. A living room that had consisted of a couch, an old beat-up TV and a trunk filled with just under a million dollars. But now there were only two pieces of furniture and neither of them looked even remotely like a trunk. He closed his eyes and could see it there, in his mind's eye, exactly where he had left it. But no matter how he envisioned it, whenever his eyes peeled open, the trunk was still missing.

The urge to vomit hit him forcefully. There wasn't any food in his stomach, so most of what surged out and onto the torn fabric of his Salvation Army couch was clear and mucousy.

I was robbed? That's it. Somebody broke in and stole my money.

But the door hadn't been forced nor his apartment ransacked. Only the money was gone. But who knew about the money?

Skip

His best friend?

But that was impossible.

First of all, Skip didn't have a key. No one had a key, apart from Tyson.

Then another thought occurred to Tyson and his legs started moving even before he had time to fully work out the details. Right before his lunch with Skip, he had thrown Han and Chewy into the top drawer of his dresser; the place where he kept all of his important documents and other knickknacks.

Tyson yanked the drawer clean out and up-ended it over the bed. Dozens of documents, paid bills and faded receipts fluttered to the bed like oversized snowflakes.

He sifted through the debris like a crime scene investigator looking for clues. He finished combing the pile twice before he was forced to admit the truth. Han and Chewy were gone.

So either he had just been robbed by a money-hungry toy collector, or something else was going on.

Tyson reluctantly picked up his cell to make what he knew would be a painful call.

The phone rang briefly before Skip picked up.

"Tyson, tell me you're just calling to chat."

"I wish I was."

"What is it now?"

"The money. I had it in a big old fashioned trunk right beside my coffee table and now it's gone."

"That million bucks you say you found? All of it gone, just like that?"

Tyson couldn't say that Skip's tone sounded contemptuous, just much closer to a 'of course your imaginary pot of gold isn't there anymore. That's what figments of your imagination do, they vanish into thin air.' If Skip had said anything even remotely like 'easy come, easy go,' Tyson would have driven to his house and throttled him. He didn't. "Did you call the police?" he asked instead, but that patronizing tone in Skip's voice was still there.

"What am I going to tell them?" Tyson replied. "Hey officer, a big pile of money that materialized from a dream I had just went poof. Can you put out an APB on a run-away steamer trunk for me please? Thank you."

"Materialized from a dream?"

Tyson looked at his watch. Fifteen minutes until his meeting with Stevens. "Skip, you'll have to take my word for it when I say you wouldn't believe me even if I laid it all out for you. Not even sure I believe it myself."

"If you can't trust your best friend, who can you trust?"

Tyson sighed. "All I can tell you is that since I've been taking that drug, things from my dreams have started... appearing. Childhood toys. Then the money." Tyson thought about last night and the muddy footprints and the ceiling thick with swarming flies. "And last night..." he paused, wondering if he hadn't already said too much. "I'm still not sure what happened last night. Look, I know what you're probably thinking, but you'll have to believe me when I say these things are real. I'm not cracking up. I spent all morning yesterday counting stacks of money and I still have the chaffed fingers to prove it. I need that medicine, Skip. I need it because otherwise something really bad is gonna happen."

"Everything will be fine, buddy. Has ol' Skip ever let you down?"

Tyson ran a sweaty hand through his hair. "No."

"Tell me, how exactly do you know these things are from your dreams?"

"Well, they don't always show up as they appeared in the dream. Sometimes they're just close. Other times they're exactly the same."

"But dreams fade, so are you sure there isn't another explanation?"

Fade

The thought struck Tyson so suddenly he wasn't sure why he hadn't thought of it before.

His money hadn't been stolen.

The objects had hitched a ride back with him from the dream world, that much was clear. For a time, they were real, tangible things. But with time even dreams fade, don't they? They lose their consistency drop by imperceptible drop until eventually they disappeared altogether.

The idea made sense, but the accompanying despair that came with the realization was making it hard to focus.

That money had represented a new beginning for Tyson. A rebirth of sorts from a lifetime of failed opportunities. And now all that had been snatched away. No worse than that. The bad dreams were coming back, and they felt stronger now than ever. He saw the old woman's face again, pale and haggard, drawing closer in the darkness of his mind and he recoiled. If Stevens had any kind of heart, he'd give Tyson at least a few vials to see him through the next few days. It seemed like something of a tall order for a pompous, self-serving butthole. There was a far better chance Stevens would tell him to fuck off in the dismissive way that seemed to be the hallmark of all arrogant pricks. And then what would he do?

"Tyson, you still there?"

Tyson looked at his watch and gasped. "Skip, I gotta run."

"Be safe," was all Skip managed before Tyson hung up.

Chapter 17

In spite of an uncommonly sweltering spring heat, the air inside the clinical trial space on Fourteenth and Houston was as cool and dry as a Pharaoh's tomb. Stevens had to peel the FDA sticker back to get in. But that was no big deal really. Not for a man who had the kind of pull he had. Flickering on the lights, he couldn't help but be amazed at how many real and figurative doors those two tiny letters had opened for him over the years. The rush he still got from watching people snap to attention when he dropped the Dr. bomb hadn't diminished a single bit.

Overhead, the neons danced and wavered before they finally flickered on. The trial had started amid such a flurry of activity that it was strange now seeing the place so deserted. No, strange wasn't quite it. It felt eerie.

"Hello?" Stevens called out, to be answered only by the dull echo of his own voice.

Two rows of hospital beds lined the in-patient wing. Privacy curtains fastened to semi-circular wall mounts. Beds unmade. A disquieting silence hung in the air, and for no longer than a split second, a peculiar thought came to Dr. Stevens that made his arms prickle with gooseflesh. It was more of a feeling really. A perverse notion, but the strength of it prevented him from ignoring the thought completely. In that moment, he wondered if in stepping through the front door, he had really taken a step into some other world. One just out of phase from the real world where nurses were still scurrying about and ghostly patients were laying in beds awaiting fresh doses of medication.

Stevens quickened his step, trying to outrun the long spindly fingers of panic that were crawling up the back of his neck.

Further on, past the cafeteria, past the twin boardrooms and the nurse's station, was the product storage facility. Stevens liked to use the term product storage facility because it sounded far more impressive than the mundane reality. In truth, the majority of the Noxil was kept in a cabinet by the incinerator that was secured by a single lock and key. A key only he had.

Only a handful of people knew that Noxil phase one had started as a little blue pill. They were nearly a hundred thousand units into production when they realized someone at the plant hadn't calibrated the machines properly. The pill was seventy-five percent sugar. Not even good enough to use as a placebo. That's when some VP in corporate decided to switch from pills to jet injectors, designed to fire vials of the drug straight into the bloodstream. Rumor was he had watched a rerun of Star Trek, saw Bones spike someone in the neck and let's just say the idea had gotten him rather excited. Barely a month later, Noxil phase two was born, but guess who was left to dispose of the nearly 85,000 little blue mistakes that had already been shipped? None other.

As head coordinator, it was his job to keep his accountability logs up to date. Every pill and vial had to be accounted for and any protocol deviation would certainly mean a visit from any number of monitors from Sino-Meck. A short and fat man named Gary Corso was probably the biggest prick of the lot, but to the very last man and woman, they were assholes - one and all.

And why should that surprise anyone? Their entire *raison d'êtres* was dedicated to sniffing out and punishing discrepancies. All those corporate lackeys ever did was sit around and wait for good people to make bad mistakes. It smelled like something right out of Stalinist Russia and, as head coordinator, Stevens swore time and again that those snickering, bloodthirsty rats wouldn't ruin his chances for advancement. In a world overflowing with people who would just as soon step on your head as ask you to move out of the way, a man had to look out for number one. To that end, he had worked diligently on perfecting the somewhat creative art of bookkeeping.

As far as the pharmaceutical company and the FDA knew, Stevens had destroyed the entire stock of Noxil, both in pill and liquid form. The IP reports he had filed certainly confirmed that and from a certain perspective, it wasn't completely untrue. As a matter of fact, that's what he had been doing for most of the morning. Dumping bucket after bucket of Noxil pills into a nasty and brutish-looking incinerator called the A850. Brutish in part because it made short work of whatever pharmaceutical they threw into it. The entire process took a full twenty-four hours, and he had sent nearly two hundred pounds of the stuff into the fiery maw of that beast. He had been on his way back to Sino-Meck's head office when Tyson Barrett had called. Over a thousand dollars for every vial he could lay his hands on. Stevens was still beside himself. He had once swiped a handful of compound they were using on women with late stage breast cancer for a competitor who had paid him very well. But $30,000 cash and for far less work and even less risk. How could he say no? The only bitch of it was Tyson's poor timing. He'd just finished loading up the A850 with nearly everything they had. He'd be lucky if he could scrape together the twenty-four vials he had promised. Lucky for him, they kept a hidden emergency stock on location in case a patient lost what they'd been given. Two or three cases, stashed at the base of the drug cabinet.

Stevens plucked the key chain from his pocket. The ceiling lights still hadn't come on. Up ahead, through the dimness, he could see the glow from the incinerator. The A850 groaned and rumbled as it first melted and then turned millions of dollars' worth of research and development into a pile of smoldering ash.

Stevens entered the disposal room and was struck at once by the heat coming off the incinerator. The intensity made him wonder if he hadn't walked into a sauna. The metal cabinet where they kept the spare drugs was becoming uncomfortably warm to the touch. He jammed his key in and yanked open the heavy door.

Stevens removed a white plastic box, unsnapped the lid. Inside were three cases of Noxil. A Cheshire grin split his features. He had only expected two.

$45,000. That bastard better have enough money for all of this.

Stevens checked his watch. Quarter to three. If traffic wasn't too bad he would have just enough time to reach Central Park and the nearly fifty thousand dollar paycheck that was waiting for him there. He turned on his heels to leave and suddenly stiffened. All the hairs on his arms were standing on end. His head made a slow tilt to one side, as though this new angle might help his brain better explain what his eyes were seeing. Although the in-patient room was still dark, the overheads in the distance had started coming on. But that just made the image of what he was seeing all the more strange. All but one of the hospital bed curtains were pulled back and behind the one that was drawn was the shadow of something large. And it looked like it was moving. No, wiggling. Just then, something tickled his nose and he flicked it absently away. Another touched his hand. Then the back of his neck and forehead. Dr. Stevens then became aware of a noise that he at first mistook for the hum of live electric cables.

A tiny insect shape blurred before his eyes as it flew toward the bed with the drawn curtain and the large shape that was now writhing behind it like a giant worm. Then, all at once, his awareness seemed to open up and he saw dozens, maybe hundreds of black dots zigzagging, all of them heading in the same direction. The space above the bed was becoming thick with flies. Stevens blinked. The amorphous shape behind the curtain was getting larger. The first inklings of fear began to course through his veins and he fought to control it. After all, this was his turf and no homeless guy, however he had managed to sneak in, was going to scare him away. Stevens started toward the form moving behind the curtain. He was less than ten feet away when his nose registered an unusual scent.

Pine trees.

The scent was sweet and earthy, but Dr. Stevens' nose, tuned mostly to fine wine and caviar, had detected another scent lurking beneath the surface. One that was familiar to him. One he recognized immediately.

Death.

His hand cramped around the three cases of Noxil. Stevens pointed his feet toward the glimmer of sunlight far in the distance, past the gauntlet of hospital beds, past the boardrooms, past the nurses' station, but above all else, past whatever was undulating behind that curtain.

Risking his own skin was definitely not on the cards for Dr. Charles Stevens. You never knew what diseases vagrants were carrying these days. No, he decided, trying to ignore the panic welling up inside him. It might be best to wait until he was safely en route to his meeting with Tyson Barrett before he called the police and informed them that some disgusting bum had broken into their lab and was using it as a Holiday Inn.

The lights gave one final flicker and came on. The bed with the drawn curtain was still between him and the exit and Stevens hadn't meant to keep watching. He definitely hadn't wanted to, but his neck was turned nonetheless, as though an invisible hand was tugging at his chin.

A spurt of blood sprayed inside the curtain wall. Then another and another after that. Soon the fabric was saturated with gore. One by one, the thin metal hooks gave way. Stevens looked on in horrified amazement. He'd been an ER doctor for nearly ten years before moving into pharma. Nicked arteries and gouts of spurting blood were nothing new to him. But in all that time, he had never seen anything like this. The curtain gave one final groan and then tore away completely. What was left lying on the bed, clotted with blood, was so far out of Stevens' realm of experience that all he could do was gawk. For a moment, there was no more fear. Just wonderment. Wonderment because he was surely witnessing something no one else on earth had ever seen.

The thing on the bed had brown, scabrous skin which was covered in thick mucus. The muscular tail wiped back and forth and it was then that Stevens began to recognize what he was seeing. It looked and moved like a caterpillar larvae. Scaly outer shell. A separate tail that swung in useless circles.

His fear shifted to terror. If this was some kind of giant larvae, then it begged the question: what was moving around inside? And if there was something inside, surely it wanted to get out. Almost in answer to his question, an appendage punched through the hardened outer shell.

Five fingers rose into the air and uncurled to reveal a hand. A small hand with long slender fingers.

Then the thick elastic inner membrane stretched and broke, revealing a child's face, black, syrupy liquid ran down it. It scanned the room with large insectile eyes which stopped when they found Stevens. Stevens took a staggered step backward. The blood in his veins dropped by a steep ten degrees. The hairs on the back of his neck were standing painfully on end.

He watched in mute horror as the tiny form with the impossibly large eyes slid off the bed and onto the floor. A stream of purplish liquid coated the floor as the inner membrane gave way and emptied. It used its hands to push itself off the floor and the first thought that fired through Stevens' mind was: It's a boy.

The second: The flies are gone. The ceiling had been swarming with them not more than a moment ago and now they were gone.

The third made all of the strength go out of his legs.

Ahriman.

Stevens took an unsteady step backward and nearly tripped over a discarded bedpan. The demon from Persian mythology who came to earth in the form of a fly. He writhed before Stevens, ready to lunge at him. Before the demon could, Stevens took off running. Not toward the front entrance, which now seemed like it was a hundred miles away. He didn't get farther than a few feet when he heard the creature grunt and felt it clawing up his leg. He turned in time to see the creature's jaw unhinge and clamp down on his thigh, could feel the flesh and bone coming undone. He howled with a pain more excruciating than he had ever known. A soupy stream of dark bile poured from the creature's mouth. Stevens howled as the acid tore through his trousers and ate away at his flesh. He looked down in disbelief as his lower leg detached and dropped away from the rest of his body. It seemed to have just melted away. Stevens tumbled to the ground. The case with the vials flew from his hands, some of them shattered, littering the floor with blue liquid. Dark red blood pumped from the stump where his leg had been only moments before.

He had been heading for the room with the incinerator. If he could only make it inside and lock the door behind him. Maybe then he could stem the bleeding and wait until help arrived. The small form with the large black eyes still had his leg in its mouth, watching him, almost playfully, the way a dog gnawing on a ball might look at its owner. It wanted to play and when it propped itself up on both hands, Stevens swung out with his one remaining leg. The sound of snapping twigs was like music to Stevens' ears and he watched with glee as the creature crumpled.

Then Stevens had another idea. Clawing frantically at the tiles, now slick with his own blood, he scrambled toward an IV stand. The wheels rolled with ease and he brought it over to where the creature lay. It was trying to stand up on broken arms. Stevens spun around into a sit up position and gripped the IV stand like a giant ax; he swung it onto the creature's head with what remained of his strength. He had already lost so much blood, but he knew he couldn't stop the bleeding until this thing was dead for good. On the third swing, Ahriman's head came apart and the demon stopped moving. A pile of clean bed sheets sat in a bin near 'bed one' and Stevens made his way there. With shaking hands he tore the sheets into long strips and then fumbled for the cell phone in his pocket. He put it on speakerphone and dialed 911.

"Nine one one, what is your emergency?"

Stevens tied off the tourniquet. "I've just been attacked and I'm bleeding really badly, please send an ambulance."

"What address are you at?"

"The medical clinic on the corner of Fourteenth and Houston." Stevens' vision swayed in and out of focus.

"I need your name, sir."

"Doctor Stevens. Are you sending someone, you silly bitch? I'm bleeding to death here."

"I've already dispatched emergency personnel. I need to know if your attacker is still there, Dr. Stevens?"

He looked over the bed frame he was using as a back rest and noticed the creature wasn't moving.

"I think I killed him." A fly landed on Stevens' phone and then flew off. Another fly tickled his nose as it tried to climb inside. He flicked it away. "Oh, no," he said.

"Mr. Stevens, please go someplace safe until the authorities arrive."

Stevens could already see the creature's fingers beginning to twitch. He'd left the IV stand next to it and there was no way he could get back there in time. Stevens dropped the phone and headed for the room with the glowing light, his hands making frantic slapping sounds as he struggled for purchase. Behind him, Ahriman was getting up. The sound of broken bone and cartilage snapping back into place. Wet sounds, horrible sounds, and Stevens wished he could plug his ears and stop himself from hearing anymore. But right now he needed his hands to drag himself into the incinerator room. On the floor behind him was his cell phone; he could still hear the 911 operator asking him what was happening.

The incinerator room door was less than five feet away. The blood streaming from his body, the fiery pain that fought for his attention with every pounding heartbeat. All those things weren't important. Right then, the room with the warm glow and the door that would close between him and this thing was what mattered most.

Stevens crawled inside and spun himself around so that he could get his hands on the base of the heavy metal door; the words 'incinerator' were stenciled in bold black letters and below that in blood red the word 'caution.' He pushed and the door began to swing on its hinges, powered by the adrenalin surging so furiously through his system. In another fraction of a second, Stevens would be safe. But the door stopped short with a sickening crunch. Stevens' eyes grew wide and his heart seemed to freeze over and shatter into a million pieces. Above him, he could see a man's leg jammed in the door. Attached to that leg was a foot with a shoe remarkably like his own. The cuff on the slacks identical to the ones he had stepped into as he hurried to dress for work that morning. The notion that the leg was his own seemed like some vague and distant concept or the punch line to some horrible joke.

He tried to keep the door from opening, but he wasn't strong enough. The creature with the bulging eyes forced its way in.

It slithered over to the A850 and paused. In the bright room, Stevens could see it clearly now for the first time. It had the upper body of a child but where its legs should have been was just a stubby tail.

The roar from the incinerator was deafening. The demon studied it as though it were some new toy. Stevens watched in horror as it balanced its weight on the end of its tail and rose up so it could close a hand around the lid, which it opened, filling the room with intense heat. Stevens could feel the moisture around his eyes being sucked away.

He's gonna try and throw me in there. He's gonna throw me in and close the lid.

But the creature did something that shocked even Stevens. It reached into the scorching inferno with its bare hand. Its arm jammed in all the way, its chest

114

pressed against the smooth metal surface as though it were fishing for something inside.

This is my chance, Stevens thought desperately. He clawed at the ground in front of him. His plan was simple. Grab hold and flip it into the incinerator. He reached for the rough bristly flesh around its waist when it turned. Ahriman had something in his hand. The arm that had been moving around inside the A850 was seared and blackened and Stevens could see in places where the flesh had been burned away completely. The stuff in his hand was dark blue and it ran between his long skeletal fingers like a clump of melted bacon fat.

Noxil.

Thousands of pills, destroyed and useless. But what could he want with that? Stevens wondered numbly.

A second later Stevens got his answer when the monstrosity that had slithered out from a blood squirting cocoon rammed the dripping sludge into his mouth.

Chapter 18

Hunter was in Bowes' office again, peeling open the doors to the metal cabinet where his boss kept the scrapbook, the one with the article clippings.

The last time he had been here, Al Quinlan, the janitor, had almost discovered him sticking his nose where it didn't belong and only Hunter's quick thinking had allowed his escape. But maybe escape wasn't really the right word. Hunter had seen a touch of suspicion on Al's face as he tried to explain that his office had been flooded by a leak from the ceiling. At the time, with his heart hammering wildly in his chest, Hunter was sure that pouring the cooler water onto the floor had been a stroke of genius, but he had quickly realized his error. Crusty guys like Al might not look like much, but their brains were storehouses filled with useless information. The men's bathroom on two needed hand towels. The hallways on four and five weren't waxed on Friday since Dan Cromley had to leave early to take his little boy to the emergency room. All the water jugs on six were replaced on Monday. And here was Hunter's sitting half empty just a day later.

Hunter could see Al's suspicion growing more acute every day as the man's computer-like brain tried to make sense of the parts that didn't quite add up.

"I was in your office last night, looking for that leak you mentioned. I gotta tell you, it was the darndest thing. No sign of water damage whatsoever."

Hunter had done his best to look confused, even bored. "That's strange. Water must have come from somewhere."

"Only thing I can think of is that water jug of yours musta sprung a leak, cause I'd filled her up only the day before. Unless you're in the habit of drinking more than a gallon and a half of water a day, that is."

Hunter had shrugged, but a thought was dawning on him. That Al was playing dumb, the way Detective Colombo on TV played dumb, when he knew all along exactly who the killer was. As long as no one could tie him to Bowes' office after hours, then a leaky water jug was all it would ever be.

Hunter sat on the floor in Bowes' office and crossed his legs, the leather scrapbook resting comfortably in his lap. He flipped through the pages, trying to find where he had left off the last time, navigating by the dim sickly light cast from the banker's lamp on the old man's desk.

He flipped a handful of pages and there it was.

Grisly Scene Stuns Quiet Neighborhood
Jack Bicman

Police responding to a domestic violence call came upon a disturbing scene yesterday afternoon. Brenda Barrett was taken into custody by Columbia County sheriffs for the attempted murder of her five-year-old son Tyson Barrett.

Hunter laid the book down, pushed himself up on achy legs and searched Bowes' disastrously messy desk for a pen and a scrap of paper. On it he wrote: *Tyson Barrett. Still alive?*

117

Then he sat back down with paper and pen and continued reading.

But it was inside one of the bedrooms that police made the most shocking discovery. The partially mummified remains of five-year-old Alexander Barrett.

Hunter paused. Where had he seen the name Alexander before? A flashbulb of recognition went off in his head. Brenda's diary and the spider that lived by her bed. Alexander was what she had named him and she had loved and doted on the insect as if it were her own flesh and blood.

Coroner Paul Shuute wouldn't speculate on the cause of death, citing that nothing could be confirmed before an autopsy was completed. He also wouldn't say how long Alexander had been in the room. He would only say that the dead child was born with a rare disease called sirenomelia; a condition where an infant's legs fuse together in the womb.

Alexander was found dressed and posed in a bedroom that Sheriff Johnston said "looked like some kind of shrine. In all my years in law I've never seen anything like it."

Police have also taken Frank Barrett in for questioning. As per friends and neighbors, Frank was frequently away on business and of late had become estranged from his wife on account of her strange behavior.

Police continue to scour the house for any additional bodies, although Brenda Barrett claims there aren't any others to find.

Hunter added two names to his list.

Frank and Sheriff Johnston.

He flipped the page and found an article from the New York Times called "When Mothers Kill." In it, they used Brenda's trial and subsequent imprisonment at Sunnybrook to highlight the point that fathers who murder their children are often considered evil and put to death, while mothers are assumed to have severe mental illness and sequestered into institutions. One final point from the article would stay with Hunter for a while after he finished reading it: ninety percent of infant deaths under the age of five were due to infanticide. And ninety percent of those were committed by women. Hunter would have to check those figures of course, but if they were right, they would make a dynamite opening for the research paper he was going to write on Brenda.

Hunter was outside Bowes' office pulling the door closed when he heard his name being called.

"Elias?" The surprise and confusion in the woman's voice was unmistakable. He peered over his shoulder, trying to force the moisture back into his mouth. Cindi was marching up to him with that labored waddle of hers and Hunter felt the sudden urge to put her head through the door.

Her face was all squished up. "Whatchu doing in the big man's office?"

"Nothing." The words no sooner came out that he realized how childish he sounded.

"Well, I guess if he's okay with it."

"Sure he is. Asked me to check on something he forgot to take home with him."

"Oh." That harsh quizzical expression on her face was slowly giving way to the empty grin he was accustomed to. "Dr. Bowes is rather forgetful, isn't he?"

"What are you doing here so late?" he asked, hoping to divert her attention.

"Filling in for Alice, but I'm done now." Cindi cupped her elbows. "I hate staying here after dark."

"Me too," Hunter lied. But the truth was, he felt at home here. Maybe more at home than he'd felt anywhere else. When the sun went down, that feeling only became stronger.

"You finished?" Her eyes were bright.

"Yeah," he answered reflexively.

"Great!" What would you say to that drink at TGIF?"

That plastic smile Hunter worked so hard to perfect was back and doing the job as good as ever. "I'm game."

• • •

Two hours later, Cindi was leading Hunter into her bedroom, her hand clamped around the buckle of his belt and he could feel his hips being jerked forward with every tug. Ahead was the shadowy confines of Cindi's bedroom. Even with a smattering of light he could see that the floor was littered with dirty laundry. A stack of 'Hello!' magazines kept the door propped open. Two stained nurse's uniforms lay crumpled and forgotten in the corner.

They were by the bed now and Cindi's nightstand was covered with empty Wagon Wheel wrappers. She pulled the drawer open, dipped her hand inside and emerged with an orange condom. The level of Cindi's precision left him with the impression he wasn't the first victim she'd lured into her lair. They had sat for no more than three, maybe four drinks apiece, but he could smell waves of rum from the daiquiris rising up at him from the crotch of his pants where she was fumbling with the latch on his belt. After failing to make sense of the mechanism, she opted to unzip Hunter's fly. In went her hand, poking and prodding as though she were searching for a stray Wagon Wheel that had tumbled to the bottom of her purse. A meaty set of fingers curled around the shaft of his penis and for a moment he was aroused, but all that changed when Cindi tried pulling him out through the zip hole, scraping every jagged tooth along the way.

"Fuck!"

"Oh, I'm sorry," she whimpered, peering up at him like a scolded puppy. He could tell she was genuinely sorry, and Hunter wondered if this was how she sounded when she tightened the restraints of the patients at Sunnybrook.

"I think you tore a strip off." He was limp as hell now.

"Nurse Cindi'll make it all better." He could sense her smiling even in the darkness as she took him into her mouth. She was swirling her tongue and sucking madly and Hunter wondered if she didn't have a gobstopper in there somewhere.

Five minutes of the same and his cock was still about as firm as a strand of cooked spaghetti. It wasn't so much the fumbling or the trashed apartment any more than it was Cindi's shapeless body that was killing his erection. He had been with heavier women. Hell, there was something he even preferred about them. Maybe it had something to do with the little known truth that hot women were boring as hell in bed. Somehow they felt entitled to sit back and enjoy a free ride.

This whole evening had been a sham from the start and he knew it. He had tried to fool himself at first, tried to pull the wool over his own eyes about why he was standing in Cindi's room with his pecker out. And every which way he spun it, the answer came back the same.

Hunter was scared of the fat girl with the shiny eyes and the fingernails worn down to nubs. Scared shitless that she would rat him out about being in Bowes' office. And because of that he'd felt he had no option other than to give her exactly what she wanted. He'd caught the signals of her attraction easily enough, there was no faulting his radar. No, that piece of equipment was working just fine. It was another piece of hardware—or in this case software—that was letting him down.

He watched the top of her head rocking back and forth. She wasn't giving up. And in a weird kind of way, it made all the sense in the world. At this stage, Cindi's self-esteem was on the line. For Hunter, however, he stood to lose a great deal more than a blow to his ego. His job at Sunnybrook for starters and certainly any hopes of writing that career altering research paper on Brenda Barrett. But what seemed to burn the most was the idea of losing free access to Brenda's room and to the treasure trove of resource material waiting to be read on the shelves of her library. He imagined Brenda lying in her bed. The tubes and hoses weren't there anymore and she was beckoning him forward. She wanted him to lie down next to her and that's when it happened. Cindi was starting to moan. Her hands and her mouth were moving faster. Rhythmically. Hypnotically. Hunter could feel himself becoming fuller, harder. He knew he could do this. As long as he closed his eyes and thought of Brenda, he knew everything would be just fine.

Chapter 19

The Duane Reade's pharmacy on Broadway and 125th street was bright and cold and reminded Tyson of the stereotypical Judeo Christian vision of heaven: whitewashed and devoid of any hint of personality. Tyson's fists were curling into tight balls and releasing, almost in time to the pacifying sound of the Muzak belting out over the PA. He had heard once, and he couldn't remember where, that the crap they passed for music in the large chain stores was laced with mind numbing subliminal messages.

Relax… keep shopping… we're watching you… relax…

It must be a lie, he knew now, because he'd never been less relaxed in his entire life.

He was still steaming mad that Stevens had stood him up. Tyson had waited by the Three Dancing Maidens for well over an hour, all the while feeling his gut working itself into knots and his temperature rising every time he dialed Stevens and got the little prick's voice mail.

Hi, this is Doctor Charles Stevens at Sino-Meck. I'm either away from my phone or on another call…

When he finally accepted the fact that he'd been played for a fool, he'd jerked himself off that park bench and yelled "FUCK" at the top of his lungs. A young couple sitting nearby had risen almost in unison and walked briskly away, the man looking over his shoulder, worried that a slavering and foamy mouthed Tyson might be shambling after them. The yell had done something to dampen the anger he was feeling at the time, but not a thing to assuage his fear. Without Noxil, his only option was to hit a Duane Reade's for the strongest non-prescription wake up pills they had. This wasn't like the old days, he thought painfully, where he could count on an hour, maybe two of sleep, before he would wake up screaming. The situation had grown infinitely worse. He had run through the possibilities hundreds of times and the odds always came out the same. There was a fifty-fifty chance that stopping the Noxil would effectively slam shut that door connecting the dreamworld to reality. But what if he was wrong? What if stopping the Noxil only brought his nightmares back? What if something else was keeping that door from closing? The rotting foot of some unimaginable thing wedged in the frame, trying to push its way inside.

An image flashed before him and it made the skin on the top of his head ripple with gooseflesh. The ragged hospital gown worn by the woman he somehow knew was his mother. It had been soaked in gore and he could tell by the look on her face that she wanted his head against her blood soaked breast. Wanted to take all his pain away.

Come to Mommy!

Disturbing as the image was, lying in a woman's arms was exactly what Tyson needed right now and he knew it. His immediate inclination was to pluck the cell phone from his pocket and start thumbing in Ruma's number, but he stopped himself, his finger hovering over the send button.

Long ago, he had come to understand that relationships are essentially made up of doorways. Once they were closed, it was nearly impossible to open them again. Ruma's felt as tightly sealed as they came.

After the first few months, when the nightmares and the lack of sleep had started slowly taking their long grueling toll on Tyson, he had eventually sought help. Mostly because of Ruma and Kavi. Even then, he could see how much his behavior was hurting them. The 'let's see who can shout loudest' game he and Ruma were constantly playing. Kavi trying to come between them, his tiny arms raised.

Stop hurting Mommy! Stop hurting Mommy!

Tyson's gut clenched with grief. Imagine, a five-year-old telling his parents to behave. He hoped to God that one day Kavi would see that that wasn't really his father doing those things. You deny someone sleep for long enough and their personality begins to bend and warp at an exponential rate and before long, all the qualities that made them human had been swept entirely away.

He plucked three bottles of Picmeups from the shelf and scanned the directions. He had learned very quickly that most of the nonprescription stuff out there didn't do a whole lot to keep you awake, other than to get your heart beating at a hundred miles an hour. The problem was that once you came down, and you most definitely would come down, you were apt to fall asleep exactly where you stood. No doubt about it, this would only be a temporary solution.

Even before the Noxil, he knew the key to avoiding the nightmares was simply refusing to sleep. But one month of playing that game had only compounded his symptoms and increased the ferocity of his nightmares. At the time, it almost seemed as though the darkness was punishing him for trying to escape it. But now, dreaming didn't have nearly the same implications as it had even a week ago. Back then, he might wake up from a bad dream and find himself screaming; today, there was a chance that even dozing off for the briefest of naps might mean waking up next to something clawing his face off. He was still holding the bottle of Picmeups when he heard a woman calling his name.

For a moment he expected to turn and find the haggard face of his mother glaring back at him. But it wasn't his mother. The hand with the pills fell by his side and he hoped out of view.

"Judy Stahl," he said, and the surprise in his voice couldn't have been more genuine.

Her mouth curled into a beautiful smile. Gleaming white teeth. She must have had braces. "I didn't recognize you with your shirt on," she said.

"Yes, Skip's cottage." His palms had begun to sweat.

"I spend most of the year in the city, of course," Judy said. "Spring and summers at... you didn't think I lived up there all year round? You did, didn't you?"

Tyson laughed and there was a touch of guilt there. "I admit, the thought had crossed my mind."

"You just reminded me of something from grade school," she said, switching her shopping basket to her other arm. "I had this teacher named Mrs. Martin and at ten years old, I was convinced she slept in the classroom at night because she wore the same plaid skirt and blazer every day."

Even in Duane Reade's flat, dead lighting, Judy's eyes sparkled like sapphires. During one of his epic all-nighters, Tyson had read in a National Geographic that eye color was a product of Darwinian evolution. Natural selection intended to help attract a mate.

Judy seemed to notice the shift in his expression. "I'm rambling," she said starting to blush. "I've been told I'm a rambler."

"No, I like it."

126

Judy looked down at her feet and then back up at Tyson. "I guess I'll see you up at Skip's sometime. Did you finish pulling all those old dusty sheets off the furniture?"

"No, not yet. Can't say I'll be back up there any time soon, either." For Tyson the memory of his mother's leering face in the window and her shambling trek through the kitchen was still too fresh in his mind. In fact, he was sure her muddy footprints were still there. Irrefutable proof, if ever he needed it, that he was being crushed between two worlds.

"Catch you around then, Mr. Tyson Barrett."

The way she said his name, her chestnut hair seesawing just enough to reveal the soft nape of her neck, left him feeling warm and rubbery. She was gorgeous, there were no two ways about it. Was it any wonder that he felt an almost irresistible force pulling them together?

"What are you doing tonight?" he heard himself ask and right away his gut clenched with all the hallmarks of residual guilt. In spite of the fact that Ruma had left him, he had always accepted the plain fact that he had pushed her away. Her adultery and her lack of faith in him aside, he couldn't fault her for what she'd done. The sad truth was, he had left her long before she had packed up his things and set them neatly at the door. The last six months had merely been the final straw.

Judy was smiling at him. He almost swore he had heard her say "I'm free." But he couldn't exactly be sure, since the thought burning like a wild fire through his tired mind was how familiar she seemed.

More than likely, he had spotted Judy in one of the eight million pictures Skip kept strung along the walls of his apartment.

Her smile had triggered the connection and he hated to even think that she and Skip might have been lovers at some point, the consequence being that it would render her immediately out of bounds.

Stop throwing up road blocks in the way of a normal life. Who cares if she had a fling with Skip? Hell, Skip's been with half the women in New York City.

"Great," he replied and now he too was smiling. Two identical smiles staring at each other under the dead, pale lights of a Duane Reade's pharmacy.

● ● ●

"Oh, this is fabulous!"

"You think so?"

"Oh yes. It's nice to meet a man who knows his way around the kitchen."

Judy had stopped and was staring at him. She was holding her fork between her index finger and her thumb and it was swinging back and forth suggestively.

"How is it a man like you hasn't been snatched up yet?"

He glanced down at his left hand, almost instinctively. He wasn't wearing his wedding ring and he felt a momentary sting of guilt.

"I was snatched. But now I'm unsnatched."

Judy let out a burst of laughter and then stopped abruptly. "I didn't mean to laugh, it's just the way you said it."

Tyson smiled.

"What happened, if you don't mind me asking?"

"I hit a bad patch and I wasn't there like I should have been. No one to blame but myself."

"Relationships are rarely that one sided. I mean, so long as you weren't cheating on her or beating her with a billy club."

"No billy clubs, too soft."

128

She grinned. "Then stop torturing yourself. Life is tough enough as it is." Judy must have sensed his unease because she changed the subject almost at once.

"You grow up in the city?" she asked.

"No, upstate. Small town. One of the lucky few who made it out, I guess."

"There's something about the way you talk. You were a mama's boy, weren't you?"

He could see the expression on her face shifting from sweet playfulness to deep concern.

"Oh my God, I'm so sorry, has your mother passed away? I'm such an idiot. Always sticking my foot in my mouth. You made a nice dinner and here I go ruining everything."

"No, not at all. My mother…" Tyson paused. "My mother died a long, long time ago."

She put her hand over his. "I'm sorry to hear that. I started a minor in early childhood development at Columbia U a few years back. I almost graduated too, but I found the case studies too difficult to deal with. I can't imagine how hard it must have been growing up without her."

Tyson contemplated that last part of what she said.

"Growing up without her was the one thing that saved my life."

Judy frowned.

Tyson's phone rang, breaking the atmosphere.

He looked down at the number. It belonged to Dr. Stevens.

Chapter 20

"Tyson Barrett?"

"Speaking."

"This is Detective Anderson. I hope I'm not disturbing you."

"Well, I'll be honest, I'm a little disturbed. This number belongs to Dr. Stevens."

"Yes, we know. That's why we're calling. I need to know where you were this afternoon between three and four o'clock?"

Tyson's heart kicked up a notch. A tangle of jumbled thoughts were firing off in his head. He knew that soliciting Stevens to buy a potentially hazardous drug the FDA had slated for destruction wasn't exactly legal, but he would never have expected getting a call by the NYPD.

"I was in Central Park."

"We found your number on Dr. Charles Stevens' phone. I see here you called him fifteen times today. That sound about right?"

"Yeah, he was supposed to meet me in the park at three and he never showed."

"What was your meeting about?"

Tyson could feel the room getting hotter. Beads of sweat were forming on his forehead. "We had some business to discuss."

"Enlighten me, please."

"He was bringing me some Noxil. I'd run out. What's wrong, is he under arrest?"

"No, Mr. Barrett, he's not under arrest. He's been murdered."

The words rolled onto him like a pile of heavy boulders. Tyson couldn't breathe. His lungs began constricting violently. He reached into his pocket for his inhaler and found nothing but loose change and pocket lint.

On the phone: "Mr. Barrett? Are you still there, Mr. Barrett?"

Judy shot out of her seat.

"Tyson, what's wrong?"

Tyson was fumbling through his pockets, gasping for air. His chest was expanding and contracting wildly, but he still felt like he was suffocating. Judy grabbed the phone.

"I don't know who this is or what you told him, but he's having an asthma attack." She set the phone down.

Tyson was pointing off toward the bedroom. Judy rose to her feet, kicked off her pumps and ran. A minute later she returned with the inhaler. Tyson was on the floor, hands clamped around his throat, looking like his head was about to explode. Judy flipped off the cap and put the mouthpiece to his lips and pushed the inhaler with her thumb. Tyson heard it fire off, but nothing happened.

"Tyson," Judy said. "On the count of three, breathe in. One… two… three…" She squeezed again. Tyson breathed and the expression on his face immediately started to relax. He lay on the floor, Judy holding his head. She was rocking him back and forth singing softly to him. Tyson's phone was still on the table and from far away he could hear the detective.

Tyson sat up and took the phone. In his other hand was the inhaler and he reprimanded himself for not keeping it in his pocket.

"Detective Anderson."

"It wasn't my intention..."

"No need to apologize. I've had this since I was a child and every once in a while it creeps up and gives me a scare. Listen, how was Dr. Stevens ki... how did it happen?"

"I'm not at liberty to say. But I can tell you that in all my years I've never seen anything quite like it. The state of the body... You ever been in the country, Mr. Barrett?"

"Sure I have."

"You know the way coniferous trees smell?"

"You talking about pine trees?"

"Yeah, that's it. All I can say at this point is that the whole bloody place stunk of pine trees."

Tyson didn't say a word.

"That mean anything to you?"

"No," Tyson lied. "Should it?"

"You take care of yourself, Mr. Barrett. We'll be in touch."

The line went dead.

Tyson's face was the color of old linen. He looked at Judy, certain she was wondering what she had just got herself into. He half expected her to get up and head straight for the door. No doubt she'd be perfectly justified in doing so. But much to his surprise and delight, she didn't move a muscle.

"What happened?" she asked somberly.

It was a simple enough question without a simple enough answer. More than anything, he didn't want to drag her into this mess, especially when he wasn't sure himself what exactly was going on.

"Have you ever had a dream," he asked her, "that was so awful you woke up thanking God it wasn't real?"

"Sure. Who hasn't?"

"Lately, I've been living that nightmare and then you came along like a ray of warm sunshine washing away everything that's bad about the world."

Judy was holding him again and Tyson felt the one thing he had been lacking for so long. The comfort only a woman could give.

But all the comfort in the world couldn't remove this terrible new weight that had settled on top of him. Somehow, earlier today, his mother had gone and killed Stevens. Of course, crazy as it seemed, the very thought had crossed his mind the second Detective Anderson mentioned Stevens' death. But it was that last thing the detective had said, about the cloying scent of pine needles, that left no room for doubt.

His failure to stop his nightmares from spilling out into the real world was no longer about shielding the people he loved from his short temper. If his mother, or even a subconscious facsimile of her, had followed him back to the real world like some kind of ephemeral stowaway, then emotional bruising was the least of his concerns.

If she was real and had come through, the way that big trunk full of money had come through, then the first chance she got, she'd start killing everyone close to him and when she was done with them, he would be next.

Chapter 21

Sunnybrook Asylum came into view not long after Ruma turned off the interstate. The hour long drive had given her enough time to conjure ideas in her head about how she thought it would look, but seeing it now, over the crop of trees that lined the road, Ruma knew she had been wrong. Sunnybrook wasn't new and sleek and covered with tempered glass windows. It looked far more like a set piece from a Rob Zombie movie than it did an actual asylum with patients. Gothic. That was the word that came most easily to mind. Judging by the way the weather had eaten away at the walls, they might once have been the color of polished Portland, but were now dark and layered with a hundred years of pollution, the place in desperate need of a makeover.

Kavi sat beside her, looking up at the Tudor-style battlements, his eyes wide, his thin lips slightly parted.

This was nowhere for a kid to be. She knew that. She also knew that coming all this way would never leave her with enough time to pick Kavi up from preschool. And she would let hell itself freeze over before calling on Tyson for help.

Can you pick Kavi up today? I need to head upstate and meet with a doctor to find out once and for all if you're going looney like your mother.

Skip had called her late last night and Ruma found the tone of their conversation extremely unsettling to say the least. Tyson's cryptic phone calls from the cottage, accusing Skip of having planted things in order to mess with his mind. And then Tyson's subsequent assertion that objects from his dreams were somehow showing up in his waking life, only seemed to confirm the worst.

Ruma wasn't completely clear on how this Dr. Bowes was going to help her or her son. She had spoken to him months ago over the phone and hadn't learned a whole lot more than she already knew. But this time it was Kavi she was mostly worried about. That the doctor might sit her son on an examining table, flash a light in his eyes and say "aha!"

Of course, he wouldn't. Since Tyson's slow dive off the deep end, however, she had become increasingly concerned that a genetic abnormality might be conspiring against her ex-husband and, perhaps by default, her son. There was also a second reason for heading to Sunnybrook. One that fit far more neatly into the morbid curiosity category than it did her concern about the possibility of genetic insanity. She wanted to see the woman who had single handedly destroyed her husband's chances of having a normal life. The woman who had also managed to destroy their marriage. She wanted to see the monster for herself.

Ruma pulled into a parking space near the entrance, took Kavi's hand and made her way to the asylum's heavy oak doors. Inside, a guard sat quietly at a large desk, dwarfed by the console of monitors and electronics around him.

The guard glanced up at her. His nametag read Terrance.

"I'm here to see Dr. Bowes," she said assertively. Ruma was a woman of slight build, but she'd never let that stop her from getting what she wanted.

He nodded, picked up the phone and spoke very quietly into the receiver.

"He'll be here in a moment," Terrance said. "Please have a seat." He motioned to the row of chairs against the wall. They were dated, the fabric ripped. The orange stuffing had been pecked at by nervous hands.

Kavi sat beside his mother.

"Honey, you okay?"

He glanced up at her and nodded, but she knew by the way his eyes were darting around the shadow filled lobby that he was afraid.

When Dr. Bowes finally appeared, the man was far shorter than Ruma had imagined him. For one reason or another, the deep pitch of his voice over the phone had made her think he was well over six feet tall.

He stopped and peered down at Kavi.

"Hello there, young man. And how old are you?"

Kavi stood staring up at Dr. Bowes. Eyes wide. The expression on his face flat and tight. He'd clamped one tiny arm around his mother's leg. Every mother in the world knew what that meant.

"He's a little frightened." She directed her first sentence at Dr. Bowes, and her second to Kavi:"Be polite. When an adult asks you a question, you answer them."

Kavi swallowed and held up all the fingers on his right hand.

"I'm five."

Dr. Bowes smiled and patted Kavi's hair. "No need to be afraid. If I'd known you were bringing your son, I'd have brought him a lollipop. Would you like a lollipop, Kavi?"

Kavi nodded vigorously.

"I can't say I've ever known Brenda Barrett to have visitors."

"To be quite frank," Ruma said, "I can't say I've ever been to an insane asylum."

Dr. Bowes stiffened slightly. "Mental health facility is how we refer to them nowadays."

"Oh. I didn't mean to offend."

"No harm done," Bowes replied and looked at his watch. "I have a staff meeting in less than an hour. What would you like to tackle first?"

Ruma pretended to think it over, but of course, there wasn't anything to contemplate. "I want to see Brenda."

● ● ●

On the way up to the eighth floor, Ruma explained to Bowes the reason for her visit.

"You must remember," Dr. Bowes said almost apologetically, "there are names and labels we use to explain her psychosis. Terms like obsessive compulsive, sociopathic, psychotic and megalomaniacal. Each of them sheds some light on why she does some of the things she does, but when those terms are held up against the woman as a whole, well, we find they fall far short of providing any kind of complete picture."

"Are you saying that you're not really sure what's wrong with her?"

Bowes smiled again and Ruma noticed the muscles around his mouth tense. The elevator doors groaned slowly apart. All three stepped out.

"To put it in the simplest terms that I can," he paused, "Brenda has something the old timers used to call a God complex."

Ruma's face was half covered in shadow. "That doesn't really sound all that bad to me."

"I suppose that might be true, considering the popular view of God nowadays. A protective being who loves us unconditionally. But that God isn't who we're talking about here. Have you read the Bible, Mrs. Barrett?"

"I'm Hindu, so I can't say I have more than a passing knowledge of it."

"There are two Gods in the bible."

"Are there? I always thought there was one."

"Are you familiar with God in the old testament?"

Ruma paused. "Only that he's rather grumpy."

Bowes laughed. "A man like Richard Dawkins would call that a grave understatement. He was a maniac who wiped out any man, woman, and especially any child, who displeased him."

Dr. Bowes stopped before Brenda's room. Ruma rose on her tip toes and peered through the curved glass porthole. There she saw a woman lying amidst a sea of machines.

"Vengeful and bloodthirsty. That's the kind of God Brenda Barrett would be."

The doctor led them into the room where Brenda's heart monitor pinged steadily.

"If you're really asking me whether there's such a thing as an insanity gene," Bowes chuckled, "I'd have to say no. From a purely scientific point of view—an evolutionary point of view—I can't see how there'd be any benefit."

Ruma couldn't take her eyes off of Brenda's contorted face. The heavy tube in her throat pried her lips into a queer, almost menacing smile.

"Granted, Dr. Bowes, it's been a while since my days at NYU, but aren't abnormalities also part of evolution?"

"To a degree, yes," Bowes answered. "But with issues such as infanticide, it opens up a whole series of other problems. You see, Darwin's initial theory…"

Ruma was suddenly aware that Kavi's tiny arms were no longer wrapped around her leg and a momentary panic seized her. Her eyes darted over Bowes' shoulder and there she saw him standing stiffly beside Brenda's bed. That wasn't strange, in and of itself, but Kavi's lips were moving as if he were speaking with someone.

Call her crazy, but from here it looked like he was talking to Brenda. Her eyes found the dancing blip on Brenda's heart monitor. When they had first entered the room she remembered that trailing dot had been moving along at a steady pace. Now it was bouncing up and down wildly. Ruma saw her son lift his hand in the air and spread out his fingers, saw his lips mouth the word five and knew that something *was* terribly wrong. The skin at the top of Ruma's head seemed to suddenly shrink wrap around her skull.

"Kavi, get over here right away. Kavi!"

The boy turned and took an almost automatic step toward Ruma, then he stopped and looked back at Brenda, as though this new friend had one final thing she needed to tell him.

"Kavi, now please, Mommy is speaking."

Dr. Bowes turned with a puzzled look on his face.

Kavi came and wrapped his arms around Ruma's legs and looked up at her sheepishly.

"What were you doing?" Ruma asked him.

"Nothing."

"Tell Mommy, I won't be angry."

Bowes was over by the heart monitor now. His face turning a dark shade of purple. "Never play with any of this equipment, young man. It's very important. Do you understand?"

Kavi's tiny face followed Bowes as he stormed across the room and pushed a button on the wall. A minute later a tall man with dark circles under his eyes came rushing in. He stopped before Bowes, breathing heavily.

"What happened?"

"I'm not sure yet, Dr. Hunter. It's Brenda's heart monitor. The boy must have pressed a button."

"No," Ruma piped in defensively. "I could see him quite clearly the whole time and I know he didn't touch a thing."

The tall doctor's glassy stare fell on Ruma and the strange look on his face made her feel uneasy.

Bowes was fiddling with the heart monitor as he introduced them. "This is Brenda's daughter-in-law and her grandson."

Ex-daughter-in-law Ruma almost said and stopped herself.

A strange jumble of emotions washed over the doctor's face. Was it recognition?

Then Dr. Bowes broke the spell.

"Dr. Hunter, go find a spare EKG unit." No response. "Dr. Hunter!"

Hunter tore his gaze from Ruma and left the room, his eyes dark, sunken pits. For a moment, he looked to Ruma more like one of the patients than he did a doctor.

The hour long drive back to New York felt like it would never end. Kavi was sitting quietly next to her, driving his *Hot Wheels* fire truck along the leg of his pants. He hadn't said much since they'd left. Kavi's habit of withdrawing into himself had become far more pronounced after Tyson had started 'coming unglued.' Ruma had even started to see hints of Kavi's anger over his father's absence. Calls home from kindergarten for hitting other children. Disruptive behavior. One day she'd left work to pick him up because he'd tried to put a plastic bag over another kid's head.

She knew that Tyson loved Kavi. Remembered how he had held her hand throughout the entire eighteen-hour delivery. The memory of it felt old and dusty. Tyson had been about as devoted to Kavi as any father should be. And then Tyson's life had started coming apart. The bond that had held the entire family together began to weaken. Before long, Ruma had started to wonder if it had ever been there at all.

"Mommy, who's tie-son," Kavi's speech was slow and careful as though he were going over a new word for the first time.

Ruma glanced over at him. His soft brown eyes looked heavy and tired.

"Do you mean Tyson?"

"Yeah, tie-son. Is that Daddy?"

"Yes, honey. That's your daddy's given name."

"It's not my name, right?"

Ruma laughed. "No, of course not. Why do you want to know?"

"It's just that lady in the bed…" Kavi trailed off the way children do when they assume adults know exactly what they're talking about.

Ruma's pulse quickened. "The woman at the asyl… I mean hospital? Is that who you mean?"

"Yeah, her."

"What about her, honey?"

"She kept asking if I was tie-son. I kept telling her no, but she wouldn't stop."

Icy fingers danced up Ruma's spine.

"Honey, that woman's in a coma. That means she can't speak or move her body. Those machines you saw around her; without them she wouldn't be able to breathe. That tube you saw going into her mouth; well, it

141

goes all the way down her throat. She couldn't possibly have spoken to you. Are you sure you didn't imagine it?"

Kavi grew quiet. Slowly Ruma's attention drew back to the road. Trees whipped by, lush with new leaves. The solid yellow line of a country road twisting and turning ever so slightly. Her inner thoughts were beginning to bubble up again when Kavi spoke.

"She did it because she loves me."

Ruma glanced over at Kavi. "Beg your pardon?"

"The woman in the hospital, she said she only put the bag over my head because she loves me so much."

The hairs on Ruma's arms were standing on end. "Kavi, I don't like this game you're playing. I don't like it one bit. That woman you saw lying in that bed can't speak, honey. She can't open her eyes or get up or walk around and she certainly can't talk. Now tell me you're lying." There was a pleading quality in her voice.

"But Mommy, she was asking me where we lived... said she wanted to come see me."

"Oh, no honey. What did you tell her? Kavi, what did you tell the woman?"

"You told me to always answer adults when they ask me a question. You said that. Didn't you always say that?" Tears were welling up in Kavi's tiny eyes.

Ruma's stomach made a slow lazy roll and she pulled the car over so she could throw up.

Chapter 22

Elias Hunter was pacing outside the Newburgh Bank of America on Lake Street, waiting to use the payphone. Inside the booth was a round little Mexican woman who hadn't the faintest idea of the importance of the call he was about to make. She couldn't, because otherwise she surely would have ended her sorry excuse for a conversation and stepped out of his way.

Old school as it was, the phone booth was a ten minute walk from Sunnybrook but probably the safest option for the kind of call he was about to make. Bowes' lack of discretion had once again worked in Hunter's favor. On his desk Hunter had found a big fat note reading:

Ruma Chaudhuri
Phone number: 212-555-7474

He had copied down the number when Bowes had sent him off to look for another EKG monitor. And if anyone had caught him sneaking into Bowes' office this time, he had an excuse. Albeit a piss poor one, because everyone knew the EKGs were stored in the basement. The one thing Hunter hadn't been able to determine was whether phone numbers dialed out of Sunnybrook were recorded in some kind of directory. He had posed the question to Terrance in what he thought was a rather casual way but saw nothing but suspicion cloud the black man's normally serene features.

"Why do you need to know that, Dr. Hunter?"

"I just do."

"Well, it just seems like a strange question."

"Do you keep a list of outgoing numbers or not?"

"I'm not sure. It might help if you told me why."

Hunter had paused, perhaps just a second too long. "I think someone's been using my phone."

Terrance's eyes widened. "You sure about that?"

Hunter was kicking himself. Telling a security man a lie like that was sure to blow up in his face, but he hadn't expected any resistance. He hadn't been able to think of a reasonable lie fast enough. "Seems like every morning I come to work my phone's been moved," he said trying to recover.

The muscles in Terrance's face relaxed. "Well, that could be Al cleaning your office. Maybe he shuffles things around a bit when he dusts."

"Yeah, maybe you're right," Hunter said, happy to be backing away from a sticky situation.

"But I'll have a word with Al," Terrance said. "Make sure he's not calling any sex lines at night." The security guard was laughing now and Hunter joined in, but neither man found the joke all that funny and both had some sense that a mutual dislike was fueling their joviality.

"No need to bother Al. But I would appreciate if you could look into it and let me know what you find."

Terrance smiled and tipped his hat. "Will do."

Hunter was sure that after the exchange they'd be keeping a close eye on the calls he made. His paranoia increased to a level that he didn't even trust using his cell phone anymore.

Outside the bank, the fat Mexican woman was reaching into her pocket and pulling out a handful of quarters. The operator must have come on and told her to start feeding the slot if she wanted to continue speaking. Hunter slammed the booth with the palm of his hand. The booth shook violently, but it was the booming sound that made the woman spin around. Her eyes found Hunter and her mouth fell open, the naked terror in her eyes unmistakable.

Heavy threads of emotion were peeling off of her and trailing into him. He could almost see it. He was feeding off of her like a vampire, sucking her dry. But instead of drinking her blood, he was drinking her fear and he was savoring every drop of it, the way a starving man might savor a juicy steak dinner.

"Get the fuck out, bitch!"

The woman scrambled out of the booth. Inside, the receiver swung back and forth like a noose. She walked briskly away, looking back over her shoulder as though Hunter were some red faced demon. He picked up the receiver. On the other end a voice was speaking rapidly in Spanish.

"This is the operator. She wasn't fast enough with the quarters." Then he flicked the actuator. In went four of the Mexican woman's own quarters and he dialed Ruma's number.

"Hello? Yes, this is Dr. Elias Hunter over at Sunnybrook. We met when your mother-in-law's heart monitor had that little mis… Yes, I know your son didn't touch any of the buttons, Ms. Chaudhuri. There was a faulty sensor in her EKG monitor so it was nothing more than a technical glitch… I'm sorry, I missed that, can you repeat… No, of course Mrs. Barrett can't speak, she's in the deepest coma possible. Level three on the Glasg… That means no motor functions of any kind… your son what?"

Hunter pulled the phone away, gripping the receiver until his knuckles turned white. "The reason for my call today, Ruma. Can I call you Ruma? The reason for my call is that I'm laying the foundations for a research paper on Brenda. The idea's already received tremendous interest from The American Journal of Psychiatry. That is to say, I believe there are aspects of her psychological makeup that need to be understood and documented. Cataloguing behavior is the basis of modern psychiatry and I believe it's imperative that I meet with you, your son and even your ex-husband. Especially your ex–husband... I don't understand. This research. The paper will help thousands of... five minutes of your time, Ruma, that's all I'm asking, just five... Hello? Hello, Ruma are you there? Hello?" A crimson flush was slowly rising up Hunter's neck and into his face. "Are you there? Goddamnit. Hello!" The phone was beeping rapidly. Hunter's fingers curled around the receiver. In a single, blinding movement, he brought the end of it down against the cradle. Shards of metal and plastic filled the air around him. He brought it down again and again. The feeling was nothing short of pure exhilaration.

And why stop there? a woman's voice said from somewhere inside his head. It was Brenda. He could feel her with him more and more lately, flitting through the wiring and circuitry of his brain, plucking at the loose ends of his central nervous system like the frayed strings of an old guitar. Never mind that he had never actually heard her speak; in ways that he didn't quite understand, the two of them had moved beyond the vulgarities of base human speech. That thought took form again in his mind.

Why stop there?

Oh the pleasure he would get from watching it all burn. Who the fuck was Ruma to stand in his way? She was going to help him, oh yes she was. She just didn't know it yet. And that's when he saw the fat Mexican woman. She was coming back. Back for round two and this time she had a cop with her. Hunter ducked out of the booth and broke into a brisk run. He was heading back to safe confines of Sunnybrook Sanitarium.

Chapter 23

Tyson was scrubbing the bathtub in his apartment for the third time that night. Not that it was dirty. You could probably eat a meal off of his kitchen floor and find fewer germs there than you would on the average person's dinner plate. But cleanliness wasn't the goal, it was only the byproduct. The real goal was staying awake and Tyson was prepared to accomplish that goal by any means necessary. A fat painful blister had formed on the inside edge of his right thumb and the stinging bolt of pain that shot through his hand every time he pressed down on it was excruciating. Tyson was thankful for the pain, since it acted as a sort of poor man's cattle prod, jarring him awake with every single movement of his tired, aching arms.

He was also jacked up on caffeine pills, which meant that his heart was clip clopping a furious jig in his chest. The major concern, apart from cardiac arrest of course, was how long he could keep this up for. In the living room, Bill O'Reilly was preparing to tear into a former DC prostitute turned business woman. On the opposite wall, the stereo was hammering out Guns and Roses' "Welcome to the Jungle."

He was trying to distract his mind from Stevens' death, without much success. He wanted to believe so badly that the man's murder had simply been a case of 'wrong place at the wrong time.' Perhaps he had startled thieves or druggies, ransacking the lab. A man like Stevens surely had a whack of enemies, all waiting for an opportunity to pounce. Or maybe some other poor soul who was also part of the study was suffering the same effects as Tyson and couldn't afford the hefty price tag Stevens was charging for a few rogue vials? Oh how he wanted one of those theories to be true. The alternative was almost unimaginable. It was enough to send streams of thick bile rushing up his esophagus.

The question he still couldn't answer was: why Stevens?

He needed someone to bounce ideas with. Someone who might be able to view his situation with a fresh set of unbiased eyes. Ruma was out of the question, as was Skip. That left one person. Judy. Tyson knew he might be coming slightly unhinged, but he could still tell when someone thought he was downright crazy. But wasn't one person's crazy another person's sane?

To say that his mother was crazy felt like a profound understatement. In one way or another, she had continued to hold a grip on him all these years. Even when he figured she was dead and buried, a tiny part of him was always positive she would come back, to reclaim what was her's. Because in her mind, Tyson belonged to her. A piece of property, that's how she'd always thought of him. He also knew that if there was any way she could come slithering back into his life, however improbable it might be, she would find it. And the frightening possibility that she might have managed to do just that left him feeling like that terrified five-year-old boy all over again.

He was reaching into his pocket for his cell when he realized he didn't know Judy's number or where she lived. She had mentioned something about having an apartment in New York, hadn't she? Up at Lake Harmony, he felt fairly confident he could find Judy's cabin. Hell, a single dirt road circled the entire lake. But he wasn't up at the lake anymore and neither was Judy. To make matters worse, the last thing on earth he wanted to do right now was call Skip and ask for her number. He couldn't forget the way she'd stayed by his side through his asthma attack and the news that Stevens had been killed. She was perhaps the only one who could give him anything in the way of help. The question which remained was whether, after everything she'd seen the other day, she would still want to?

Chapter 24

The X-ray room at Sunnybrook was dim and Hunter couldn't help but wonder why Bowes had called him in here.

Ruma filed a harassment complaint against you.

The thought kept racing through his head. He was going to be fired and Bowes had chosen a nice dark room to dampen what the old man expected was going to be a heated exchange. Except the funny look on Bowes' face wasn't stress. It was a look Hunter had seen that very first time they'd gone into Brenda's room. The same mask the Mexican woman had been wearing when Hunter banged on the telephone booth.

The old guy was scared out of his wits.

Hunter could feel strands of fear coming off of him and he lapped them up with delight.

"You're probably wondering why I've called you here," Bowes said.

Hunter nodded. The dark circles under his eyes looked heavier in the soft pool of light cast by the X-ray viewer.

"What I'm about to show you must remain under the highest confidentiality."

The grin plastered on Hunter's face wavered.

Bowes reached into a manila envelope, removed an X-ray and placed it on the view screen. The X-ray showed a bone that looked about as porous as a honey comb.

"This is a bone sample doctors removed from Brenda after her first hip transplant back in '03. I'm not sure how much you do or do not know about Brenda's medical condition, but she suffers from acute osteoporosis. Even if she could get up and start walking around, she probably wouldn't get more than five feet before falling flat on her face and breaking every bone in her body."

"I didn't know that," Hunter said, still wondering what Bowes was driving at and whether the old fuck was ever going to get there. "Not that I *would* know, since I don't have access to her medical or psych files?"

Bowes didn't seem to catch the dig, although Hunter suddenly realized that by ignoring Brenda's medical history, he had been overlooking a huge and significant part of the equation.

Bowes put up another X-ray, presumably from sometime further in Brenda's past, because this bone sample looked healthy and strong.

"How long ago were these taken?" Hunter asked.

What little humor remained in Bowes' tanned face was now completely gone.

"These were taken this morning."

Hunter took a step back.

"Dr. Hunter, when was the last time you saw Brenda?"

"Uh, the day her daughter-in-law and grandson came by, I suppose." Which made perfect sense, for although Bowes had hired him with the express purpose of pawning off his responsibilities on the eighth floor, he had continued jealously keeping Brenda all to himself. At least as much as he could.

"I made a point of seeing her first thing during my rounds this morning," Bowes said. "Given the problems we had with her EKG monitor. I was about to begin the usual series of response tests when I noticed something about Brenda's face that was different."

"What do you mean different?"

"What I mean is that I wasn't sure right then and there. Have you ever seen a woman who's come straight from the hairdresser? You might not be able to put your finger on why she looks different, but you know something about her has changed."

"So Brenda got up and went out to have her hair done?" Hunter crossed his arms over his chest. He was beginning to worry. If Bowes was going where he thought he was going then the old man might be on the verge of usurping the research paper Hunter was planning on writing. Perhaps his one chance to make a name for himself, in a discipline brimming with insecure, egocentric assholes. Suddenly, everything he'd been fighting for felt on the verge of being swept away.

Bowes pointed to the X-ray. "It was the bone scan that settled it for me. I've seen a lot of strange things in my four decades here. Fifteen years ago, we had a patient who could make blood roll down his forehead just by thinking about it.

"Dr. Hunter, every year we see a new batch of patients come to Sunnybrook. If they don't manage to off themselves within the first six months, there's a chance they could actually reach something like old age and if their luck holds, they might just die a peaceful death in their sleep.

"There's something about this place that eats away at you. I've seen young doctors fresh out of school, like yourself, looking weathered and ready for retirement after less than ten years. I've seen it time and time again, but I've never seen anyone at Sunnybrook like Brenda. I've never seen anyone come here and grow younger."

"Pardon me?" Hunter wasn't sure if he believed what he was hearing. "I'm sure there's a rational explanation."

"I hope there is, Dr. Hunter, because three months ago Brenda had her seventieth birthday, and judging from these test results, the woman lying there now isn't a day over fifty."

But it was what Dr. Bowes said then that chilled the very blood in Hunter's veins.

"What's happening to Brenda is nothing short of a medical miracle. Of course, we don't believe in miracles, but I see you've developed something of an interest in Brenda's case and so I wanted to let you know—"

Hunter rose to his feet. "Wanted to let me know what?"

"I'll be using Brenda as the subject for a research paper I intend to submit to The New England Journal of Medicine. The initial paperwork's already been filled out. At this point it's really a question of data collection, but there's a slight problem."

Suddenly Hunter felt the room spinning in slow nauseating circles. He cupped his forehead.

"There isn't much time left," Bowes said. "You see, patients in a class three coma aren't permitted to remain on state-funded life support indefinitely. There's a six month grace period I believe and Brenda has just slipped past that."

Hunter's hands came away from his head. "I don't believe what I'm hearing. First you steal my research paper and now you're telling me that once you have what you want you're going to just unplug Brenda's life support."

"Your research paper? Need I remind you, Dr. Hunter, I've been a member in high standing at

Sunnybrook for over twenty years. And no one can cease Brenda's life support without the proper authorization. We'll need consent from surviving next of kin. The proper forms need to filled in. It's an entire process and in the meantime you're going to help me get the data I need. I'm not asking you, I'm telling you."

"Get it yourself," Hunter said and stormed from the room, slamming the door behind him. He could hear the glass rattling in its frame as he stalked down the hall. A single thought was running through the twisted corridors of his brain, again and again.

"Over my dead body."

• • •

Hunter had spent the last two hours staring at Brenda in disbelief. The most noticeable change in her appearance was the tightening of the skin around her eyes, cheeks and chin. If Hunter didn't know better, he would almost have sworn she'd had a face lift.

He'd performed the usual response tests and the results were the same as always.

Nil.

But how wonderful would it be, he thought with a beaming heart, if one day soon she just opened her eyes and sat up in bed?

An imaginary Hunter straightened his tie.

Good morning, Brenda. My name is—

Hello, Dr. Hunter. I know who you are. Thank you for looking after me. You've been so very, very caring. How can I ever repay you?

Hunter had come out of that one with an erection the size of the Eiffel Tower. Not long after that, the reality of his situation had started to settle over him. Even if Bowes meant what he said about writing his own paper, it didn't mean Hunter was out of the game entirely. At least not yet. He certainly had a head start, especially when you considered the treasure trove of information he had stumbled across in her bookcase. Sure the sudden shift in her medical condition was staggering, but what sense would it make if you didn't understand the woman as a whole.

He was sitting on the floor of her room, a copy of 'The Very Hungry Caterpillar' snuggled in his lap. The contents of this one were new to him. Brenda was beginning to enter uncharted territory. She had mentioned something about children trapped in a school, their flesh burning until it became crisp and blackened. The newspaper article Hunter had found in Bowes' office—the article the head doctor kept hidden in a ratty old scrapbook—was the first thing that had come to mind. There, Bowes had set two clippings side by side. One citing how Brenda had lost her job at Collingwood Elementary and the other detailing the subsequent fire which had left five children dead.

In Hunter's mind there wasn't any question about whether Brenda had set the fire. On a professional level, his main interest lay in understanding how she could have justified such a savage act. The further he read, the more confident Hunter grew that he was about to hit pay dirt. He flipped the page; the words he saw scrawled along the margin of that page made the skin around his scrotum tighten painfully.

Unplug me.

His head snapped in Brenda's direction, not entirely sure for a panicked moment whether he'd find her in bed or on the ground, slithering toward him. He had to focus for a moment before his brain registered that she was exactly where she should be.

Hunter went back to the children's book and turned the page.

Unplug me, Dr. Hunter.

Hunter flung the book across the room as if it were a hissing snake. Heard the pages fluttering wildly before it hit the wall and fell limply to the floor.

He speared the crumpled book with his eyes, half expecting it to get up and lunge at him.

Sudden movement in his peripheral vision. He looked over and gasped.

From where he sat, it looked like Brenda's eyes were open and glaring at him.

But that's impossible.

He felt a thought pop into his head and knew it wasn't his own.

UNPLUG ME, YOU FUCK!

"No!" he screamed and scrambled to his feet. "You'll die. I swore an oath never to do harm... I swore an oath… no, there's nothing I can do."

He was staggering into his car when the full weight of it finally hit him. He would never let anything happen to Brenda. Not because of some archaic oath he had sworn—an oath he had already managed to break at least once. No, that was just an excuse and he knew it. Brenda was fishing around inside his head and he knew he was powerless to make her leave. But Hunter had no intention of obeying Brenda's order, because he couldn't stand the thought of living without her.

Chapter 25

Tyson came awake with a start. He'd been dreaming. He remembered sliding onto the sofa just after nine. The intention was to wash down a half dozen caffeine pills with an espresso chaser, that would surely have kept him hip hopping until morning. He glanced down. In his right hand was an empty mug. His lap was brown and sticky. It looked like a Chihuahua with a bad case of the runs had been sitting on his knee and Tyson knew from the smell that he probably hadn't managed to get the espresso past his lips before his eyes had sealed shut. The clock on the wall read quarter past nine.

Tyson breathed a sigh of relief.

Fifteen minutes, he thought. I *couldn't have been out for more than fifteen minutes. Surely even that wasn't long enough for anything to...*

The tapping sound drew his attention toward the balcony. A fly the size of his pinky nail was bouncing off the sliding glass door. It was trying to get outside. The breath hitched in Tyson's throat and he stood, trying not to think about where that fly might have come from. He hadn't taken more than two steps when he felt something crunch between his toes and the sensation was like walking on spilled cornflakes. He glanced down. On the floor were thousands of dead flies.

His mind was whirling with images from Skip's cottage and the ceiling of the master bedroom; a black swarming mass. Something from the other side had crossed over that night. Since his very first dose of Noxil, whatever mechanism normal people employed to keep their waking and dreaming worlds in check, had broken inside him.

And wasn't it the morning after he left Skip's cottage that Stevens had been found dead? Tyson felt his insides twisting violently into painful knots.

His lungs were beginning to tighten. He headed for the kitchen and the pot of coffee he hoped would still be warm. Next to that were the remnants of his caffeine pills.

A little shot of adrenaline, he told himself. That's all he needed. Just to smooth out the edges so he could think straight and figure out what to do next. It was only when he was half way there that he found himself hugging the wall and avoiding the center of the living room.

Good boys always listen to their mothers.

He couldn't remember how her young face must have looked to him as a child, but that queasy feeling that bit deep down in his gut every time he did something wrong had never gone entirely away.

That was a long time ago, he told himself. *You're an adult now, have been for a long time. Hell, you practically raised yourself. You aren't bound by those rules anymore.*

He was in the kitchen now, about to tip back his coffee when the brown shape under the table caught his eye. He squinted. His tired mind kept trying to form it into an overnight bag, but that was impossible because the sides were dark and slick with some kind of ooze. The top had been peeled back and folded over into three even flaps, like the ends of a rotting banana. As though something inside had pushed its way out. He touched one of the slime-covered flaps and retracted his hand almost at once. The word cocoon kept popping into his head and each time he tried to brush it away. Except each time he tried to make sense of what the hell he was seeing, that word kept glowing brighter and brighter, as if lit by a bulb inside his head.

Eventually it was blazing across his mind's eye in blinding neon flashes.

Cocoon.

But a cocoon for what?

The scratching sound was soft at first, barely audible above the ambient din in the room. Then it grew louder and Tyson couldn't deny what he was hearing. It was definitely coming from the short hallway that led to the front door. A set of claws scraping at wood. Then he became aware of the trail. Blood mixed with snot. It snaked out from the cocoon, through the dining room and around the corner to the front door of his apartment.

...on the quietest nights, if you hold your breath, you might just hear his nails scraping against the door...

Tyson scanned the kitchen, fear bubbling up through his pores. He searched frantically for a weapon. Beside the stove sat his John Lewis knife block. Inside were six knives.

Cleaver for chopping or the Sashimi?

Sashimi in hand, Tyson crept out of the kitchen and past the dining room table, where only yesterday Judy had saved his life. He pressed his back against the flimsy gyprock wall that separated the dining room from the hallway.

He waited to hear the scratching again, unable to build up the nerve to see what was making the sound. Seconds felt like hours. His heart pounded inside his chest and he could feel his breath as it quavered in and out of him.

Scrape scrape scrape

There it was.

Definitely at the front door. The more closely he listened, the more it sounded like a dog scratching to be let out for a piss. Except this dog didn't want to piss, did it? No, whatever monstrosity had slithered out from that cocoon in his kitchen wasn't interested in pissing at all. It wanted to kill.

Tyson peeked quickly around the corner and then retreated back behind the wall.

Holy fuck.

Oh, there was something there all right and it was hairless and dark brown and lying at his front door, scratching to get out. But that wasn't an animal, was it? Although his rapid-fire glance had lasted barely a nanosecond, he had seen enough to know that it was human, or at least part of it was.

But why is it on the ground? he wondered skittishly. And then it dawned on him. He couldn't remember seeing any legs. He was getting ready for another look when the scratching stopped. This time he waited nearly a full agonizing minute before he had the courage to look again. Tyson held his breath and peered around the corner.

Empty.

But both the bathroom door and the hall closet were open. Had they been like that before? Goddamnit, he couldn't remember.

He stepped into the tiny hallway that faced the front door of his apartment, the business end of the knife leading the way. On his right was the closet, jammed with winter coats and boots and a tangled mass of heavy shadow. Tyson slid the closet door shut with his free hand. Behind him was the bathroom, and unless this thing could walk through solid objects then it must be in the bathroom. Tyson flicked on the light. The fan overhead buzzed loudly, startling him. Since it was too big to be under the sink, the only other place was behind the shower curtain. The drape was dark blue, but right now he would have given his left nut for a nice boring curtain, made from clear plastic. Tyson grasped the plastic edge in a tight fist and swung it aside. He yelled as he did so and swung the knife around wildly.

Empty.

That's impossible.

He turned and the sight before him made his skin crawl. The sliding closet door was open again. Inside, he could see one of his winter coats swaying back and forth. Tyson reached for the door, and that's when it came at him, pulling itself along the floor on two skinny arms. Tyson only had enough time to feel the pressed wood and peeling paint on the bathroom door before the creature had knocked the knife away and was on him. But on him wasn't exactly right because it was scaling up his clothing, pulling at handfuls of loose fabric as it came at him. In the sheer terror that gripped him, Tyson could see it clearly now for the first time. The creature's skin was brownish gray. And it looked human. At least, it had the trunk of a human body, with impossibly thin arms. Its eyes bulged out of its sockets and its lips seemed to have receded, drawn back so the sharpened teeth that filled its mouth were constantly bared. Below the waist, apart from a thick tail, Tyson couldn't see anything resembling legs. Sure, at a quick glance, it looked human enough, but Tyson knew whatever this was, it had stopped being human long ago.

The creature was still scrambling up Tyson's shirt when he slid a hand under its chin and curled his fingers around the thin leathery skin of its neck. He wasn't sure what it intended to do once it finished climbing on top of him—maybe it only wanted to give him a big kiss—but he certainly wasn't going to stand around and find out.

Tyson cocked his right arm back and let it fly. He was aiming for what resembled a nose. His knuckles landed squarely in the creature's face and it made a snorting sound. He punched it again and blood began pouring down its face. After the third strike, he felt its grip loosen and he laid his free hand, smeared now with a kind of dark, cadaverous blood, against its abdomen and shoved the thing back into the hallway. It flew through the air, its arms scrambling madly for purchase. It hit the floor with a wet thud and went sliding into the closet.

Tyson wasn't going to wait around to see if he had killed it or not. He sprang for the front door of his apartment, swung it open and charged into the hallway, glancing back over his shoulder briefly as he took off running. That's when he heard his name being called out, about a second before the collision. Tyson went sprawling onto the ratty hallway carpet, entangled with whoever or whatever he had just crashed into. He scrambled to his feet.

"Judy!"

She was shaking her head. Above her right eyebrow was a thin trail of blood.

"Oh Judy, oh I'm sorry."

Tyson looked back and gasped. His only thought had been of escape and he saw now that he hadn't even bothered to close the door to his apartment. The half man half creature was pulling itself into the hallway, thick streams of dark blood running down its face. It looked angry.

As Judy rose to her feet, Tyson saw her eyes grow wide. "Is that a dog?" she asked.

But instead of answering, Tyson grabbed her by the arm. Run!" he shouted.

Tyson burst through the metal door into the stairway with Judy close behind, heading for his car in the underground parking garage. Jumping the stairs two and three at a time, Tyson was searching desperately through his pockets for the keys to his car. Above them the stairwell door fired open and slammed against the wall. Even from here he could hear the thing grunting as it dragged itself down the stairs. They were going as fast as they could and yet somehow, the thing without legs was catching up. He could hear the air being knocked from its lungs as it hurled itself from landing to landing.

Just ahead stood the door to the parking garage. As Tyson yanked the door open and pulled Judy through, he saw the creature scrambling down that final flight, its arms outstretched, reaching for them. He slammed the door in its face, certain that if he didn't stop soon he would surely drop to the floor with another asthma attack.

● ● ●

At 9:30p.m. Cindi Jaworski was finishing up her rounds on the eighth floor. A strange tangle of random thoughts had been roaring around her head for most of six and all of seven, but it was only as she entered through the doors onto the eighth floor that those thoughts had started to become dark and sinister. At first she'd assumed it was from the way Dr. Hunter had rushed past her earlier that evening, without so much as a hello. There was an air of excitement in his step and she couldn't help but wonder, painful as the idea might be, whether he was heading off on a date with some other girl.

But now she knew that wasn't it at all. She was starting to see flashes pulsing through her brain. Horrible snapshots of something unspeakable grunting as it pulled itself down a set of stairs on its belly. In her mind, she could tell that it was after someone and it wanted them very badly.

As Cindi approached Brenda Barrett's room, the images were becoming stronger and she now knew without a doubt why no one wanted to come here after dark. Just about every staff member at Sunnybrook could tell you a story or two about the eighth floor that would surely make the hairs on the back of your neck stand on end for a week. And most of them agreed that the funny feeling, like someone knocking around inside your brain, had to be coming from Brenda's room.

When Cindi rose up on her tippy toes to peek through the curved glass portal, she saw the EKG by Brenda's bed pinging madly. In fact, all the machines seemed to be going haywire. The sight of it frightened her, but it was the next thing that nearly made her scream: Brenda sitting up in bed, her arms stretched out before her as though she were grasping for something just beyond reach.

Chapter 26

"I want to thank you for coming all this way to meet me," Ruma said, sipping at her coffee. Sheets of rain drummed outside the tiny café and for a moment Ruma wondered if she was back in the slums of Calcutta during monsoon season.

"I know when we spoke the last time I didn't give you the warmest reception…"

"Don't give it another thought, Mrs. Barrett."

"I go by Chaudhuri now."

"Oh yes, that's right. I forgot."

Ruma studied the dark circles under Dr. Hunter's eyes, not entirely sure what to make of them. She was feeling desperate though. Desperate because something had occurred for which she had no logical explanation and she needed to speak with someone. Anyone. There was a time when Tyson would have seemed the logical and definitely the preferred choice. But that was a long time ago and if nothing else, their separation had helped to give her the kind of strength and emotional independence—successful career or not—that she'd always craved.

Sitting here now, however, the rain outside pounding the place to hell, she wasn't quite sure at what price this meeting had come. It was like inviting a Jehovah's

Witness in for a chat because you wanted some company. They'd be more than happy to oblige, but after they filled your head with crap for thirty minutes, you'd begin to wonder how you got yourself into this mess in the first place. Then you'd remember your momentary lapse of judgment.

Hunter regarded her with a detached, almost clinical expression. "What is it you wanted to talk about?" he asked.

"My son, Kavi, isn't prone to making up stories; I just wanted to start by laying that out."

"I know perfectly well he had nothing to do with Brenda's—"

"That's not why I asked you here," Ruma said. "Frankly, I don't care about that. I know it sounds cruel, but if he had hit a button and switched off her life support, I think the world would be a much better place."

The change in Hunter's expression was so startling that Ruma grew quiet for a moment.

"I know you're a doctor and you probably hate hearing when people say things like that, but she's brought a lot of misery to my life. Indirect misery, of course, but misery nonetheless. Whatever it was she did to Tyson, and I'm not only talking about what the papers reported that day they found him with the plastic bag... I'm talking about what it must have been like day to day. Tyson's never been able to move past that trauma. He's still a scared little boy, trapped in a man's body."

Hunter fiddled with his coffee cup, spinning it in a slow circle.

"But none of this was why I called you here. Something strange happened when Kavi and I went to see Brenda at Sunnybrook and I haven't been able to set it straight in my head since then."

Hunter raised an eyebrow. "Strange?"

"Well, from what I understand, people in a deep coma can't communicate at all, right?"

"Right," Hunter replied and even Ruma caught the way he had drawn the word out, as though he knew exactly where this was headed and wasn't sure he wanted anything to do with it.

"I know it sounds... well... crazy, but when we were in there, I swore I saw the two of them having a conversation."

"The two of who?"

"Brenda and Kavi. I saw him speaking to her. Standing by her bed as though she was asking him questions and he was answering them."

"Is that it?"

"I know how all of this must look. In Calcutta, the streets are brimming with Swamis and superstition. Must be an East Indian thing. But I assure you, Dr. Hunter, I'm a levelheaded, skeptical woman. I'm certainly not blind and when I see something that doesn't add up, I need to understand it."

"So it looked to you as though your son was speaking with Brenda?"

"In the car on the way home, he brought it up on his own. I never asked or prompted him in any way. He just came right out with it."

Hunter moved the coffee cup aside and leaned closer. "Tell me exactly what he said."

"He said she asked for his name, said he looked an awful lot like his father did when he was young. Then she wanted to know where we lived. She asked for our address and when I heard that, that's when I lost it."

"And did Kavi give it to her?"

"Yes."

"Has Kavi been demonstrating any unusual behavior since then?"

"Unusual?"

"Talking to himself, imaginary friends, nightmares…"

"That's partly what I'm afraid of. It's the reason I went to Sunnybrook in the first place. You see, my ex-husband's been suffering from nightmares and insomnia for over six months now. Last week he joined a drug trial that was supposed to treat PTSD and he's been acting strangely ever since. I'm afraid that whatever psychosis he might be suffering from..." Ruma's voice trailed off. "I'm afraid Kavi might inherit it."

"You said your husband's nightmares started around six months ago?"

"Yes, in September."

"Can you be more specific?" Hunter asked, taking her hands. "Think. It's important."

"Labor Day weekend. I remember because we were at my parents' and on the Friday night, Tyson woke up screaming. Scared the heck out of me. My parents never approved of him, they're very old fashioned, and that night I just chocked it up to nerves."

Hunter's jaw slacked, his eyes staring off into empty space. "Labor Day fell on the sixth this year, didn't it?"

"I believe so. Is that important?"

"I'm not sure, maybe. September sixth was the same day Brenda Barrett slipped into a coma."

Chapter 27

Tyson punched the end call button on his cell phone with his thumb and swore. "Why isn't she picking up?"

He and Judy barreled down Columbus Avenue, travelling a fair bit over the speed limit. A black minivan pulled out suddenly and Judy gasped.

Tyson swerved, narrowly avoiding it. Judy grimaced, clutching the passenger side handle.

"Slow down or you're going to get us killed," she said.

Tyson nudged his foot off the accelerator by a hair. Then he pulled out his cell phone and rang Skip.

"Skip, I need your help."

"Tyson?" The concern in Skip's voice was unmistakable.

"I need to get a hold of Ruma. I think she and Kavi may be in danger."

"Ty, Kavi's here with me."

An inexplicable and blinding sting of jealousy suddenly gripped Tyson. "Is Ruma there too?"

"No, she's meeting with someone. Asked me to watch Kavi for a while. I'm not great with kids, Ty, you probably know that better than anyone, but I gave him some chocolate ice cream and he seemed real happy after that. He's sleeping in the other room now. He's perfectly safe."

"Yeah, chocolate ice cream's his favorite. Skip, would you do me a favor and check to see that he's all right?"

Skip paused for no longer than a second and it seemed to last ten minutes. "Sure," he said.

"Thanks. Listen, don't go anywhere, Skip. Judy and I will be over in a few minutes to pick him up."

"Judy?" Tyson heard Skip start to ask, but he'd already hit the end call button and Skip's voice floated away.

Tyson was a mess. His mind was swirling madly. His hands shaking, his mouth bone dry. He felt like a junkie again. But he hadn't had a chance to take the caffeine pills that were still sitting on his kitchen counter. He knew the signs well enough to know he was about to come crashing down.

He pushed on the accelerator and flew across West Fifty-Seventh Street at record speed.

Judy looked over at him in the darkness. She was beautiful, and he could see that even in his peripheral vision. "I think it's about time you told me what the hell is going on here," she said. "You're not some kind of drug dealer, are you?"

Tyson let out a nervous giggle. "I wish it were that simple."

But Judy didn't even crack a smile. "Why don't you pull over at the corner here and let me out. I'll take a cab home."

"I don't think that's safe. That thing you saw at the apartment—I have a feeling it's not just after me. It may have already killed the one person who could make all of this go away. If I'm right, there's no telling who it'll go after next. Look, I know it might not sound like much, but right now you're all I have."

"I'm flattered. Really I am. But ten minutes ago something I don't have words to describe was chasing us down the stairwell of your building. I can't stop hearing it grunting. I feel like I'm stuck in a nightmare I can't wake up from."

"You are," Tyson said without a moment's hesitation. "You're stuck in my nightmare."

He could see her staring at him, as the lights from the oncoming traffic flickered across his face.

Tyson slowed the car to a stop before a red light. He was gripping the steering wheel with both hands.

That's when he decided to tell Judy everything he knew. How it had started was perhaps the clearest thing of all. The nightmares. The months without sleep; the way his life had started falling apart. Finally, he broached the craziest sounding part of all; that people and things from his dreams were somehow finding their way into his waking life. That mixing Noxil with other powerful pharmaceuticals had done something to his brain to open a doorway to another reality. One he had no idea how to close. The only saving grace was that whatever came through didn't seem to be able to stay for too long. Losing the million dollars and the Star Wars action figures he'd loved as a child had been proof positive of that.

"You know those drug commercials where they show you people running through the streets having the greatest day of their lives? And you have no idea what the commercial's about until you see the picture of a pill or something."

It looked like Judy was still trying to absorb everything Tyson had been telling her. "Yeah, what about them?"

"Well, right now I'm the schlep who ended up as one of those statistical anomalies they rush through at the tail end of the commercial. You know that last bit about 'may increase the risk of cardiovascular problems, heart attack, ruptured spleen, and death.' Maybe if I hadn't been so rash I might have remembered the golden rule."

"You mean do unto others…?"

"No. Nothing in life is free."

● ● ●

"Where's Judy?" Skip asked Tyson who was busy fidgeting with the pencil in his hand, wagging it between his fingers like the tail of dog, happy to see its owner.

"Down in the car," Tyson said. "She had to make a phone call. Where's Kavi?"

"Still sleeping."

Tyson went to move past him, but Skip didn't budge.

"You've put me in a real awkward spot here, Ty. What's Ruma gonna say when she comes by to get him and I tell her 'oh he's gone with his daddy'? You damn well know she's gonna blow a gasket."

"I wish I had the time to explain everything right now, ol' buddy, but if I don't get out of here in the next few minutes, something's gonna come waltzing through that door that'll turn your hair white as snow. Keeping you as far away from Kavi and Ruma as I can is the only way to keep you safe."

Skip stepped aside.

Tyson found Kavi snuggled in a tiny corner of Skip's king-size bed. He shuddered at how young and vulnerable his son looked. When Tyson scooped him up, Kavi stirred in his arms.

"Mommy?"

"No, it's Daddy. We'll see Mommy soon enough."

Skip stood by the living room window, looking out at something on the street down below. "I don't know what you did to Judy up at the cottage, but she hasn't been returning my calls lately."

"I didn't know you two had a thing."

"We don't," Skip answered sheepishly, "but that wasn't from lack of trying."

"I guess she knows a real man when she sees one."

Skip smiled. "I guess so. Give her my best, would you?"

"Will do. And lock this door after we leave and don't open it for anyone you don't know."

Skip crossed his arms over his chest. "Tyson, you're really starting to scare me."

Tyson looked back at his friend. "Good."

Chapter 28

Hunter sat in his car, parked in front of Ruma's house, and the only emotion he could feel was disgust. Disgust at himself for following her home, for acting like a two-bit stalker. He honestly didn't know why he had followed Ruma from the coffee shop. If a cop had tied him up to a lie detector and given him the third degree, he probably would have passed with flying colors.

"Why did you follow Ms. Chaudhuri home?"

"I don't know."

Long pause.

"Looks like he's telling the truth."

Maybe he wanted her address and didn't think Bowes had stashed it anywhere in that junk heap he called an office. Or maybe there was something about a woman at the height of vulnerability that excited him.

Earlier tonight at the coffee shop, Ruma had been talking about her strange experience at Sunnybrook and nearly the entire time he had been fantasizing about tying her up and hurting her. Not sexually. No, it wasn't quite the sex he was after, but something far more interesting. Far grander. Communion with God. Wasn't that how Brenda had put it in one of those little journals of hers? But which God was he courting?

Hunter thought of that patient he had tortured with the needle and then of the Mexican woman in the phone booth and couldn't help wondering what special kind of monster he was becoming.

Inside the house, Ruma was heading into the kitchen. She was...

● ● ●

...still reeling from the bombshell that Dr. Hunter had laid out for her. But what could it mean? Ruma fingered a scrap of paper. A note to herself. One of the few she had made during her meeting with Dr. Hunter. On it was a date: September sixth. And below that: "Tyson's nightmares and Brenda's coma. What are the odds that both started on the same day? Coincidence?"

The idea that Brenda might have something to do with it—her remote location and physical condition aside—had seemed like the kind of mumbo jumbo her own mother would often babble on about. Black magic, she called it. You couldn't take a step through the streets of Calcutta without meeting someone who was dead certain they were being cursed. But here? In America?

That acute sense of unease had magnified as Dr. Hunter told her how Brenda's brain waves were off the chart. She'd apparently always been an exceptionally intelligent woman, only now her readings were so far beyond that. But the biggest question that begged to be answered: how was Brenda's coma connected to Tyson's nightmares?

She had kept all this from Tyson because, quite frankly, she wasn't sure what she would find after visiting Sunnybrook and then after meeting with Dr. Hunter today. She knew now she couldn't keep it from him any longer. He would be angry with her for going behind his back, but more importantly, he might be the only one who could make sense of what Dr. Hunter had told her. Her attention shifted to the kitchen phone where the message light was blinking.

Ruma lifted the handset and dialed her retrieval code. As she waited, her nose curled at the strange scent in the air.

Smells like... Christmas trees.

The woman from the phone company was asking her to hit one at about the same time that she saw the dead flies on the kitchen table. Ten of them. And they formed a perfect circle and Ruma felt that vague disquiet return in full force. The same one she'd felt in Brenda's room the other day and again, on the way home, when Kavi had told her about the conversation he and Tyson's comatose mother had been having. The conversation where she had asked Kavi for their home address.

Seeing Kavi's smiling face in her mind's eye made her heart skip a beat. She had been so preoccupied with meeting Dr. Hunter, and then afterward, with the consequences of what she'd learned, that she'd forgotten to pick Kavi up from Skips' place.

She was about to hang up when the first message started playing. It was Tyson and he sounded out of breath.

"I've been trying to reach you forever, Ruma. You and Kavi could be in grave danger. I don't have time to explain right now. Take Kavi to a motel and call me when you're safe."

Tyson's next message nearly sent Ruma into hysterics.

"Kavi's with me. I picked him up from Skip's just now. Whatever you do, don't go home."

Ruma's first inclination was to call Skip and give him the biggest bitch out session of his life. Her hands were trembling. She had entrusted Kavi to him and what had he done? Turned him over to the one man who might just be on the verge of losing his mind. And this by Skip's own admission.

The piece of paper with Skip's number on it was fastened to the fridge with an old Pizza Hut magnet.

When she turned to grab it, she spotted something that made all the blood drain from her face.

It was coming up from the basement. A single paw—or was that a hand?—planted on the kitchen tile as though it were playing a game of statue and it was Ruma's turn to close her eyes.

Her first thought was that the Anderson's Pit Bull from next door must have wandered in through an open basement window. Except her basement didn't have any windows and whatever was connected to that hand was no Pit Bull.

It emerged and Ruma screamed. The face staring back at her was human, albeit barely. Its skin looked gray and worn. Its lips were receded and corpselike, revealing a set of sharp-looking teeth. But it was the long curving claws on the creature's hands that made the greatest impression. She stood watching it, with an acute look of horror on her face. Ruma realized she was in a world of trouble.

The creature pulled the rest of itself into the kitchen with its long skinny arms and Ruma saw for the first time the reason for its strange form of locomotion. Where she had expected to see legs, the creature had only a compact and stubby tail that swished from side to side.

A thick line of what looked like afterbirth trailed behind it and as it came forward, she could see it sniffing at the air. Sniffing at her. Was it confirming it had the right person? A legless corpse. That's what it looked like and she wanted to scream, but somehow her mouth wouldn't open.

The man thing was less than five feet away when she broke free from her paralysis and ran.

She could hear it behind her, breathing hard, almost grunting, as it scrabbled after her, its claws clicking and scrapping against the hard brown tiles.

Ten feet from the front door, she realized her mistake. East Harlem hadn't been a dangerous place to live for years, but the worry wart in her had insisted that each of the front door's three deadbolts be latched. Now that little obsession for safety was taking on a deadly and rather ironic new twist, since with the door so securely bolted shut, she knew she would never get it open in time. Ruma spun on her heels. There was a blur of motion as she came about and it took her panic-stricken mind what felt like an eternity to realize that it had leapt in the air after her. She ducked and the creature went careening over her head.

The creature crashed head first into the door and collapsed to the ground. Ruma scurried to her feet and saw that it wasn't moving. Its face was bleeding profusely, and she realized with a chill that its jaws had been open as it sailed through the air.

But it isn't dead, she thought hysterically. It's playing possum. Wants me to walk over there and pull it away from the door and that's when it'll strike.

Blood oozed down the creature's face.

Blood meant it could be hurt and hurt meant it could be killed. Ruma knew she had to find something she could use to bash its brains in. She stumbled into the family room, numb from the waist down, her eyes scanning from left to right and seeing nothing. She staggered over to the fireplace and plucked up the black iron poker which sat resting against the hearth. It felt solid in her hands and well suited for the task.

Ruma was still weighing the object in her hand when she became aware of the noise behind her. Long nails scuttling along the hard wood floor. She spun. Nothing was there. Even the small patch of hallway she could see was empty.

Her hand gripped tightly around the poker's hard metal handle. She wanted to take a look in the hall, to see if it was still lying there, but a little voice inside told her it was gone.

There was a phone in the kitchen, the same one she had been about to use when she'd seen the thing coming out of the basement. But to reach it, she would have to cut through the hallway and once there she would be vulnerable. No, she would make a break for it and go across the street to the Henderson's.

Heart pounding, Ruma crossed the room and stopped. The noise she heard was faint and hard to identify, but it seemed to be coming from Kavi's room.

Except he wasn't home... right?

For a moment her stomach churned with doubt. He was with Tyson. She'd heard the message on the machine, right? But what if Tyson was in the throes of some mental breakdown? Maybe Skip had just dropped the boy off moments before she'd come home. What if Kavi was sleeping in bed and that thing was in there with him?

Oh God!

How could she ever live with herself if she knew she'd left him to die? And if she was wrong and it was only the creature, then she would gladly cave its head in with the poker. She didn't have a second to lose.

To her right was the front door. It was damaged and around it lay bits of broken glass and wood, but she saw no sign of the monster that had leapt at her. To her left was Kavi's bedroom and she headed in that direction.

She walked on the balls of her feet as quickly as she could. If it was there she might be able to sneak up and put its light out forever with a single well-placed blow.

Ruma nudged open the door and gasped. For a moment, she blinked, unable to comprehend what she was seeing. Her initial scan of the room had produced at least one positive result: Kavi wasn't there. The covers on his bed were still neatly folded, the way she'd left them that morning. On the floor, the large plastic container where Kavi kept his Hot Wheels had been dumped on the ground. But instead of a huge pile, the tiny cars were lined up neatly in three tight rows. And hanging over these rows was the man-thing, a toy car clutched in each hand. It was playing with them. Lining them up exactly the way Kavi liked to do. Maybe even the way Tyson had done when he was young. For a moment, the man-thing no longer seemed like a man at all. Suddenly Ruma realized it was a young boy.

It was only when it looked up at her and snarled that she snapped back to reality. She was staring into the infinite depths of its inky, soulless eyes and in her mind's eye she could see it hovering over her dead body, the same way it was hovering over those toy cars.

Ruma raised both arms over her head, the poker scraping the ceiling as she did so. The creature lunged at exactly the same moment. This time Ruma hadn't quite been expecting it and for a split second, she forgot what had happened in the hallway, not five minutes before. She was clubbing a baby bird with a broken wing, that was all.

She was at the top arc of her swing when its jaws closed solidly around her left shoulder. A gush of foul smelling liquid jetted from its mouth and Ruma screamed and writhed in agony. Her entire shoulder seemed to melt and almost immediately her left arm fell to the floor, twitching, the severed flesh still bubbling under the cotton blouse she was wearing.

But the boy-thing was still on her. It would go for her neck in a moment and then it would all be over. She still held the poker in her right hand, and through the blinding pain, she stuck the point against its throat and rammed it home with everything she had. The creature let out a hoarse cry and fell to the floor. This time, Ruma didn't hesitate. Up went the poker before she sent it arcing through the air and into the thing's skull.

Spittle flew from her lips as she hit it again and again. Soon the seams in its skull had come apart completely and a blackened, sickening mess that might once have been a brain came spilling out. Even then, its hands continued to claw at the ground, pulling itself toward her. Her last swing connected with the vertebrae at the back of its neck. There was a noise like dry twigs being snapped over someone's knee and it finally lay still.

She was exhausted and bleeding excessively from a gaping wound where her arm had once been. Ruma collapsed next to her severed and she looked at it queerly. Slowly the adrenaline was seeping out of her system and with it came the onset of excruciating pain and the stark realization that if she didn't do something quick, the creature wouldn't be the only one lying dead on the floor.

Every movement sent lightning bolts of pain coursing through her body. Slowly, Ruma rolled onto her good side and as she propped herself up with the poker, something drew her attention. In the dim light of the room she could barely make them out, but then again she didn't really need to because she could hear them and there probably wasn't a person on earth who didn't know exactly how they sounded.

Flies.

She wasn't sure how they'd gotten in nor how they had caught the dead creature's scent so quickly, but there they were, dozens of them.

They were landing on the creature's shattered head, seeming to be melting into it. And it couldn't have been longer than a minute before that head stopped looking like a torn sack filled with bloody meat. No, it was starting to fill out, to look like a head again and the more flies that landed, the more its skull seemed to stitch itself back together.

Ruma tried waving them away with her hand.

She stopped abruptly when she saw the thing's fingers start to twitch.

"But I killed you," she said out loud and imbedded in her tone was the sense that some golden rule had been broken. The creature was cheating.

Get up, Ruma! Get up and get out of here as fast as you can!

Ruma clambered to her feet. Her intention had been to buy herself some more time by whacking at it before she fled.

The creature vetoed that when its hand grabbed the poker before Ruma could firmly plant her feet. But strangely she wasn't thinking about herself anymore. She was thinking about Kavi. Wondering if he was with Tyson. Hoping he was safe, if there was such a thing as safe from a thing like this.

The creature rose up on two spindly arms. Its head was grotesquely misshapen. One eye was gone completely and most of its teeth were broken, but it was smiling. It could see the look of terrified disbelief plastered on Ruma's face and that made it happy.

● ● ●

Hunter was sliding the car into drive when he heard the loud booming sound coming from Ruma's townhouse. Then he noticed the odd shape of her door. From here it looked like it was bowing outward. And was that light from inside spilling out through a series of cracks? For a moment Hunter wasn't sure what to do. He sat watching that door, transfixed, somehow expecting it to keep pushing out like some great lung until it exploded. But it didn't. The house was quiet and Hunter nearly talked himself into driving away. It didn't take a genius to realize something was fundamentally wrong. Drawing on an increasingly distant and vague sense of humanity, he found himself stepping out onto the cold, hard pavement and moving toward Ruma's house.

If he had been thinking clearly he might have had time to talk himself out of it. He might have listened to that little voice growing louder in his head now telling him not to interfere. Telling him to get back into his car and drive away.

Brenda?

The townhouse was just ahead. The door had been badly splintered. Only something very strong or very angry could have caused that kind of damage.

He brought his eye to one of the cracks and peered in. A long hallway with what looked like rooms on either side, but no Ruma. He was about to call her name when he heard an unearthly shriek. In med school he had read about battlefield surgeries during the Civil War, where surgeons had been forced to perform amputations without any anesthetic. Those haunting shrieks of pain had stayed with those doctors for the rest of their lives and Hunter thought he knew now what they had tried in vain to describe.

He kicked at the door. It was slowly coming apart. Too slowly. Finally with a well-placed blow, he was inside and running down the long corridor. On the wall were pictures of a woman and her young son. Ruma. A man in some of them. Was that Tyson? No time, he scanned each room as he passed. Kitchen. Family room. Bathroom. The whole time he was acutely aware of the disquieting silence and what it might mean.

One room remained at the end of the hall and he was now certain that was where the horrible scream had come from.

Hunter stood in the doorway, his eyes slowly

adjusting to the darkness. Then the muted shape of a body lying on the floor began to come into view. Light brown skin, black hair. The body was horribly mutilated, but still he knew it was her, if only because she'd been wearing that same suit when they'd met earlier that night. Hunter had seen his fair share of dead bodies before, that was nothing new, but this…

Less than an hour ago they had been speaking and now… now Ruma barely looked human.

Hunter's pulse raced, but guilt dulled his fear. If he'd only got here sooner.

You'd be dead too, Brenda's voice said from somewhere inside him.

The realization that whoever had done this was still there chilled him. He was turning to run when a thin band of light from the hallway cut across the bed. Something was lying there, hiding amongst the child's plush toys. But what really caught Hunter's attention were the thing's eyes: black and soulless, they were shark's eyes. Hunter blinked and the next thing he knew the creature sprang from the bed and knocked him off his feet. Hunter's head hit the floor and he saw stars dancing before his eyes. But even through the haze he could still make out his attacker; a hideous creature with a faintly human face and the deformed body of a monster. In another second he would look like Ruma, torn open and spilled out onto the floor. He had seen how it had shattered the door and knew he didn't stand a chance of escaping.

The creature studied him with those two bottomless eyes. Its head tilted, the way a dog's head might tilt when it isn't sure what to do.

Its jaw came slowly unhinged and Hunter saw rows of serrated triangular teeth, all bent back. Hunter's first thought was that whatever this was, the shape and angle of those teeth told him one thing: this was a carnivore.

He expected the teeth to clamp down on his neck with excruciating pain and for the world to go black shortly after, but instead, the creature leaned forward, extended its thick putrid tongue and dragged it up his cheek. Then in a blur of speed its long arms snapped out, grabbed hold of the door frame and propelled it from the room. Hunter could hear it grunting as it clawed its way down the hall. He had just enough time for one quick glance before he saw it disappear into the night.

Only then did he notice that instead of legs the creature had a short little tail. And seeing that tail jogged something loose from his research into Brenda's past. When the police had found young Tyson, clinging to life with that plastic bag around his head, hadn't they also found the remains of his older brother, Alexander, sitting placidly on a child's bed, surrounded by plush toys? And hadn't that brother suffered from sirenomelia; a rare genetic mutation where a child's legs fused in the womb to produce a tail-like appendage? *But that child had died years ago*, Hunter thought. The creature couldn't possibly be him.

Chapter 29

The man at the desk didn't look up from the magazine he was reading until Tyson stepped into his light.

"N'I help you?"

"I'm here to see my wife."

A strand of the man's thinning hair slid out of place as he fixed Tyson in the crosshairs of his beady little eyes. He licked the pads of his fingers and coaxed the rebellious hairs back into place. There was a ledger beside him with bold black letters which read "Kings County Medical Examiner." He pulled back the cover and leafed through pages the way a hotel clerk might leaf through a register.

"Her name?"

"Ruma Barrett."

The clerk ran his finger down the page and then stopped. "No Ruma Barrett here. I have a Ruma Chaudhuri, and a Rumena Carter, but—"

"Chaudhuri," Tyson replied, trying to ignore the giant fist squeezing his insides to jelly. The man with the thinning hair rose, the expression on his narrow face had inexplicably morphing from indifference to sympathy. Tyson wondered if the man had seen the look of pain on his face and could find little solace in playing the asshole anymore.

The clerk's hands trembled as he closed the register. "Right this way, sir."

Tyson followed the man through a set of wide double doors which read 'Authorized Personnel Only,' when it dawned on him. That hadn't been empathy Tyson had felt trickling out of the man's pores like hot wax. The clerk was frightened. Maybe it had something to do with the state of Ruma's body. He could see it now, laid out before him on a cold metal table. She had been zipped into a plastic bag like a sandwich. The bag was opaque and Tyson noticed the pink and brown mound of flesh within. Not enough yet for any kind of positive ID, which was the reason he'd been called in the first place, but more than enough to tell that something awful had happened to her. A sick feeling rose up from the depths of his bowels and he fought to suppress it. The clerk pulled at the zipper and mercifully stopped just shy of her neck. Tyson could see enough to know he didn't—or couldn't—take seeing anymore of the woman he had once loved with every inch of his soul. He could feel the clerk's shifty eyes burning into him. The man was waiting for his confirmation.

"That's her," Tyson said, numbness running down his spine and into his legs.

"I'll just need you to sign of few documents before you go. Just a legal formality, really. So we can confirm this is your... ex-wife."

The words stung and managed to add a level of morbid finality that somehow surpassed seeing Ruma's mangled body, lying on a cold, drafty slab.

Tyson nodded absently. His mind was retreating into a warm memory which right now felt about as welcoming as a down-filled bed. He was thinking about the day he had proposed to Ruma. Nearly four months pregnant with Kavi, her belly was already starting to show. They were in Central Park, enjoying a beautiful summer

188

afternoon when the music had started. You're the One that I Want, from the musical Grease. Ruma's favorite. Groups of picnickers had begun to rise and dance, a handful at first, then dozens. By the end, there were well over two hundred of them. The entire thing was magical to watch; all of them moving in unison, each of them fixed on Ruma and the expression of surprise and elation plastered all over her face. The song was nearly over when a little girl emerged from the crowd and handed Ruma a tiny box. In it was a ring and that's when Tyson asked her to marry him. She'd held her ringed hand in the air, fingers splayed while the sun's rays had danced off its smooth surface. He had read an article about something called a flash mob back in 2003 and the idea had always stuck with him. Of course, this little 'idea' of his had cost him over five grand, but catching Ruma off guard and seeing those tears of joy streaming down her round cheeks had been worth every penny. That day in the park she was radiant and that was how he would always remember her.

"And there is the matter of her personal effects."

Tyson felt himself jerked back into a stark, cold room and a thin little man with a pointed face.

"Beg you—"

"Her things. What would you like us to do with her things?"

"Where was she found?"

"You'll have to talk to the cops about that. I'm sure they'll be in touch."

I'm sure they will, Tyson thought.

The clerk handed a manila envelope to Tyson. He held a clipboard and pen in his other hand. "I need you to sign here, here." He flipped a page. "And here."

The envelope was light, which was unusual since Ruma never went anywhere without a purse brimming with crap.

She must have been at home when it happened and that sick feeling seemed to come back all at once.

He emptied the envelope onto the metal table in front of him.

The first item to drop was a long silver chain. Hanging from the end of it was her wedding ring. Unconsciously his hand slipped into the pocket of his jeans, his fingers finding the smooth edges of his own wedding band. He felt himself almost collapse onto the metal table, sobbing uncontrollably.

Even after everything I put you through, he thought. *You still never gave up on me.*

Tyson cleared his tears away, distinctly aware of the clerk fidgeting nearby. The envelope contained two more items. The first was a compact. This wasn't a big surprise. In spite of her natural beauty, she would never leave the house without putting on at least a modicum of makeup. He had made the foolish mistake once of suggesting she was stunning enough without it.

"Would you ever leave the house without your wallet?" she had asked him.

"No, I can't say that I would."

"Well, nor would I without putting my face on."

He looked over at her face, the one peering up at him from between the set of plastic sheets, unable to reconcile the Ruma he'd known and loved and the Ruma lying torn and mangled before him.

He would never be able to make peace with the stark and soul shattering reality that she had died because of him. He would live with the guilt for the rest of his life. His eyes started to fill with warm salty tears again. Through the blur, he saw the final item slide from the manila envelope. A scrap of paper.

It was a note, written in Ruma's hand:

September sixth. Tyson's nightmares and Brenda's coma. What are the odds that both started on the same day? Coincidence?

190

Tyson slipped the items into his pocket. But what could that mean? And how did she know the date his mother had fallen into her coma? Tyson was on his way out of the morgue—mumbling to himself—when he bumped into a man who identified himself as Detective Anderson.

Chapter 30

"Just the person I wanted to see." Anderson's bulky frame filled the doorway like an unmovable colossus. His thick hairy fingers danced along the door frame. "You saved me having to pay you a visit."

"It's been a real bad day so far, Detective."

"I'd say you've had a bad week. I only have a few simple questions for you."

The reception area of the Kings County Medical Examiner's office had a series of plastic fold out chairs and Detective Anderson motioned to two in the corner.

Tyson went over and took a seat. Anderson removed a notebook and a pen marked NYPD along the body.

"First off, can you tell me where you were last night at twelve thirty in the morning?"

"I was picking my son up from a friend's place."

"Why was he there?"

"Ruma had dropped him off earlier that evening."

"Are you in the habit of picking your son up from the babysitter?"

"No, but when Ruma didn't show up I got worried."

"Worried she was with another man?"

"No, worried she'd forgotten him."

"Do you remember leaving your ex-wife a message last night?"

Tyson paused. "Yes."

"You were warning her that her life was in danger. Tyson... can I call you Tyson?"

"Sure."

"Tyson, why was your wife in danger?"

"You wouldn't believe me even if I told you."

"Try me."

Tyson ran an unsteady hand through his hair. "Detective Anderson, do you believe in the bogeyman?"

Anderson's poker face was astounding. "You mean the bogeyman that hides under your bed, waiting to snatch at your feet? Sure, when I was a kid. Then I grew up and realized the world doesn't need bogeymen. There are plenty of people who do very bad things."

Tyson was looking at the floor. "Are we almost done?"

"Almost," Anderson said.

He had moved into Tyson's personal space now and it was clear the detective wanted nothing more than to lock him up and throw away the key. "Can you tell me why Ruma might have gone to Sunnybrook Asylum two days ago?"

Surprise spread across Tyson's face. It wasn't lost on Detective Anderson.

"No, I didn't know that she had."

"Your mother's up there, isn't she?"

"I don't have a mother, Detective. But I'm sure you already knew that."

"I see. One final question, if you'll indulge me. I know you've been through a lot already."

Tyson remained quiet, knowing Anderson's query for permission was all part of his charade of politeness.

"It's just puzzling to me that the bodies of both Ruma and Dr. Charles Stevens demonstrated a rather peculiar kind of oddity. Nothing the medical examiner had really seen before. See, in each case the flesh had been partially dissolved by a substance ten times more powerful than hydrochloric acid. A substance that we find in the natural world in only one other place."

"Yeah, where's that?" Tyson asked, knowing he was about to find out whether he wanted to or not.

Anderson watched him keenly. "The stomach of house flies."

• • •

They were on the interstate, heading for Sunnybrook. In the back, Kavi was staring off into empty space. Tyson hadn't exactly told him straight out that his mother had been murdered. He had decided instead to tell his son that Ruma had gone to stay with the angels in heaven.

"When is she coming back?" he'd asked.

"Never, I'm afraid." Tyson felt the tears welling up behind his eyes as he did everything he could to strangle the emotion.

The never part wasn't going over well. In the few hours since Tyson had told him, Kavi must have asked over a hundred times when his mother was coming home and why she'd decided to leave in the first place. The kinds of questions no parent wants to ever have to answer. Since then, Kavi had been sullen and Tyson worried that his son was burying the pain and confusion, much the way he had done as a child.

"Shouldn't you let the police handle this?" Judy asked. She was referring to their trip to Sunnybrook and Tyson's burning desire to find some much needed answers.

"On my way to the medical examiner's office I was beating the crap out of myself. I pray that you'll never have to see what I saw. But the note Ruma had on her, it put serious doubts into my head that maybe everything that's happening isn't completely my fault."

"What do you mean?"

"My nightmares started on the same day my mother went into a coma."

Tyson caught sight of Kavi in the back, watching him.

Judy had been quiet for a moment. "So her coma caused your nightmares, is that what you're saying?"

"I'm not sure. But I'm hoping that whoever Ruma spoke to at Sunnybrook might know. If this thing gets loose again I'm scared of what it's liable to do."

Kavi was still watching him. The toy car fell from his hands to his feet, forgotten.

"Did you sleep well, Buzz?" Tyson asked him.

Kavi didn't respond.

"What do you think of all these trees? Did you know there are trees in California that are over five thousand years old?" Tyson paused, waiting for a response that never came.

He raised his voice a little, hoping the sound of authority would shake the cobwebs loose in Kavi's head. "Son, I'm talking to you."

"Tyson, he's been through enough…"

Tyson ignored Judy's plea. "When an adult asks you a question, you answer them."

For a moment, Kavi's eyes seemed to clear. "Mommy said not to do that anymore, not after I talked to the woman."

"Woman? What woman do you mean, Buzz?"

Judy reached behind her and laid a hand on Kavi's tiny knee. "Tyson, what are you doing to the poor boy? In case you haven't noticed he's been through hell in the last twenty-four hours. Maybe we should just let him sleep."

"He's been sleeping since he found out."

"And the dark rings under his eyes? If you push him too far, the stress is liable to lower his immune system. He could end up catching some kind of bacterial infection or who knows, maybe even that H1N1. It's still going around, you know."

"You're starting to sound like—" The hairs on the back of his neck stood on end. It wasn't Judy's fault, somewhere deep down he knew that, but her words had sounded like a ghostly echo from a past he had never really stopped running from.

"What's the matter?" she asked, feeling self-conscious.

"Nothing. For just a moment you sounded like someone else. I guess I'm just trying so hard to make right what's happened and I don't know how else to do it."

They flew past a sign along the interstate.

Sunnybrook. 1 MILE.

Tyson pulled off the highway and onto what quickly became a gravel road. It couldn't have been longer than a minute or two before they heard the gasp from the back seat. Tyson could see Kavi's mouth formed into a perfect O. He was staring at something in the distance and it was only when Tyson followed his son's frightened expression that he saw the tip of what was surely Sunnybrook Asylum, poking through the trees.

Judy was back at her mother hen impression again "Sweetie, what's wrong? You feeling sick? Here, lemme check your forehead."

"He's been here before," Tyson said quickly.

"What?"

"Detective Anderson asked me why Ruma might have come to Sunnybrook, but he never mentioned anything about Kavi being with her."

Tyson could see that Kavi was listening and on some level probably understood what they were saying. That popular old expression about little pitchers having big ears suddenly came to mind and he chided himself for not being more careful earlier when he'd been speaking about Ruma.

"You've been here before, haven't you, Buzz?"

Kavi nodded. "I didn't hit a button, you know."

Tyson made a right hand turn. "What do you mean you didn't hit a button?"

"The man in the long coat said I hit a button that keeps the woman breathing, but I didn't."

"I believe you."

"I don't want to see her."

"That's fine. Was one of the nurses mean to you, Buzz?"

Kavi didn't answer.

"Listen, I can't help you out unless I know who you're talking about."

"The woman lying in the bed. She kept asking me all sorts of questions."

Tyson and Judy stared at each other in silence. "Are you sure you spoke to her, Buzz, she's in a coma?"

Kavi was quiet.

"Do you know what a coma is?" Judy asked, reaching for his hand.

Kavi nodded. "It's when you're sleeping and you can't wake up."

"Right," Tyson said. "Now listen, you're not in trouble, son, but it's very important. Did you speak to this woman?"

Kavi's voice was almost a whisper. "Yes."

"And what did she ask you?"

"She kept calling me by your name, Daddy. Over and over she kept saying it. I didn't tell this to Mommy when she asked me, 'cause Mommy was already mad at me, but the woman in the bed kept saying 'I miss you, Tyson, I miss you so much.'"

Tyson suddenly felt queasy. "Was that all she said?"

197

Kavi shook his head. "I don't really know what it means, but she said: I want you back."

• • •

Tyson was talking to a middle aged black man behind the security desk. "My ex-wife was here the other day, Ruma… Barr… no, Chaudhuri," he added a second later, hoping that might clear away the blank expression on the man's face.

"Oh yes, came in with a cute little boy, didn't she?"

Tyson guided Kavi out from behind his leg.

"Yeah, I remember her quite well. She was here to see Dr. Bowes."

Tyson saw the man's name tag now for the first time. "Terrance, it's very important that I speak with him."

The smile on Terrance's face withered.

Tyson frowned. "Don't tell me he's not available."

"I'm afraid Dr. Bowes hasn't been around since this morning."

Tyson's fists were clenching when Judy stepped forward and leaned in. She was smiling and Terrance was smiling now too, whether he wanted to or not. "We've come all the way from New York City," she said, biting her lower lip. "On your website, I saw a Dr. Hunter under Dr. Bowes' name. Is there a chance we might speak with him?"

Even from where he stood, Tyson couldn't help admiring the way her mouth moved when she spoke.

Terrance's eyes fell to some indiscernible point on his desk. His left hand was down by his waist, fiddling with the oversized set of keys on his belt.

"Give me a moment, folks. I'll see what I can do."

• • •

Ten minutes later they were sitting opposite Dr. Hunter. He was speaking animatedly to someone on the phone, all the while mouthing the words to them: "Won't be more than a minute." The doctor's eyes were wild and bulging in their sockets.

There was something disquieting about Dr. Hunter's office and Tyson couldn't quite put his finger on it. Wasn't much more than a glorified shoe box, really. Warm light from an antique banker's lamp should have made the place feel homely. So what was making the skin on Tyson's arms crawl? And he wasn't the only one who seemed to feel that way. Kavi was sitting on Judy's lap, his arms locked around her neck in an apparent death grip. Was the boy simply in shock after losing his mother? Tyson hadn't yet had time to digest some of the things Kavi had told him in the car, the least of which was having had a conversation with a coma patient. But how believable was that?

Probably about as believable as your nightmares coming to life and killing your ex-wife and a drug test coordinator.

It wasn't until Dr. Hunter had finished his conversation and went to hang up the phone that Tyson *knew* something was terribly wrong. Was that the operator's voice he had heard coming from the receiver as Hunter had replaced the handset?

"Please hang up and try your call again… please hang up…"

The crazy fuck wasn't speaking to anyone, was he? All this time and he was speaking into a dead line. Was this guy a doctor or a patient?

"So how may I help you?" The weak smile on Hunter's face only accentuated the premature aging lines at the corners of his eyes and mouth. Tyson guessed he couldn't have been older than twenty-eight or twenty-nine, but from here, the man appeared to be pushing fifty.

"Tyson is it?"

Tyson remained quiet.

"Terrance downstairs already phoned to announce your arrival. How can I help you?"

"My wife was here the other day…"

Dr. Hunter was staring at Judy now and something about his expression said that he had no intention of looking away anytime soon.

Tyson felt a pinprick of jealousy.

"Listen to me," Tyson heard himself say. "My wife is… gone and this was the last place anyone remembers seeing her before that happened, so you can understand I'm looking for some answers from you."

"The police were already here earlier and asked Dr. Bowes and myself a number of pointed questions. Frankly, I'm not sure there's much I can tell you that will be helpful. In fact, Dr. Bowes was so distraught with his handling by the police that he disappeared shortly after and hasn't been seen since."

Hunter's gaze was ping-ponging between Judy and Kavi now and Tyson's level of discomfort and annoyance was beginning to peak.

"How severe is this coma she's in?"

"Who, Brenda?"

"Of course Brenda," Tyson snapped. "Who else?"

Hunter's index finger tapped against the phone receiver. "Glasgow level three. The least responsive of any level."

"My son here says that he spoke with her, when he came with Ruma. That she was asking him questions. Is this possible?"

A strange look came over Hunter's face as he pretended to consider the question. Then a crooked smile distorted his already disturbing features. "We had a nurse report she'd seen your mother sitting up in bed last night,

200

but you'll have to believe me when I tell you that's quite impossible."

"Sitting up?"

"It sounds amazing I know, but frankly, in a situation like Brenda's, where you have someone lying immobile for such a long duration, it isn't uncommon for people to begin hearing strange voices and seeing things that aren't real. As humans, we're surrounded by a bustle of activity all day long, so it isn't a stretch to project that onto someone who's rather inanimate."

Tyson nodded in agreement, growing more and more certain that this guy wasn't quite right in the head. "And how long has she been like this? When did it start?"

"I'm not sure."

"I have a note in Ruma's handwriting that says it started in September; was this information Dr. Bowes gave her?"

"He might have," Hunter lied. "But why is that important?"

Because it was starting to look like ever since Brenda descended into that coma of hers, she'd been dancing a merry jig in Tyson's subconscious mind. But what was he going to do, open himself to ridicule before a man who was clearly unhinged?

"I'd like to see her," Tyson said instead.

"I'm afraid that's quite impossible."

"You let Ruma and Kavi in, so why can't I? I'm her son, goddamnit!"

"Please, Mr. Barrett. We're conducting a series of tests on her and I'd have to clear it with Dr. Bowes first."

He was lying and Tyson could almost smell the bullshit wafting in the air between them.

"Then I'd like to see her medical file."

Dr. Hunter laughed. "Only Dr. Bowes has those files and as I mentioned before, he's not here."

"No problem. Tell me where he is and I'll pay him a visit."

Hunter's face darkened and for a frightening moment Tyson wasn't sure if it was the poor lighting in the doctor's tiny office or whether that expression spoke of something far more sinister. "As I mentioned, Doctor Bowes is indisposed at the moment, but I'll be more than happy to pass the message along to him."

Chapter 31

Less than thirty minutes later, Elias Hunter was snaking through the bowels of Sunnybrook Asylum. Sub level three—or S3—was the deepest part of the hospital. The corridors were long and dark and overhead were Sunnybrook's entrails: water mains, heating and cooling ducts and an assortment of other pipes crammed in along the low ceiling. This was the last place anyone wanted to come and that was precisely the reason he was here. A few of the interns whispered among themselves about seeing ghosts stalk the hallways—the victims of psychiatry's more questionable past. One such story had it that a young male attendant was tasked with storing two broken beds in the basement when he saw a man come shambling toward him out of the darkness. He was wearing a torn hospital gown and had three small holes in his skull where the screws from a head clamp had been. The attendant had glanced down for no longer than a second to fetch the radio at his side, but when he looked up, the man was gone.

Hunter had feigned fright upon hearing the tale, but it would take more than ghost stories, clangy generators and a bunch of leaky steam ducts to scare him. It wasn't long before Hunter realized he could use the general fear and apprehension of Sunnybrook's basement to his advantage. Unlike the world above, this was not the kind of place people would be poking their noses on a regular basis.

Hunter made a right hand turn. Ahead of him, the hallway disappeared into shadow. But it wasn't far now. He had found it almost by accident. What looked to him like a secret ward, hidden away in the basement, that had once complete with beds and an operating theatre right next door. Of course, his discrete inquiries hadn't been able to shed much light on the kinds of operations that were going on down here, but Hunter thought he knew just the same. The apparition in the hallway had filled in that blank rather nicely.

Hunter came to a locked door and reaching into his pocket, he removed a single key and let himself in.

The man lashed to the chair by thick reams of duct tape turned to him at once. A length of tape covered his mouth, but that didn't stop him from trying to speak. Although from where Hunter stood, it looked far more like yelling.

"I can't hear you," Hunter said as he approached. Dried blood caked the man's face. A carpenter's drill rested on the mayo stand next to him. The man's eyes bulged from their sockets, flitting between Hunter and the drill. Hunter was sure that if he removed the tape the man would resume that annoying little habit he had developed of pleading for his life.

You don't have to do this, Elias. Stop this now and everything will be forgiven, you have my word. You have my word!

"No, Dr. Bowes. It's too late for any of that. People like you are a real menace. You wanted to cut Brenda's life support, wanted to steal my research, well, I'm sorry but you've gone too far. You're a sick, sick man and sick men require treatment."

Bowes shook his head violently.

"I've been rather enjoying these conversations of ours, I really have, but I can't keep you down here forever, can I? Sooner or later someone's bound to find out." Hunter's hand passed over the drill and he could see the tears rolling down Bowes' face.

"And to think what might have happened if you hadn't hired me. You'd probably be off playing golf right now, wouldn't you? Certainly, you wouldn't be any closer to understanding the true genius of Brenda Barrett. And to think you were so ready to cut her life support because of a little state regulation." Hunter bent down and inserted the drill's plug into the power outlet. Bowes suddenly stilled. Hunter craned his head. "No, you make a great point. Who does this new guy think he is? Hasn't been here a mere fraction of the time I have. How on God's green Earth does he think he can run Sunnybrook without me?"

Bowes grunted and his cheeks flared out. It looked as though he were having trouble breathing.

"The man who believes he's irreplaceable is destined to suffer the greatest fall. I'm not sure who wrote that, in fact, I might have just made it up." Hunter strolled over and tore the heavy tape from Bowes' lips. Maybe he wasn't as bored with hearing the old man plead for his life as he thought he was.

Drool ran down the side of Bowes' face. There was a puncture mark in his neck and on the table beside him was a needle filled with Demerol. Hunter had been jabbing him every few hours, mostly to keep the good doctor quiet and well-behaved.

He would have made a great patient, Hunter thought with no small amount of pride.

"This can't only be about Brenda. Elias, she's a lump of dead flesh; come to your senses, man." Bowes' words were slightly slurred, but Hunter could make them out just fine.

"She is not A LUMP OF DEAD FLESH," Hunter shouted an inch from Bowes' face. "You saw her brainwave activity, you saw her body slowly healing itself."

"Yes, she's getting younger, but have you taken a look at yourself lately? You've probably aged twenty years in the short time you've been here."

Hunter hadn't looked at himself. Didn't need to. Maybe didn't want to was closer to the truth. He'd already made up his mind that he wasn't going to let Bowes squirm his way out of this one. He came forward with the duct tape.

"Hold on, Elias," Bowes said desperately. Hunter thought the man's fear had all run out. He was wrong. "Just hold on one more minute. I've thought things over and if you feel that strongly then I won't push to have Brenda removed from life support." Bowes was crying now.

"And the research paper?"

"Dead," Bowes spat. "I'll tear all the forms up and put a match to them."

Hunter raised both eyebrows.

"I was wrong," Bowes continued. His face was a mess of snot, tears and dried blood. "I'm sorry. I'll also submit my resignation, effective immediately. And recommend to the board that you take my place. It'll all be yours, Elias. All of Sunnybrook and every single last one of its patients, especially Brenda, they'll all be yours. And you'll never see me again. I won't say a word, I promise."

Bowes certainly was a stubborn S.O.B. Although his boss' professional sensibilities had prevented him from admitting the truth, Hunter knew very well that Bowes understood just how special Brenda really was. That she could do things with her mind. Unexplainable things. It certainly explained the man's nervous demeanor around her. It was sad the way simple men were so deathly afraid of anything they couldn't cram into a tidy little box.

Of course, he would be lying if he said the thought of a snickering Dr. Bowes sprawled over Brenda's defenseless body, breathing his hot, diseased breath into her face as he made ready to pull the plug, didn't make him want to drill a hole in the man's head. But the old man's empty promises hadn't been what he was really after. It had taken hours of abuse and torture to finally extract the three little words Hunter had really been waiting to hear Bowes say.

I WAS WRONG.

Now came the fun part. Hunter strolled over to the heavy door and swung it shut.

Chapter 32

At first, all Tyson had was a name: Marlboro. The town where he'd spent the first five years of his life. He could find it easily enough with a GPS, but pinpointing the house where he'd lived was another matter entirely.

Truth was, he was running on instinct. Tyson hated to think of it that way, since it made him feel like a dog, lost on vacation and sniffing the wind to find his way home, but that was exactly what he was doing. The one distinct flaw with the analogy was that home, in the strict sense of the word, definitely wasn't where he was heading. To him, home was a place full of warm smiles and even warmer hugs. The kind of place you go to escape from a world that wants nothing more than to tear a strip off you. It wasn't all that long ago he used to know that kind of safe haven. But not anymore.

God how he hoped that when he came out the other side of this, Kavi might forgive him for what he'd put him through and that maybe somehow they might both find that warm, safe place again: together. Tyson looked over at Judy. Her left hand was behind her, resting on Kavi's tiny leg. She had a slight hint of a smile and for a moment Tyson wondered if she wasn't already there. Judy caught him staring and asked the very thing he'd been trying all the while not to think about.

"You ready to see your childhood home again?"

Tyson felt a bolt of tension run through him.

"As ready as I'll ever be." He smiled faintly. He decided he would keep quiet for the next bit. He needed time to dust off some old memories and sort through them in his head. Memories that felt about as far away and dilapidated as the ratty looking lunchbox he kept in the storage locker with the sole surviving remnants from his shattered childhood.

Before long they passed a sign.

Marlboro. Population 2339.

Ruma had always chastised Tyson for pushing things to the edge and now the edge was exactly where he had to go. What could be more disturbing than rummaging through the house where as a child you were nearly murdered?

Marlboro looked a depressing enough place. Signs of the recent recession were still visible. Tyson had counted no less than half a dozen going out of business and bankruptcy signs before they had reached the first major intersection.

"Any of this coming back to you?" Judy asked delicately.

Tyson shook his head. "Not really." The car slowed. He was trying to take in as much as he could. They rolled past a piece of green space. Park benches ringed the statue of an Iroquois brave holding a hatchet up over his head.

But that's not what Tyson saw. To him, that brave was holding an old plastic bread bag and its eyes were sparkling like sharpened dagger points. He could hear it whispering.

Mommy loves you most of all.

Judy's voice jerked him back. The car had veered slowly into oncoming traffic. Tyson spun the wheel and the car lurched, narrowly avoiding a beat up Ford Taurus.

The car's balding occupant had just enough time to flip Tyson the finger.

Tyson rubbed at his tired eyes and reached for his caffeine pills. He popped two out from the foil and placed them on his tongue. The bitter taste was a touch worse than chewing aspirin, but the psychological security he gained knowing he'd be up for the next twenty-four hours was worth it.

They drove aimlessly for the next fifteen minutes before Tyson found an intersection that looked vaguely familiar.

"We're getting closer," he said. "I can feel it."

They had driven past nearly a dozen split level houses when Tyson slammed the brakes.

Judy stuck her hands out to keep from hitting the dashboard.

"My goodness, Tyson, what's…?"

But when she followed his eyes to the house on their right, her words petered out.

"This is it," Tyson said.

The lawn was all weeds. The windows were shuttered with boards covered in graffiti. Even from the curb, he could see that a part of the bungalow's ceiling had collapsed. When he caught Judy's expression he couldn't help but wonder if he was seeing terror or awe.

Tyson killed the engine and stepped out onto the pavement. His legs felt like Neil Armstrong, back from a week-long stint in zero gravity.

"You two stay here," he said. All the saliva had suddenly gone out of his mouth.

Kavi was struggling with his seat belt. "Daddy, I'm coming with you."

"Not a chance, Buzzman, you stay here with Judy."

Judy's eyes were still locked on the house. "I'll keep an eye on him."

Tyson looked at her. "You're the expert on early

childhood development. Tell me, once I'm in there, how will I know when I find what I'm looking for?"

She glanced up at him, shielding her eyes from the sun. "If there's anything left inside after all these years," she said solemnly, "I'm sure you'll know it when you see it."

Tyson rolled his eyes. "I thought you were gonna say that."

Judy tried to smile. "Sometimes facing what scares us most helps to lessen its grip on us."

Although he hadn't been able to articulate it, he knew that was exactly why he was here.

To let go.

Tyson started for the house. But now each step felt like he was wadding through a raging river. There was some part of him that didn't want to go inside that house.

The front porch was an impenetrable fortress of junk: old sofas, broken tables, the eerie remnants of a baby stroller.

Had his mother pushed him around in it as a child? he wondered. Of course she hadn't, another voice shot back. She never let you leave the house.

Tyson circled around back and found a hole in a wall large enough for a child to squeeze through. He lay down in the tall grass and reached inside the hole. His hands encountered cool air and he grasped around until he found something solid he could latch onto. Sharp splinters of wood and brick dug into his ribs as he pulled himself through the grass and into the house. From there the place looked gloomy, seriously run down. If something were to come scurrying at him from out of the darkness—and by something he meant whatever he had seen scratching at the door of his apartment—it would have no trouble at all opening him up like a fat beetle trapped on its back. His hands clambered blindly and found a broken pipe poking up through a dirty shag rug and he used it as leverage to slide the rest of himself inside. He stood and dusted himself off, realizing he'd need to find a better way out than this. As his eyes began to adjust, the contours of the room took on a more solid form. Against the wall was an old TV with a set of crooked rabbit ears. Across from that, a battered sofa. Tyson went to it and placed the palm of his hand on the cushion. It was covered in plastic and the creaking sound it made under his full weight made his skin crawl. If ever there were any doubts that he had found the right house, they were now gone. And the more he looked around, the more plastic wrap he found. Forks and knives littered the kitchen floor, still in their protective packaging. Door handles looking new and pristine under years of grime and decay.

Tyson stood before a short hallway.

How impossibly long this looked all those years ago, he thought.

Seeing the door at the end of the hall made his heart begin to stutter. It was slightly ajar and Tyson stood for what felt like a full minute; *waiting.* But waiting for what exactly? Did he think it was going to move on its own? The feeling of *déjà vu* was overwhelming.

You're not that little frightened little boy anymore, he tried to tell himself.

He started walking toward the door at the end of the hall.

Be a good boy or Mommy will have to let the monster out.

He brushed the thought out of his mind as he passed a bedroom that may once have belonged to him. The room was gutted, and the memory—like so much of his life—seemed like a faded old photograph. His focus shifted back toward the end of the hall and the monster's room.

He approached the door and took a deep lungful of air as he raised his hand and placed his palm against the peeling frame. He pushed. Slowly. The door swung open.

Tyson braced himself, certain that when the room came into full view he would see something inside, waiting for him. Something unspeakable.

The room was dark, the windows boarded up. The only light came from a small tear in the ceiling, where the roof had fallen in.

Strangely, Tyson's fear quickly turned to disappointment. On some level, he had wanted to come face to face with whatever nasty thing he thought might be living here. But what he had found instead was a house filled with broken junk. He was wasting his time chasing ghosts.

Funny, he thought, *how so many of these fears aren't much more than a product of an overactive imagination.*

Of course there hadn't been any monster at the end of the hall. His mother was a sick woman, exactly the reason she was shacked up in Sunnybrook. But you didn't have to be crazy to scare the shit out of your kids so they would behave. Or at least behave the way you wanted them to.

If you're very quiet at night you can hear it scratching to get out.

The floor boards moaned under his weight.

The real danger wasn't being attacked by something twisted and demonic scuttling out from under a rotting bed. Those were the bogeymen adults used to mess with kids' minds. Here, the real danger was snooping around inside a house that was about as stable as a house of cards. He was thinking about finding a way out that didn't involve crawling through the equivalent of a glorified mouse hole, when something caught his eye. It was on the inside of the door and went from the knob all the way down to the floor. Tyson stooped down for a closer look, trying desperately to quell that cold, sick feeling rising within him that was telling him to run away as fast as he could.

He reached out and ran his finger along the marks. It looked almost as if long ago, something had been reaching up for the knob, but hadn't quite made it. Even with a darkened room wrapped tightly around him, he could still tell what he was seeing: scratch marks.

Chapter 33

Tyson had no sooner risen to his feet than the floorboards underneath him let out a final groan before giving way. His hand shot for the doorknob—at the time, the closest thing within reach—but fell just short and his nails scraped along the rotting wood of the door as the ground swallowed him whole.

He opened his eyes. A thin stream of light was beaming in from a tiny window above. Voices shouting, clammy hands grabbing at him, shaking him hard. A face came into the brightness, then another.

"Are you hurt?" his mother asked.

Tyson swung his arms out protectively.

"Whoa! Take it easy, Tyson." It was a panicked-looking Judy Stahl.

Tyson sat up and tried to orient himself. He had fallen through the floor into the basement and now Judy and Kavi were helping him. He tried to wiggle his toes, could feel each of them in turn moving in his shoes. At least his back wasn't broken, although it sure hurt like hell.

"I musta got the wind knocked out of me. I feel like I went a round or two with George Foreman."

"Daddy, who's George Foreman?" Kavi asked. "Did he make you fall through the floor?"

"No." Tyson was holding his head. "I should never have come inside."

"We were worried…" Judy started to say. "So we came in to see if everything was all right and—"

"Worried or not, I told you to stay put."

"You found something, didn't you?" Judy asked, looking around into the shadows as if something might be there.

"Scratch marks on the door."

Judy's face was blank.

"That thing that chased us from my apartment complex. The one you thought was a dog, well, I found it at my front door, scratching to get out, the very same way. I remember it made me think of the monster that had terrified me as a child. So I'm saying that maybe that thing is real or at least was real at some point and now, somehow, whenever I sleep, it follows me back from that other place."

"But Tyson, you're talking about memories from when you were five years old."

"I know, and trust me, I've spent my whole life trying to forget. The few snippets I remember feel more like the loose pieces from some disjointed jigsaw puzzle."

Kavi's hands were scrunching inside the pockets of his tiny jeans. "But you were sleeping when we found you, Daddy." He said the words as though his child's mind had connected two disparate facts. "Did you see him again when you were dreaming?"

Tyson and Judy both looked at each other. Kavi was right. How long had he been out? Truth be told, he couldn't say. Couldn't have been longer than a few minutes, but then again, it had taken less time than that for a cocoon the size of a hockey bag to form in his kitchen.

"This place isn't safe," Tyson said, not entirely sure yet if he even had the strength to get to his feet.

Judy rose and grabbed Kavi's hand. In the faint light, her face was a mask of tension. Tyson was getting to his feet when he saw the fly land on Kavi's forehead. Kavi swatted it away, almost absently. Two more buzzed past his nose.

"GO, NOW!" Tyson shouted.

Kavi's bottom lip was quivering and Judy pulled him close to her.

Tyson's legs were still weak as he made his way through the darkness. Slowly, the basement came into focus. Faded light bled down through a stairway across from them. Tyson could hear what sounded like Rice Krispies crunching under his feet and he didn't need to look down to know what they were. More than a dozen flies were already buzzing around each of them. One landed on Tyson's lips and he slapped it away and spat on the ground. He scooped Kavi up into his arms and started for the stairs.

A sound came from upstairs and all three of them stopped. The floorboards above them were moving. Something was in the house and it was directly above them, scurrying around frantically. Judy's eyes were like saucers.

"Daddy?" Kavi gasped.

"Hold on, son. You gotta keep real quiet right now, okay?"

Kavi stared blankly at Tyson.

Tyson could hear its nails scuttling along the loose floorboards. It was heading for the basement, as if it knew exactly where they were. Judy's eyes were transfixed on the ceiling. There was no escape. Tyson tugged on her shirt and motioned toward a corner in the back of the basement, behind a shelving unit. She nodded and for a terrible moment Tyson felt crushing guilt for having mixed her up in all of this.

A second later it was on the stairs and he could hear it

breathing. Rough scaly hands groped from riser to riser. Slowly, the three of them inched backward. Their only hope was to hide. Hide in the corner and hope it didn't see them. Or smell them. He knew charging past the beast wouldn't work, it would snatch one of them for sure. And what would happen to the two that were left as they tried squeezing through that hole in the kitchen wall? Would they even have enough time for a single scream, before it yanked them back inside?

Judy and Kavi were already nestled behind the metal shelf filled with junk. Piles of faded magazines. Torn off dolls' heads. An old box of matches. Judy was waving at him frantically to come. She seemed to do everything but shout his name. Surely she was wise enough to know the creature could hear everything they said? Tyson's back hit the wall. Judy's hand found his and pulled him to the ground next to her and Kavi. His legs bent and it fired off a sharp pain in his left knee, but the discomfort vanished entirely as he watched the thing clamber into the basement. The way it breathed sent gooseflesh crawling up Tyson's arms. That its legs had been replaced by a small fleshy tail, or that it moved around by pulling itself along the ground with its hands, didn't seem nearly as upsetting as the way it breathed. It had all the snortiness of a Pug. In fact, in the dim light, Tyson could swear its face had the same squashed shape.

When the creature raised its Pug face and drew in several deep breaths; Tyson realized what it was doing. Tasting the air. Sniffing for them. Its head swung back and forth in a wide arc, like a Komodo Dragon, and with each swing it seemed to narrow the angle of its search. Soon its head stopped, pointing directly at the three dark shapes hiding behind the prefab shelving unit.

Tyson's hand slipped over Kavi's open mouth. The boy tried to scream, but nothing was coming out.

It was less than five feet away. Its skin was grayish

brown and wet and Tyson was sure that somewhere upstairs was a trail of gore leading from a cocoon just like the one he had found split and oozing in his kitchen. The creature reached out with one of its hands.

Tyson's breath hitched in his throat. His mind raced. He would wait until its arm was all the way through the shelving and then he would grab hold of it and hope he could tie it up long enough for Judy and Kavi to escape. The muscles in Tyson's body tensed.

Then without warning, the clawed hand stopped and closed around something on the shelf. One of the severed doll's head. It had been reaching for the child's toy all along and now it was bringing it to its chest and cradling it as delicately as Tyson was cradling Kavi.

All three of them watched as the hand with the doll's head seemed to do a little dance and the creature's mouth, filled with tiny triangular teeth, opened and closed. It was hard for Tyson to even wrap his head around what he was seeing, but from here it almost reminded him of the way Kavi played with his toys, mouthing the words to the imaginary dialogue in his head.

The scene had been so surreal and hypnotic that even Tyson was startled when Kavi started screaming. Tyson's hand had slipped for no longer than a second, but it happened to be the very second Kavi finally found his voice.

The Pug-faced creature recoiled. The doll's head hit the ground with a hollow clop and rolled grotesquely along the floor. The temporary flash of fear on its face quickly became something ugly and harsh. It was getting ready to lunge at them and Tyson knew he had to act now or they would all be dead. In one quick motion. he nudged Kavi into Judy's arms, grabbed hold of the shelf and rocked it forward with everything he had. The aluminum unit didn't weigh more than twenty or thirty pounds and Tyson knew it would take that deformed monstrosity no more than a second to shrug it off. And that was why Tyson had gone crashing down with it. If his extra weight could keep it pinned for a few more precious seconds then Judy and Kavi might have a chance to make it out.

The creature scrambled to get free. The impact the shelves made as they landed nearly sent Tyson bouncing right into a pile of broken wood and cinderblocks. His head whacked one of the supports and his vision bloomed with a vivid starburst. But he held on. Through the pain and disorientation, his grip never wavered. He knew there wasn't any other choice. Kavi and Judy still hunkered in the corner.

A thick pool of dark blood was spreading out from the creature's tail where one of the metal shelves had split the flesh.

"Run, goddamnit! Get Kavi out of here, now!"

Beneath him, he could see the thing working to free its arms and he knew once it did, he would be torn apart. Judy scooped Kavi into her arms. The boy's face was ashen and expressionless.

The shelf bucked wildly.

"I can't hold it much longer."

Judy and Kavi were at the stairs when she stopped and turned around, a pleading look in her eye.

"Go!" he shouted.

They paused and then they were gone.

Tyson looked down just long enough to see two clawed hands reaching for him. Felt them wrap around his throat and tighten like a vice. He grabbed at its wrists; they were thin, but powerful and certainly stronger than he was. And it would keep squeezing until Tyson's world went black. He just hoped that he had bought Judy and Kavi enough time to get away.

It slowly squeezed the life from his body. As helpless as a child, an old memory began floating through his oxygen-deprived brain. Through the plastic bag pulled over his head, he could see the blurry outline of a woman smiling as she wound thick tape tightly around his neck. Black spots were bursting before his eyes and Tyson knew he was about to die. Although part of him might have accepted his fate, his physical body refused to give up. All the while he'd been gasping for breath, his right hand clambered frantically inside his pocket for something that might help.

For a moment, everything went black. Probably for no longer than a second or two, but when the lights in his head came back on, there was something in his hand and it was jingling. His car keys. He braced the long, fat ignition key against the palm of his hand, sharp end out. He cocked his arm and brought the point down against the creature's face. A long gash appeared in its cheek. Tyson's second blow went glancing off the side of its head, tearing away a flap of flesh as it went. When his hand rose again it was slick with a black, horrible smelling liquid.

His arm rose again and he thought of Ruma, of what this monstrosity had done to her. How terrified she must have been, fighting it alone as he was doing now. He swung a final time and heard the creature yelp. Through the haze Tyson could see that its right eye had burst open and part of it was trailing down the side of its face. Its head jerked wildly, the car key poking out from its eye socket. An unquenchable blood lust had seized him. A kind of insatiable primeval rage. He closed his hand around its neck and rammed the key all the way in until he heard a crunching sound. Almost at once, the pressure on his neck slackened and then fell away completely.

The creature's remaining bulbous eye looked back at him blankly. Tyson rolled off the pile of now crumpled aluminum onto his knees, gasping for air. His throat felt raw. His hand disappeared inside his pocket and came out with his asthma pump. He depressed the tab, felt the cool swoosh of air, but this time there was no accompanying comfort. His lungs were fine, albeit greedy for oxygen, but his crushed throat was the problem. Slowly he rose to his feet and padded across the dark basement toward the stairs. He was almost there when he realized he had left behind something terribly important. Buried in the creature's brain were the keys to his car.

He turned around, wondering if he'd find a crumpled heap of metal with nothing underneath it. But it was still lying there, a gray slab of meat. A pool of blood around its head.

Tyson approached. The key was still there, sticking out of its eye socket. He watched it for a moment. He had seen those scary movies. The ones where the beasty plays dead, then snatches its naive and unsuspecting victim.

His fingers closed around the hard plastic key handle. He was pulling at the key, a wet distasteful sound, when he stopped. Had he seen that other eye move? From here it seemed to be watching him, but it was dark and the thing was dead, he was sure. Tyson jerked the key in one clean movement and slid the tiny metal shape, gore and all, into the pocket of his pants.

He noticed a collection of paint cans against the far wall. Tyson kicked through them until he found what he was looking for. Paint thinner. The lid wasn't on very tight and he flung it off and doused the creature's body. That was when he noticed its fingers starting to twitch. There had been a box of old matches on the shelf before the whole thing had gone crashing to the floor. Where the hell were they? As he scrambled around looking for them, the gaping hole in the creature's eye was slowly closing up. Its clawed hand was closing around one of the metal supports when he finally found them. Tyson scooped them up and slid open the box and fumbled out a handful of wooden stick matches.

The aluminum shelf went flying and struck the back wall with a loud booming sound. The creature rolled onto its stomach, covered in paint thinner and blood. Tyson ran the match heads along the sandpaper surface and watched them bloom. He dropped those into the match box itself and flung it all at the creature as the entire box burst into flame. It struck the thing's head and a split second later flames engulfed it completely. Tyson raised his arm to shield his face from the heat. He could see it trying to claw at him, the flesh around its face and body bubbling and melting away.

He'd seen enough.

Without wasting another second, Tyson ran up the stairs and back out through the hole in the wall where he had entered, hoping to never see the place again.

Chapter 34

A thick stream of blood pumped out from the quarter inch hole in Bowes' forehead. Hunter stood watching it in amazement. Bowes lay on the ground, but he wasn't dead. Not yet. His twitching lips had worked up a thick frothy lather that ran down the side of his face. His eyes fluttered and Hunter wondered if he was trying to speak.

KILL ME!

Hunter removed a plastic bag from his back pocket and snapped it open with a flick of his wrist. It had taken a while with Bowes. The man was about as stubborn as they came, but in the end he had understood Hunter's point of view.

It was quite simple really. Bowes would forget this silly research paper idea of his, and more importantly, he wasn't going to murder Brenda.

At one point, when the drill came out, Bowes had even offered to give Hunter every penny he owned. It would have added up to a tidy sum, no doubt. But even Hunter knew you couldn't trust the word of a man with a drill bit inching toward his face. Hunter hadn't even made it completely through Bowes' skull when the old guy stopped shrieking and admitted he'd been wrong about Brenda. And this time, Hunter could tell he meant it.

Nevertheless, Hunter had pushed the drill in all the way and Bowes had let out a queer sort of scream that tapered off just as the drill bit disappeared completely into his brain.

An incredible amount of blood had followed, along with the foaming and the twitching face routine that had started once he'd removed the bit. Now, Bowes was down on the floor, begging to die. At least, that was what Hunter imagined he was saying.

Hunter scooped Bowes' head up off the ground with one hand and slid the plastic bag down to his neck with the other. He cinched the loose end and watched the bag pull in and out as Bowes gasped for air.

The old man's breathing grew more and more shallow. His eyes were starting to bulge. Then, gradually, they closed and Bowes lay still.

Hunter checked his watch and let out a little squeal. He was ten minutes late for his rounds on seven and eight. Late meant people might come looking for him. Late meant they might discover what he'd been up to.

Hunter studied Bowes' lifeless body. The plastic bag over his head, filling with blood. He would come back later, he decided, and chop him into more manageable pieces. Then he would wrap each chunk in several garbage bags, filling each with trash as he went. After that he would take a trip to the compactor.

Hunter grasped Bowes' arm and began dragging him toward the service closet. In went the drill and it made a thumping sound as it landed on Bowes' corpse.

A bright blinding flash. That was how it had felt as the drill bit burrowed into the soft tissue of his boss' brain. His communion with God.

Oh Brenda, wrathful and all-knowing, please accept this sacrifice...

Hunter's legs felt nearly as weak as when he'd imagined Brenda giving him a BJ in Cindi's messy apartment. But here was the funny part. Since the ecstasy of that orgasmic moment, his level of exhilaration had begun to fade almost at once, to the point where Hunter wasn't sure anymore if it had even really been there in the first place. He wanted that feeling again. And soon.

● ● ●

"You're safe now," Hunter whispered into Brenda's ear. "Dr. Bowes wanted to turn off your life support, said you'd passed some silly threshold and there was nothing more he could do. But I knew those rules had some room for give in them. Bowes just hadn't thought things through properly, that's all; otherwise he would have seen how foolish he was being. There's nothing to worry about." Hunter wiped her forehead with a damp cloth. "Not anymore. Dr. Bowes and I had a little chat. It took some convincing, sure, but the old curmudgeon eventually came around."

Hunter paused and tilted his head. Words blossomed inside his mind as clearly as if they'd been his own.

Where is Bowes now?

"Sub-basement 3. I stuffed him in the concierge's closet."

You killed him?

"Yes, of course. I couldn't let him hurt you." A sudden shuddering pain in Hunter's head brought him to his knees. His hands went to his temples as though he were trying to keep his brain from exploding. He moaned in agony.

I'm so very disappointed in you, Dr. Hunter. I specifically asked you not to interfere and you did just the opposite.

The pain intensified. Instead of the worst migraine in the world, his head now felt as though six-inch ice-picks had been jammed into each of his ears. She was killing him and he knew there was nothing he could do about it. He had freely let her into his mind. Let her walk about as she pleased and now she was trashing the place. Hunter slumped to the floor.

"Please," he said. It was all he could manage.

Then the pain began to slacken. The door to Brenda's room flew open and in charged Cindi Jaworski. She dropped down beside Hunter and cradled him against her great bosom. She frantically pressed the panic button next to her like an overzealous contestant on Jeopardy.

Inside Hunter's head, a final foreign thought took shape.

Next time, you'll do as you're told.

Chapter 35

Tyson pulled into the Marlboro Regional Hospital parking lot, jerked the car into the first spot he could find and killing the engine. The letters MAIN ENTRANCE were etched over a wide canopy. For a town suffering its own hardships, this place seemed to be doing just fine.

On his right, Kavi was curled up in Judy's arms, his face pale and lethargic. She was singing some kind of lullaby to him. It sounded familiar and for a reason he didn't quite understand, it made him feel uneasy.

Tyson scanned the peculiar feeling for anything remotely akin to jealousy. Was Judy becoming too protective of Kavi? And was all that nurturing highlighting his already overwhelming sense of parental inadequacy?

He could see Ruma in his mind's eye, shaking her head with disapproval. But it was too late for that now, wasn't it? The damage was already done. The doorway was open, and closing it, if that was even possible anymore, was all he could do.

Tyson looked over at Judy as she dabbed a Kleenex at the sweat forming over Kavi's brow. Perhaps there *had* been a touch of jealousy.

She reached out and ran a finger over the purple ring around Tyson's neck.

"Did you...?" She didn't need to finish for Tyson to know what she was asking him.

"Yes. You know, I half expected it to disappear. The way the Wicked Witch of the West did when Dorothy threw that bucket of water at her. It was still burning when I left."

Judy patted his arm gently.

He caught her hand and held it for a moment. "I'm okay. Course my throat feels like a fat kid mistook it for a seat, but apart from that, I'll live."

"If you're not hurt, then why are we here?"

"We need answers. Those scratches I found on the door prove there was something real in that room, not some imaginary bogeyman. Who knows, maybe my mother *was* protecting me from something.

"I have these loose snippets of memory that come tumbling out from time to time and I'm never quite sure if they actually happened or not. I remember going to sleep at night in that house, the covers up over my head because I was sure something was lurking under my bed. And I dared not look down because when you're that young, what you don't see can't hurt you. But I remember once I did look and I could swear I saw something crawling out from under my bed and into the hallway. Seeing that house where I used to live again, maybe that's what triggered the memory, I'm not sure. But I'm about as positive as a person can be that it's the same thing I killed in there. The same thing that got Ruma and maybe even Dr. Stevens. I need to know what it was after."

"Maybe it wants you all to itself, like when you were younger," Judy said innocently. Her eyes softened. "Maybe it only loves you and doesn't want to let you go."

Tyson brought the tips of his fingers to the raised and sensitive flesh around his neck. "Then it sure has a funny way of showing it."

229

The head nurse at Marlboro Regional was a busty thing, with a deep manly rattle in her voice. Tyson could see she had gone to great lengths to whiten her teeth— were those dentures?—but had ignored the yellow tobacco stains on the first two fingers of her right hand. Those two fingers twitched impatiently as though he were the only obstacle standing between her and the fix she so desperately needed.

Her left eyebrow cocked when she spotted the deep purple bruise around his neck and Tyson was suddenly not as sure this would go as well as he had hoped.

"Birth records?" she asked, as though Tyson had just asked her to pull her pants down and stand on her head.

"I was put in a foster home when I was five." He paused. "The same age as my son here, Kavi." Tyson's arm fell to his side, waiting to receive Kavi's tiny hand, but it never came. When he looked down he saw that Kavi was clinging to Judy's leg.

"So you wanna find your birth mother, is that it?"

"No, I know exactly where she is. I'm trying to find out if I'm an only child."

The head nurse's hand continued to twitch. "Records are in the basement. Go down that hall, hang a right 'til you see a set elevators. Ruth is the head archivist. If we got it on file, she'll know."

"Don't you have them on computer?"

"Good one," she said. "Computers break down. You store it properly and paper'll last forever. Just look at them Dead Sea scrolls." When the head nurse smiled Tyson was sure she was wearing dentures.

Much to Tyson's surprise, Ruth wasn't the head nurse's haggard doppelganger. Granted, she was old enough to be his mother and then some, but haggard?

Definitely not. Just looking at her bright and intelligent eyes, he could tell there wasn't much that got by this one.

Tyson told her why they had come.

Kavi was sleeping in Judy's arms and Ruth leaned over and stroked his head.

"What you're going through is perfectly normal after an early fragmentation."

"Yes," Tyson said automatically. "You know, I never thought of it that way, but that's exactly how I feel. Fragmented."

"Then you've come to the right place. If you were born here we'll have a record of it. Your name?"

"Tyson Barrett."

The sudden change in the nurse's expression was so striking that Tyson wondered if he hadn't given her a name like Adolf Hitler, or Pol Pot. Her otherwise smooth features rippled with tension.

"I'm so sorry," was all she said before disappearing through an opaque door.

Judy was running her fingers through Kavi's hair, his limp arms slung over her shoulders. She looked distressed and anxious and Tyson didn't think it had anything to do with the nurse's strange behavior.

"You don't look so well. What is it?"

"I'm not crazy about hospitals," she said. "And I don't think Kavi will be either when he wakes up. He's sleeping, but I can feel his heart beating a mile a minute. I'm wondering if we shouldn't talk to one of these doctors and get him a valium or a Prozac or something."

"Valium? I don't think that's a good idea. I mean, that's something I might have agreed to in the past, but—"

"Half a pill, Tyson. It's no big deal. Think about what he's just been through. Fact, I might take a couple myself."

"Yes and the next time life gives him an uppercut,

231

he'll be looking for his next fix."

"I'm not trying to turn him into an addict. I'm just trying to help."

"Yes, so am I. Besides, he's only five years old."

Tyson could hear the nurse coming back.

"Yes, maybe you're right," Judy said coldly, and Tyson wasn't entirely convinced she meant it.

The nurse emerged and laid a manila envelope on the desk. She was starting to act like one of those cops on TV who have the terrible burden of informing a family there's been a terrible accident.

"I think you'd all better come with me." She reached down under the desk to retrieve a sign that read: Be Right Back.

She led them into the filing room. On either side stood shelves taller than a man, not unlike the ones you'd find in a library, except these bookshelves had wheels on either end. In the corner sat three chairs and a table. Judy hoisted Kavi up on her lap. Ruth was still holding the folder.

"I wasn't out of nursing school longer than a week or so when a young woman was rushed into the emergency room. Her water had broken and she was dilated, nearly seven centimeters. I was working in intensive care at the time. Never did get a chance to see her. The head nurse was the one to tell me later, her belly was so pronounced it looked about ready to split.

"She was ranting and raving about the germs. Germaphobe was what they called them back then. Nowadays, they call it OCD. And I'm sure to some of the younger, less experienced staff, she must've looked plain old nuts."

Judy stirred and Tyson wondered if the nuts comment wasn't sitting well with her background in early childhood development.

Ruth pushed the folder across the table to Tyson. Inside were a series of faded documents. On top, one labeled Birth Certificate.

Under that, Tyson Barrett.

Date of Birth: May 23, 1974

Time of Birth: 4:35am

"This seems standard. Why the need for the sit down?" He wondered if the precautionary measure had to do with his mother's attempt to murder him.

"Turn the page," the nurse said.

Tyson complied and it took a second for the information to sink in.

Alexander Barrett

Date of Birth: May 23, 1974

Time of Birth: 4:15am

"I had a twin brother named Alexander?"

"A fraternal twin."

The nurse waited until he had scanned the rest of the page. Under the comments section was something he didn't quite understand.

"What's sirenomelia?"

"Your brother was born with a deformity."

"What do you mean de—"

"Sirenomelia is where a child's legs fuse in the womb. Most of the poor souls afflicted with the deformity die very young. Thank God. Those who survive learn to crawl on their stomachs until they're old enough to use a wheelchair. In Alexander's case, he also had a slight compression of his nasal bridge. It's a degenerative condition which means that had he lived, upon reaching middle age, his breathing would have become incredibly labored."

Tyson's eyebrows rose.

"Sort of like a Pug?" Judy asked.

"Yes, exactly."

Tyson became very quiet. His stomach roiled in slow nauseating circles. "What happened to him?"

"I guess the answer to that depends on who you ask. Most everybody in town could tell you a piece or two, but I'd be surprised if anyone apart from the police and the other members of your family have any clue what really went on. From the bits that I know..." Ruth paused, looking at Kavi.

"It's all right," Tyson said. "He's asleep, go ahead."

"Your brother, Alexander, died from neglect when he was about the same age as your son, Kavi. After his death, your mother arranged his mummified body in his bedroom as part of some sort of shrine. I'm sorry, all this must be terribly difficult to hear."

Kavi's head was pressed against Judy's chest and Tyson hoped he was still sleeping and hadn't heard any of this.

Tyson flipped through the pages and stopped when he came to an old photograph from the hospital's nursery. On one side was a pink newborn baby, wrapped tightly in a blue blanket. In the isolette next to it, a ghastly sight. Bulging eyes, long skeletal fingers and legs bound by dark gray flesh into a horrible looking tail. And now Tyson had a name for the creature that had kept him awake as a child terrified to look out from under the covers. The same fear that now kept him from sleeping, but for a vastly different reason.

Alexander.

That thing he had fought in the basement of his old house. The thing that seemed to want nothing more than to tear them apart. Could that really have been his brother? No, of course not, his brother had died years ago. If not his brother, then what had followed him back from the dream world, groping and clawing out some horrible cocoon in his kitchen? If not a real being,

Tyson reasoned, perhaps it was a symbol. A facsimile of a childhood trauma. Everyone has their own bogeyman, don't they? How could he forget entering the dim confines of Alexander's room as a child, on that horrible day so long ago? Seeing something recently dead staring back at him from the bed, where all the stuffed animals were neatly arranged. His mind kept returning to something on the scrap of paper he had found on Ruma's body. What are the chances that his nightmares could have started on the same day his mother fell into a deep coma in Sunnybrook? Then he remembered what the nurse had said about Alexander's breathing problem and suddenly it all made sense.

Chapter 36

"There's no way I could have known."

Judy was crossing the living room of Tyson's apartment, heading for the kitchen. She'd just come from checking on Kavi, who'd slept for most of the ride home. She poured herself a drink and sat down next to him.

"What do you mean, couldn't have known?"

"That thing from my nightmare, that's been chasing us, that killed Ruma."

"His name was Alexander."

"Yes, but that's what I'm saying, it's not the real Alexander."

Judy stared at him intently.

"The real Alexander died more than thirty years ago, right?"

"Yes, of course," she said.

"And this… this perversion that pushed its way out from the darkest part of my subconscious. Wouldn't you also agree that it's nothing more than a kind of projection of a childhood fear? Hell, my mother used to threaten to lock me up with whatever was in that room. So you can imagine what was going through my mind as a child when that thing was under my bed in the middle of the night or when I saw it sitting in that room, the flies swarming over its corpse." Tyson stopped and leaned against the wall. He'd just made the connection between the flies he had seen buzzing around the rotting flesh of his brother's dead body and the same insect that acted as a warning sign of the creature's arrival.

"I'm not sure I see where you're heading, Tyson."

He stood before Judy now and took her by the shoulders. "If those things coming back are from some deep dark pit of experience buried somewhere inside me, then nothing should be there that wasn't a part of that experience, correct?"

"I guess."

"When that thing chased us from this apartment, it was grunting and snorting."

"Yes, I remember. It made me think of a dog."

"That nurse at the hospital, Nurse... Ruth, she said that Alexander had a degenerative problem with his nasal cavity."

Judy's eyes lit up.

"Alexander died when he was five years old. So I couldn't have known about his breathing problem if it hadn't kicked in yet. It wasn't something that I'd ever heard as a child, the scratching at the door sure, but the heavy breathing? Never. And yet sure enough when he shows up, there it is."

"So then where did it come from?"

"The Alexander that's been coming back from that other place isn't coming from me. Not entirely. There are things I couldn't have known about. I mean, part of it is me, the way I remember seeing him. The rest, well, the rest is being supplied by someone else."

"But who?" And as she spoke the words Tyson could see the inevitable realization slowly begin to dawn. "No, it couldn't be."

"Why not? As crazy as it sounds, when you take everything we now know, there's no other answer."

"But how could she?" Judy asked.

"There was a scrap of paper I found with Ruma's things when I was at the morgue. She'd written a note about two events, connected by a single date. The first was the onset of my mother's coma and the second was the beginning of my nightmares.

"When you add in Alexander's breathing defect, something only she and a handful of nurses knew about, there's no other conclusion you can draw. Look, we still don't even completely understand what happens to people in comas. She lives in a dreamscape and maybe she's finally found a way to finish what she started thirty-three years ago."

Judy's hands were shaking. Tyson slid his arm around her and pulled her close to him. "I'm so sorry I involved you in any of this. Never in a million years did I imagine things spinning out of control the way they have. If you want to leave, I completely understand."

She put her arms around his neck. Her hands were soft and he welcomed the warmth of her touch. "How can I?" she said. "I've spent most of my adult life secretly wishing for something I thought I'd never find." Her eyes were shining.

Tyson drew her moist lips to his.

The sound of shrieking from the other room sent a violent jolt racing up Tyson's spine.

"Kavi!"

Tyson sprang to his feet, numb with fear. Scared to death that he would fling open the door where Kavi was sleeping and find a mess of blood and gore. Ruma's mangled corpse was being projected inside his mind as he burst into the room. Scanning frantically through the darkness, Tyson was certain he would see the creature he killed in the basement of his old house, grinning back at him, Kavi's blood smeared all over its burnt face. But when Tyson flicked on the light, he saw Kavi sitting up in bed.

He was crying.

Tyson went to him and curled an arm protectively around his son's tiny frame. His hairline was wet with perspiration. Tyson was patting him down, looking for blood.

"Bad dream?" he asked, when he was finally confident that his son was unhurt.

Kavi nodded, his eyes were fixed on some point in the distance. It had been so long since Kavi had looked at Tyson and really seen him. Judy stood in the doorway.

"Just a bad dream," Tyson said. "He'll be fine."

"I'll put some warm milk on. It'll help you get back to bed. Would you like that, Kavi?"

Kavi nodded. "Yes, please."

Tyson stood, making ready to leave.

"Daddy, I don't want you to go."

Tyson stopped.

"You want me to stay 'til you fall back asleep?"

"I don't want you to go to that place."

"What place? Where don't you want me to go, Buzz?"

"To the hospital. The old lady told me you were coming and I think that something bad is going to happen."

A cold, dead hand seized his heart. "Which old lady is that? Do you mean Nurse Ruth?"

"No, not her," he said drawing the words out, the way kids do when adults just don't get it. "Your mommy."

Thedead hand squeezed harder.

"Is that what she told you when you went there with Mommy?"

"No."

"Can you tell me when?"

"Just now."

"When you were sleeping?" Tyson asked, trying

to control the sudden fear rising in his voice.

Kavi nodded.

Tyson's eyes fell to the shadow beneath the bed. He dropped down on one knee and scanned the darkness. Nothing. He was in the middle of checking the closet, cursing his frayed nerves when Judy reappeared with a mug in her hand. Soon he was satisfied they were safe and the two of them sat with Kavi while he drank his warm milk. Studying his son's delicate features, Tyson wondered what kind of a person would want to harm a face like that.

"You know Daddy loves you more than anything in this whole wide world. I'd never let anyone hurt you."

Kavi rolled his eyes and smiled. "I know."

When Kavi was done, Tyson took the mug from him, hugged his son one more time and went to the door. He left the bedside light on so Kavi could sleep. The door was half way closed when Kavi spoke.

"Please don't go to the bad lady. Please Daddy, promise me you won't go."

Tyson's eyes fell to the door handle. He was suddenly very conscious of a thin layer of grime on the metal polish. His mother's solution to that had been to vacuum seal the entire house in plastic wrap.

"I promise," he whispered and as he spoke the words, he hoped Kavi couldn't tell he was lying.

Chapter 37

The day after Bowes' disappearance, Hunter had ordered a fresh battery of tests on Brenda and the results had surprised him. He'd also had to deal with a terrified Cindi Jaworski, who'd sworn up and down she had seen Brenda sitting up in bed the other night. Of course, he wanted it to be true, more than anything else in the world, but none of the tests he'd just performed bore out her wild story.

Part of what he'd been hoping to find was something that might shed light on Brenda's impressive mental abilities. It became clear, once he had been able to peruse Brenda's medical records, that she hadn't always been special. Bowes had mentioned on that very first day how Brenda's brain waves had gone off the chart after she had slipped into her coma. But Hunter wasn't convinced the coma was to blame. Lots of people were in comas and none of them could hold a candle to Brenda's uniqueness. There had been a mix up with her medication. That's what induced the coma, Bowes had said, but it was more than that. Hunter was beginning to suspect that very understandable error had altered the very chemistry in Brenda's mind.

What the tests revealed, however, was that Brenda's age regression, which had been so startling after Ruma and her son's visit, had slowed to a virtual crawl.

In the last few days, Hunter would sometimes see ghostly images of the boy, flickering through his mind like some kind of residual image seared onto his cornea after staring at the sun for too long. They had grown stronger since the boy was last here. It reminded Hunter of the way Clifton Walker in C-14 would beg for food right before lights out, fearful he would starve to death before morning. Was that why ghostly images of the boy were flitting through his head? Was Brenda begging for something to eat? Not physically, of course. This was Sunnybrook, after all, and not some backwater UN outpost in Central Africa. The physical changes in her had been remarkable after Kavi's visit. But if that were so, then how was she continuing to feed now that Kavi was gone? If not on the boy, then on who? She must have a proxy. The thought made Hunter smile and he felt his dry lips split in three places. Hunter saw the pale, translucent flesh on his hands and suddenly knew then that she had chosen him; the realization left him positively gleeful.

A series of pictures began forming in Hunter's mind, like a video of bursting soap bubbles played in reverse.

Brenda was speaking again.

She was showing him her room, the one he was in now. She was lying in bed. The sun was gone and heavy shadows played against the walls. Her son, Tyson, was padding determinedly across to Brenda's body. In the daydream, Tyson stopped and examined the equipment. He was poised over her body for several moments before he plucked the sensors off her chest and attached them to his own. It all seemed so strange to Hunter until he saw Tyson pulling the feeding tubes out of her nose. He pressed on her chin with the fleshy part of his thumb until her mouth opened and he removed her breathing tube. He was killing her, removing the heart sensors and

242

attaching them to his own chest suddenly made sense. Tyson was making sure that none of the attendants knew there was a problem until it was too late.

Brenda's body hardly moved. The machines had been the ones breathing for her and now that Tyson had stopped that, Brenda's chest had simply fallen and failed to rise again. Hunter shook his head, mumbling to himself and it was a minute before the words finally took some kind of coherent form. "You know I love you more than anything in this whole wide world," Hunter whispered. "I'd never let anyone hurt you."

The images flashed again in his mind, this time more rapidly, more emphatically.

"No!" he shouted. "I will not let anyone hurt you, not again." For the first time, he became consciously aware that he was speaking out loud. He also had her cold, limp hand clasped in his own, but to Hunter it felt warm and full of life. For a reason he didn't quite understand and would never be able to accept, Brenda wanted to die. He knew that he would never be able to forgive himself if he stood by while the woman he adored was summarily executed. The images were cycling through at the speed of light now; each time reset and played back a second faster. And now Hunter could see there was something different. Tyson's face had melted away, replaced by his own. She wanted him to do it. Wanted him to end it right now.

"Never," Hunter screamed again and then grabbed his head, doubling over. The pain was excruciating. A thin stream of blood seeped from his left ear. He had time for one last thought before he collapsed onto the floor. Before the world went black.

He had one more person to kill, to make her safe.

Brenda wasn't nearly as powerful as she used to be and the pain in his head gradually eased and then stopped altogether. He righted himself, brushed the dust off his lab coat and kissed her hand.

Not long after, Hunter was down the hall seeing to a schizophrenic named Joel Marsh; a middle aged man who had hacked six of his relatives to death because the letters in his alphabet soup had told him to.

Cindi Jaworski came in, doing her rounds and desperately trying to play hard to get. Hunter hadn't returned a single one of her twenty-eight phone calls since the night he had... done what anyone else in his position would have.

Cindi was emptying Joel Marsh's biohazard bin when she said, "Al's still looking for the key to that storage closet on sub level 3. He's been bitching about it all morning, driving us bat shit." She was trying to make some form of conversation to fill the cavernous silence in the room and it took a full second for the significance of what she had just said to register. Hunter felt the muscles in his face suddenly stiffen. Hunter had stashed Bowes' body in sub level 3 and the demands of his work day had made it impossible to return to dispose of it properly. Oh no. The keys Al was talking about had come from the janitor's own ring. Hunter he had found them in the maintenance lunch room and tried each key until he had found the one that worked. Then he had returned the chain to where he had found it, minus the single key he had been searching for.

"Yes, I know how stubborn Al can get," Hunter said, "when the smallest thing is out of place." He was trying to sound calm and agreeable.

Cindi smiled weakly. "Well, knowing how impatient Al can be, he might just use a crowbar to get in."

Her eyes locked on his face and for a moment Hunter could see she was disturbed by his haggard complexion. A thin film of sweat was forming over Hunter's brow.

"What's his goddamned rush?" he asked.

"Oh, I don't know, 'parently there's some kind of master water valve or something he needs to get at." She swapped the bag to her free hand. "You sure you're all right? You really don't look so good."

Hunter smiled and his thinning lips pulled back from a set of darkening teeth. "Never felt better."

Chapter 38

"Look Ty, we've known each other for how long now?"

Tyson eyed Skip suspiciously as they stood in his friend's living room. "Fifteen years, at least."

"Things have been... difficult lately, I know that."

Skip was choosing his words carefully, Tyson could tell, and normally his friend's deliberate sensitivity was a welcomed thing. Between the two of them, Skip was always more thoughtful and responsible and it didn't have anything to do with the fact that Skip was a few years his senior. Of course, Skip had always been more than a close friend. He'd been a surrogate father, but right now Tyson didn't need a father. He needed a friend.

"I'm worried you're about to go and do something very stupid," Skip said slowly. "I've seen that look in your eyes before and it's usually a sign you're about to do something you'll regret."

"I never expected you to believe me when I told you what was happening."

"I didn't, not at first. Then I remembered our lunch at Le Bernardin and that thick stack of twenty dollar bills you threw at me after the meal." Skip was keeping his voice down because Kavi was in his bedroom, watching Toy Story for the nine hundredth time.

Tyson shook his head. "I'm sorry, Skip, I wasn't trying—"

"I only ended up needing about half of them," Skip cut him off. "Stashed the rest in an old jar above the fridge and I kept meaning to remember to give them back to you each time you swung by, but you were always in such a... rush." Skip went into the kitchen and returned a second later with a jar in his hands. He held it up for Tyson to see.

"It's empty," Tyson said.

"Then I remembered you telling me how the money had vanished from your apartment. How it had faded, the way dreams start to fade after you wake up."

"So you know now I'm not crazy."

"Money, toys and then people coming out of dreams. I can't believe it, Tyson, but I also don't see how I can deny it."

"You know, up until now, Judy's been the only one to stick by me and I've known her all of a week. I'm glad we're not alone anymore."

Skip smiled. "And where is Miss Perfect? I'm starting to think it's some kind of conspiracy with you two."

"Not on my part. Look, Skip, right now, I really need you to look after Kavi while we go and do this thing."

"You still won't say what it is you're up to."

"I don't feel that I can. Not yet, at least. I just need for you to trust me on this."

Skip set the jar down on the kitchen table. "After what happed to Ruma, I don't want anyone else to get hurt."

"Only one more person's gonna get hurt and then everything will be back to the way it was before."

Skip slumped silently into a chair. After a moment, he spoke. "You know you've just gone and made me an accessory."

Tyson was shaking his head. "I wish there was some other way…"

Tyson's phone vibrated in his pocket. He removed it and flipped it open.

"I'll be right down."

The voice on the other end surprised him.

"Pardon me, Mr. Barrett?"

"I thought… who is this?"

"This is Dr. Elias Hunter. We met the other day when you came by Sunnybrook."

Tyson was suddenly gripped by a horribly irrational thought.

She knows. Somehow she's read my mind and she knows what I'm about to do.

"What is it I can do for you, Dr. Hunter?"

"There's been a change in your mother's condition."

"Oh, what kind of a change?"

"One for the worse, I'm afraid."

Tyson was quiet.

"At this point, she's well past the state's time allowance for patients in Glasgow level three comas. I'm sorry, but we don't have any other option than to terminate her life support."

Tyson switched the phone to his other ear. "You have my permission, go ahead."

"I'm afraid it's not quite that easy. You see, there are legal issues to observe, paper work to fill out and signatures. Lots of signatures."

The line was quiet for several moments.

"As her only surviving relative…" Hunter went on.

"My father," Tyson spat. "He's gotta be around

somewhere."

"I'm sorry to inform you that he passed away not long after your mother arrived at Sunnybrook."

Tyson checked his watch. "Then it's gonna have to be today."

"Very well, Mr. Barrett."

"See you in an hour," Tyson said and slid the phone back into his pocket.

Skip was shaking his head. "Looking at your face right now, I can't decide if you're happy or scared shitless."

Tyson ran Skip through his conversation with Dr. Hunter.

"And you think killing your mother will stop these things from coming out of your dreams?"

"It has to."

"I never got along with my father," Skip said quietly. "I certainly don't have to tell you that?"

"Course not."

"I can remember getting the call from a doctor over at Lennox Hill hospital after my parents' car crash. They never were able to figure out quite how it happened, but the one thing the cops could see was that the ol' man was probably hitting my mother just before they went off the highway. One of his hands was off the wheel, probably along with both of his eyes. She went through the windshield and well, you know the rest. His catatonic state lasted only a week before they said he was brain dead. A stopped heart can be started again, but when the brain goes... Even though I knew what the ol' man had done to her, pulling that plug was still the hardest damn thing I ever did."

"Because you still loved him?"

"Hell no, I hated the son of a bitch. But he was the only family I had left. Never had any kids to come home to."

Skip stuck his hand into the pocket of his sports coat and came out with a fountain pen.

"This pen you bought me for my birthday, I've started to grow attached to it."

He handed it over to Tyson.

"Skip, I can't."

"Take it. For your sake, I hope you'll have an easier time signing your name than I did." Tyson took the pen and was staring at it when Skip continued, "Maybe after all this is done you'll be able to get some real sleep."

Tyson smiled. "I think I'll sleep for a month."

Skip came forward and grabbed him in a bear hug.

"You look like shit, not sure if Judy has the guts yet to tell you."

Tyson left a few minutes later, feeling an odd mixture of apprehension and euphoria. Furthest from Tyson's mind was the possibility that this was the last time he would see his friend alive.

Chapter 39

It was evening when Tyson and Judy arrived at Sunnybrook. They had sat for nearly an hour on the Henry Hudson Parkway at a near standstill, hardly saying a word to one another. They were both deep in thought. For all Tyson knew, Judy was probably wondering why she couldn't have met a normal guy.

The parking lot at Sunnybrook was deserted. Above them rose the asylum's imposing battlements. It almost felt as though they were about to enter a fortress. But the entering part wasn't what worried Tyson; it was the leaving.

The Eagles had written a song about that back in the '70s. *Welcome to the Hotel California. You can check out any time you like, but you can never leave.*

A cracked lamp cast a pool of shadow over the front doorway.

Tyson turned to Judy and saw the tension in her face.

"I don't trust this Dr. Hunter," she said.

"Neither do I, which is why you're gonna wait in the car."

"Tyson, I didn't come all this way to wait in the car," she snapped.

"Listen to me," Tyson said, taking off his seatbelt. "I might be blowing all of this way out of proportion…"

"Yes, I think you are."

"And if I'm not?"

Judy was quiet.

"If I don't come back out I want you to go to the police."

"And tell them what?"

"That I've gone missing and this was the last place you saw me."

"And after what's been happening, they'll think you're right where you belong."

Tyson burst into a fit of laughter. He felt all the blood rush to his face. When he settled, the tension had dissipated a little.

"See what happens when you get yourself worked up over nothing," she said.

He slid his hands behind her head and brought his lips to hers. Then he forced himself to pull away and rubbed his hands together against the cool air creeping in from outside.

"It must be something about this building," Judy said somberly, staring at Sunnybrook. "I hate it."

Tyson watched a shadow flit past one of the second story windows. "Me too."

● ● ●

If Tyson had found Sunnybrook unsettling during the day with the sun beating down from above, and doctors and orderlies filling the asylum's guts like bacteria, what he saw now was nothing short of frightening. The only soul was an emaciated security guard on the front desk named Joe, who pointed him toward a bank of elevators.

"Dr. Hunter's new office is on the eighth floor."

Hunter must have told him he was coming. It was beginning to look like the sort of place where you didn't stick around after your shift was over. The kind of place you ran from as soon as you could, maybe never completely sure why you were running in the first place. The elevator doors opened onto the eighth floor and right away Tyson could hear someone screaming. Couldn't tell if the voice was male or female and frankly he wasn't interested in finding out. Someone else was calling for help. Then he heard a small voice, like a child, sobbing.

Help me. Somebody please help me.

The smell of disinfectant was strong and the odor made Tyson's nose curl. He associated it so strongly with his mother it might as well have been the perfume she wore.

He came to room H-16. Beside it was a name. *Barrett.*

Tyson stopped and peered into the concave porthole. The room was empty.

Along the far wall was a bookcase and near that a simple wooden chair. But his mother was gone. Even her bed was missing.

This Hunter's one efficient S.O.B., he thought. *I guess for him signing those papers isn't much more than a formality.*

Three doors down, Tyson came to Hunter's office. He studied the name plate before knocking.

Elias. What kind of a name was Elias? Sounded like his parents were a couple of Bible nuts. And then he saw the tiny Post-It note clinging to the door; tiny curling letters spelled out a message he practically had to knock his head against the door to read.

Mr. Barrett,

Please meet me in room 373 on S3.

Regards,

Dr. E. Hunter

Tyson tore the note from the door. "Where the hell is S3?"

He was heading back to the row of elevators, suddenly aware that the screaming had stopped. He depressed the descending button and waited as it called the elevator. The silence was hard to ignore, as was the overwhelming sensation that he was being watched. He glanced down the corridor. It seemed to stretch on forever. At the end was an emergency exit and the dull red glow from the light overhead. It was empty and Tyson felt a tinge of relief wash over him.

Figure or no figure, that uneasy feeling wasn't going away. His scalp felt tingly and far too small for his head. He had a sudden, burning urge to look behind him. God, the elevator was taking so long. There wasn't anyone here, why was it so slow? The disquieting feeling was growing stronger.

A buzzing noise started in his ears and he felt his breath begin to quicken. He fingered the reassuring contours of the inhaler in his pocket and hit the elevator button again in the illogical hope that mashing it over and over might get it here sooner. That urge to look behind him wasn't going away. Count to ten, isn't that what they say? Tyson felt his head begin to turn almost in spite of himself.

The face staring back at him almost made him scream. Distorted by the concave glass, she was thin and old, eyes sunk deep into her skull. That's exactly what she looked like, a smiling cadaver. The dark lines under her eyes were heavy and Tyson couldn't help thinking about how they looked like the purple smudges under his own eyes.

It had nearly been a week now since he had slept at Skip's cottage and he knew it was catching up with him in a big way. Increased heartbeat, inability to concentrate, frayed nerves. All the old symptoms were there all right, and then some. Tyson's new friend was still watching him. A thought popped into his head but he dismissed it almost immediately.

Could that be Brenda? Somehow awakened from her coma and walking about?

It could be, for all he remembered of the way she looked, but this woman was far too young. Brenda would be approaching seventy. The chances were strong that she was lying in some room, hooked up to a dozen life support machines, hardly aware the end was so near at hand. Better yet, if this Dr. Hunter had done what Tyson hoped he had, she might very well already be dead.

Tyson heard a clang as the elevator doors slid open. Something compelled him to look down the hallway again. That's when he noticed that, as far down as he could see, patients were watching him from nearly every porthole, their faces twisted up against the glass. For a moment a curious thought flitted through his mind and it had to do with the way they were watching him. As though he was the crazy one, a freak of nature. Maybe they had a point. On the eighth floor in Sunnybrook Asylum, he was the odd man out.

He stepped into the elevator, scanned the panel and pressed a button labeled S3. The doors were sliding closed when it started again. Somewhere, a genderless voice was screaming at the top of its voice. Beneath that, the sobs of another, a young male, begging for someone to help.

● ● ●

Exiting the elevator onto S3 didn't do anything to put Tyson's mind at ease. It looked like a maintenance area, more than anything. Long shadowy hallways, exposed piping overhead and each step made him more certain that something wasn't quite right. The clanging of a heavy generator bellowed out from behind a set of double doors. On each was a picture of a man, head back, feet well off the ground, his arms splayed in each direction and a bolt of lightning about to cut him in two. You didn't need to be a genius to tell that whatever was in there could give you a nasty shock if you weren't careful.

Ahead was an open door, spilling warm light into the hallway. A faint pinging sound was coming from inside and he knew right away what it was. The slow steady beat of a heart monitor.

Tyson slowly approached and peered inside. The basement of an asylum was the last place he expected to find his mother, but nevertheless, here she was and a million electrified thoughts were jostling through his head.

He was about to step inside and paused. He hadn't laid eyes on her since he was five years old, not that he remembered what she looked like. But if he couldn't pick her out of a police lineup, then how could he be sure this was the right person?

He went to the side of her bed. A piece of tape on the heart monitor settled his concerns.

The name on it read: Barrett, Brenda.

Her face was old, contorted by tubes and wiring. But he had seen this decrepit face before, hadn't he? At Skip's cottage. That haggard face in the window and then hovering over him in bed. Seeing it now gave him a chill.

"Now it's my turn to put a bag over your head," he whispered.

On the wall was an electrical socket where the life support machines were keeping her alive. All he needed to do was pull it from the wall and it would be over.

That old expression about pulling the plug was closer to the truth than he had ever realized. And then he was struck by another notion.

It was one of the many idiocies of life. That pulling the plug now would be tantamount to murder while waiting for Dr. Hunter to sign some papers wouldn't. He had learned the consequences of being impatient the hard way, of wanting a solution right away. That was what had gotten him into this mess to begin with, wasn't it? Maybe counting to ten and fighting the urge to yank the cord out of the wall would mean the difference between a life in prison and a life watching Kavi grow up.

As Tyson's eyes followed the line that traced the rhythm of his mother's heartbeat, a terrible thought occurred to him.

What if she wakes up before the paperwork goes through?

It was one thing to pull the plug on someone who was for all intents and purposes dead, but the idea of plunging a knife into someone's heart, well that was another matter entirely.

Studying her face, he could almost swear it looked like her eyelid had twitched. The way eyelids tended to twitch when someone was playing dead, waiting for the right moment to spring up and yell, *Surprise!*

"She's magnificent, isn't she?"

The voice from behind him nearly made him jump. Tyson turned on his heels to find Dr. Hunter standing in the doorway. He didn't look well at all. Tyson had watched a program about people who were addicted to methamphetamines and Hunter could be their poster boy. Eyes receding into his skull, cheekbones high and protruding. He might have been missing teeth, judging by the way his thinning lips curled inside his mouth.

"Why the hell was she moved down here?"

"Merely a formality, I assure you." Hunter said. He was lisping. "We try to remove patients whose life support is about to be terminated from the general population so it doesn't upset the others."

Hunter smiled and in the dim light of the room he looked more ghoulish than ever. "So Mr. Barrett, should we get this over with? I still have mountains of work ahead of me."

Tyson nodded and was walking toward Hunter when his eye caught something he hadn't noticed before. He had been so overwhelmed with seeing his mother after all these years that he hadn't taken a moment to take in his surroundings.

To his left was the door to what looked like a utility closet and running out from beneath the crack...

"Is there a chance," Hunter asked, "that when all of this is over and done with I could ask you a few questions about your childhood?"

...what looked like...

"That isn't being too presumptuous, I hope?"

...a thin stream of blood...

Hunter set a briefcase on the table and removed a series of documents.

"Why don't we get started then?"

For the first time since he had arrived, Tyson felt the walls closing in around him. His breath narrowed to shallow gulps. His senses suddenly kicked into high gear. Everything around him slowed to a crawl, the way car accident victims later describe the moment of impact. Something or someone inside that closet was dead and it didn't take much to realize Dr. Hunter had something to do with it. The doctor was closing the door and the loud noise it made reminded Tyson of a jail cell door swinging shut.

"Maybe this isn't the best time," Tyson heard himself say, vaguely aware that his mouth had gone terribly dry.

"Nonsense, you've come all this way."

"Maybe I wanna give it some more thought."

"Mr. Barrett, there's nothing to think about. It's

the state that pays for her care, not you. After six months in a comatose state… well, it's a matter of policy really."

"Yeah, well then you don't need me," Tyson said as he reached for the door. But Dr. Hunter was there, right in his face and in one hand were the documents, bunched into a tight fist. He was holding them up as if he were a waiter challenging a customer who was refusing to pay. In Hunter's other hand was a syringe filled with a yellow liquid and he plunged the point into the fleshy part of Tyson's neck. Tyson yelped and swung his left arm to knock Hunter away. Hunter had been trying to depress the plunger and inject the yellow substance into Tyson's neck, but now there was a snapping sound and the needle went skidding across the floor.

The point was missing.

No, not missing, it was sticking out of Tyson's neck and the pain was excruciating. Hunter couldn't have had time to inject more than a few drops of whatever was in that needle, but still, Tyson felt his vision becoming glassy. His limbs suddenly felt heavy and sluggish.

Tyson took an unsteady step away from Hunter, who was coming toward him determinedly, his arms swinging madly. A wild punch connected with Tyson's left cheekbone, rocking his head backward into a cloud of starbursts. Another punch and this time he had enough sense to raise his arm to block the incoming blow. But Hunter's fists were flying at him faster than he could avoid them and he was caught by a left hook and went spilling onto his mother's prone form. As he struggled to clear the grogginess, something hard hit the side of his skull and he fell to his knees. Hunter stood over him, grinning. In one hand he held a metal bedpan with a sizeable dent . Tyson was on all fours, trying with everything he had to stay conscious.

Hunter motioned to the utility closet.

"The old man and Al the janitor didn't have the

fight in them that you have." His skeletal face broke into a gap-toothed smile. "You had me worried there, for a moment. Anyway, it isn't you your mother wants, but I'm sure by now you've already figured that out."

Hunter took a step forward and as he did, Tyson remembered the parting gift Skip had offered him. He reached for the fountain pen, nestled inside his pocket beside his asthma pump, not entirely sure if his hands would cooperate. Hunter was on top of him now, saying something but his words not making sense. Just then, the bedpan tumbled out of Hunter's grasp and hit the floor with a metal clang. The fingers of Hunter's left hand rose to his temple. Then his right. He seemed to be having some sort of aneurism. Behind them, Brenda's heart monitor was going crazy.

Tyson flicked off the cap of the pen with his thumb and plunged the Mont Blanc into Hunter's belly, just above the navel. He pulled down, using the leverage to get one of his feet planted firmly on the ground. The piercing scream that emanated from Hunter's open mouth sounded animalistic. A gush of blood gushed out from what was now a six-inch gash. Tyson pulled the pen out and swung it again, this time twelve inches higher. It tore through his doctor's lab coat and made a sick noise as it bore through his chest cavity and punctured his heart. His hands clamped around Tyson's neck, but he had lost whatever power he once had. Hunter sucked in a final breath before his eyes turned up to whites and his knees buckled. Tyson fell on top of him, his chest heaving. The world was swimming away from him and he knew in another few seconds everything would go black. How ironic would it be, he thought, to have struggled to stay awake for so long, only to succumb a few feet from his goal. If he failed now, there was no telling what might come through.

Less than three feet away, past Dr. Hunter's

convulsing body and the pool of blood that was forming around him, lay the plug that powered his mother's life support. Her heart was beating rapidly and he could hear the distant pinging of the machine beside her. For a second his eyes closed and he slapped his own face until his vision settled. Couldn't have been more than a few drops of that yellow shit swirling through his system and he wanted nothing more than to sleep.

Two feet now.

He could hear his mother's breathing quicken. She was dreaming. Somehow he knew that. But about what he wasn't sure.

One foot.

His eyelids each weighed a thousand pounds and he was only seconds from losing the battle. The wires were within arm's reach. He saw a hand—his own?—grasp both cords and when his eyes closed—this time for good—he hoped to hell he had managed to pry them loose from the wall in time.

Chapter 40

I gotta say, Ty, you certainly don't waste any time, Skip thought when he heard the knock at the door. He and Kavi were eating cookie dough ice cream and playing a game of Uno. He swung open the door without bothering to check the peephole. The young woman before him was beautiful. At least she could have been beautiful, if it wasn't for the queer blotchiness of her skin and the fact that large chunks of her hair was missing.

"Where is he?" she croaked.

Skip tried to slam the door shut, but the woman's foot stopped it dead.

"Who are you?" Skip shouted.

"Don't fuck with me, old man! Where is he?" The knife in her hand was a Sashimi and right away Skip recognized it as the one from Tyson's kitchen.

He backed away into the living room, trying to buy some time, hoping for an opening where he could lunge for the knife and overpower her. The woman slammed the door behind her. The loud boom must have startled Kavi, because he came running around the corner, eyes wide, holding his ice cream bowl.

They both saw him at once.

Skip reached out a hand when he saw her stalking toward him. "Kavi, get back!"

"I told you not to fuck with me," the woman said and slashed a deep red line across Skip's throat.

Skip's hands clamped around the wound but thick ropes of blood slipped between his fingers as he tried holding the loose flaps together.

But the woman wasn't done, not by a long shot and Skip knew he had no other choice. He charged and tackled her. The back of her legs hit the sofa armrest and both of them tumbled over it and onto the ground. Skip's hands locked onto her face and she swung the blade in a frenzy. A single thought pulsed through his head: *rip her apart, or you and Kavi will both be dead*. The thumbnail on Skip's right hand cut through the flesh of her cheek and when he pulled it away, a chunk of flesh the size of his fist came with it. But the woman didn't scream, she just swung the knife in a wide arc, burying the blade in the top of Skip's head. It made a strange sound, like whacking a wet pile of rags with a stick. His mouth opened almost as if he was about to say something, but his eyes went dull and his body went limp. The woman pushed him off her and stood up.

Kavi's hand was on the doorknob. One turn and he'd be in the hallway. An ice cream bowl lay shattered at his feet. The woman approached him cautiously, almost maternally, telling him everything was going to be all right, that he didn't need to be afraid. The boy could see her teeth through the hole Skip had torn in the side of her face and her teeth were black.

Chapter 41

Black spots dotted Tyson's vision. He rubbed his eyes with his palms and waited while the room around him slowly came into focus. His first overall sensation was an auditory one, or at least it was the lack of sound. That loud clanging from the generator room next door was gone, but that wasn't all. So too was the soft symphonic pinging from Brenda's life support.

The first image to form before Tyson's eyes was the electrical socket. Both slots were empty and the eerie silence suddenly made sense. He had managed to jerk them from the wall before he hit the ground like a sack of dirty laundry.

But she didn't die right away, did she?

Dr. Hunter lay nearby, face down. A creeping puddle of wet and sticky blood pooled around him.

Tyson used the railing on Brenda's hospital bed to haul himself to his feet. With his legs unsteady and stiff, he wondered how long he'd been out.

Before him lay his mother, mouth ajar, her body still and lifeless. He felt her wrist for a pulse and found none. Her skin was cold, the color of raw dough. The surge of happiness he had expected never came and for the life of him, he couldn't figure out why. Maybe it had something to do with the dead man lying on the floor next to him, Tyson's Mont Blanc jutting from his chest.

Tyson grabbed a handful of Dr. Hunter's bloody lab coat and rolled him onto his side. He looked away as he curled his fingers around the handle of the pen and pulled it out.

But the whole time he'd been watching his mother's lifeless body, certain he would see her eyes snap open.

Come to Mommy. You know how much I love you. Tyson, don't make me ask you twice.

Then he remembered the utility closet. He crossed the room and opened the door.

The bodies of two men were inside. One wore a doctor's coat and had a clear plastic bag over his head. The name embroidered near the breast pocket read: Dr. Bowes. Tyson removed the bag and was sickened to find a hole had been drilled into the man's forehead. The second man wore a janitor's uniform. His name tag read: Al Quinlan. Beneath his left ear was a puncture mark; quick and painless.

Tyson was out in the hallway, preparing to leave, when he noticed his shirt was covered in Hunter's blood. There wasn't a chance in hell he would make it out looking like that.

Only one of the three dead men in the room wasn't soaked in blood. Tyson returned and undid the upper part of the janitor's overalls. He wore a filthy white T-shirt and it reeked of rotting flesh. The janitor's body had been in the closet long enough that he'd begun to bloat and his shirt now bore the undeniable smell of death. Plugging his nose, Tyson pried the shirt off the cadaver. At this point he wasn't in a position to be picky.

If he managed to make it past the guard, Tyson hoped Judy would still be outside waiting for him.

He slowly made his way out of the labyrinth, and up onto the main floor. Joe was still at his desk. The guard looked up when he saw Tyson walk by.

"Excuse me, sir. Sir…"

Tyson stopped and slowly turned around. The muscles in his cheeks and forehead and around his lips were twitching and he was sure Joe could see that. The guilt on his face was unmistakable. And the blood. There had been so much of it surely he had missed some. A spec or two on his collar was all it would take.

Tyson's eyebrows rose.

"I need you to sign out," Joe said with a touch of annoyance.

Tyson approached the desk, his heart jack hammering in his chest. There was a booklet on the desk and a free line underneath departures. But of course he couldn't put his own name. Tyson quickly signed a name, then smiled and made his way to the front door.

Joe scanned the signature. "Thank you, Dr. Stevens," he said. "Have a great day."

But Tyson was already gone.

The sun had come up. He scanned the parking lot for any sign of Judy. In the distance he saw a woman walking briskly away from him and something about her gait made him pause. It wasn't Judy. No, this woman was short with dark hair and the way she bounced ever so slightly with each step made him think of Ruma. Tyson rubbed his eyes and the act of lifting his arm made the needle mark in his neck sting. Of course it wasn't Ruma, he told himself. After whatever Dr. Hunter had just tried to pump into his jugular, it was a miracle he wasn't seeing flying pink elephants.

There were no more than five or six cars in the parking lot but none of them belonged to him. Tyson's heart sank with the realization that Judy had left. How long had he been unconscious?

266

Tyson struggled down the steps and began heading for the road.

They had arrived in the evening and now it was early the next morning. He couldn't blame Judy, since he told her to go to the police if he didn't return. And he was sure that's exactly where she was, telling the police a story they would never believe in a million years. He had really just assumed he was going to sign a document to have his mother's life support cut. Tyson certainly hadn't counted on leaving Sunnybrook with two dead bodies behind him. Four, when you counted the ones in the closet he was sure the police would try to pin on him.

Tyson took in a deep breath, and for the first time in days felt as though an enormous weight had been lifted off his shoulders. He thought of that tiny metal lunchbox in the storage locker of his apartment. He hadn't opened it in years and could barely recall what it held—a few old toys and pictures maybe. The sad remnants from a childhood that no kid should have to experience.

He removed his cell phone from his pocket and dialed Skip's number. It rang for a while before the voice mail picked up.

Hi, you've reached Skip Williams, I can't take your call right now, but if you leave your name, telephone number and message... beep ...

"Listen Skip, I need you to keep an eye on Kavi a little longer, there's one more thing I need to do."

For some reason, while his mother was alive, he had always been too afraid to look inside that box and perhaps even more afraid to throw it away. Now that she was gone for good, he would do both.

Chapter 42

Two hours later, Tyson was sitting by the fireplace in his apartment, a Star Wars lunchbox in his lap. The wood was dry and crackled as he watched the flames flicker. He was waiting for the right moment to lift the lid. A thick layer of dust obscured the cover image and when Tyson wiped it away, he could finally make sense of what he was seeing. Darth Vader's TIE Fighter had just fired his lasers across the bow of Luke Skywalker's X-Wing. Inside the dented tin box, loose objects rattled around like distant memories.

He had hailed a cab to the closest car rental shop and driven straight to his apartment, somehow expecting, or hoping, to find Judy there waiting for him. When that hadn't happened, he grew more and more certain that she had gone to the police, just as he had asked her to. And the very idea was starting to really scare the crap out of him, what with four dead bodies awaiting discovery in Sunnybrook's basement.

Tyson tried to ease his mind that she would show up again before long. But her way of popping in and out of his life, even over the short amount of time he had known her, wasn't doing anything to calm his nerves.

After undoing the metal latches, Tyson opened the lunchbox lid. For a moment, he examined the contents without touching a thing. The heat from the fireplace made the skin on his cheeks tingle as he took a mental inventory of the lunchbox. In the background, the television set was desperately trying to convince him that a new Lexus would somehow make his life complete.

Tyson reached down and began removing items one at a time. First an old yellow Volkswagen Transformer he still recognized as Bumblebee. He studied it for a while before tossing it onto the fire. It spat and crackled as the plastic slowly came undone and began to drip down in thick globs. Next was his favorite GI Joe action figure, Shipwreck, and after that a pair of red dice. Tyson held each of them for a moment before throwing them into the flames. Then came Han Solo and Chewbacca. Han's left arm was missing. On a whim he stuffed those into his pocket, but in went the other toys, each flooding him with powerfully mixed emotions. On the one hand, seeing them again brought back all the old childhood wounds he had buried long ago. And on the other, these toys had been the only real source of joy in a difficult life.

Underneath the toys were a set of photographs. Most of them were of the house and the pristine condition his mother had kept it in. He examined each one in turn before tossing them into oblivion, and as he did so, he released a deep breath. The load he had been carrying around for so long was becoming lighter with every flick of the wrist. Catharsis, he was beginning to understand, wasn't really about facing the difficulties of life head on, it was about learning to let go of them.

Somewhere in the back of his mind, on an almost alien frequency, came something from the television.

State troopers say they've found...

More pictures of the house he grew up in and this time with him, dressed in a tiny suit, standing by the front entrance, alone. No smile. Off it went.

...the body of a woman...

Another one of him at the kitchen table. Laid across him was the shadow of whoever was taking the picture. There was a smile here, but Tyson couldn't help but sense the tension in his young face.

...up in the Catskill Mountains.

He was about to toss it into the flames along with all the others when something hit the ground. It was another picture. The two must have been stuck together. It seesawed quickly to the ground and landed right side up. The picture of a beautiful young woman in her mid-twenties...

The victim, a woman in her early fifties, has been identified as Judy Stahl. Police say she was strangled in her home, a remote cottage where she lived year round.

Tyson turned toward the television, hardly aware that all the muscles in his face had gone completely slack and that his jaw was hanging open.

The coroner's office says the woman had been dead for nearly a week.

The newscast flashed a picture of what Judy Stahl had looked like in life, but it was a face Tyson had never seen before. That wasn't his Judy.

His eyes fell to the picture on the ground; his mother in her early twenties. The room was starting to spin.

This was the Judy he knew. Young, attractive. Not the dead woman on TV.

Something about this building, he remembered her saying about Sunnybrook. *I hate it.*

Course you do.

Tyson sprang to his feet, sending his old Star Wars lunchbox clanging to the floor. He fished his cell phone from his pocket and frantically dialed Skip's number. Voice mail again. Tyson's heart slammed against his chest. He wasn't sure if he quite understood the totality of what was going on, but he was damn sure about one thing. And the very thought of it was almost too much. If his mother had found a way to stick around after her physical body had died, then Skip and perhaps even Kavi might already be dead.

Tyson snatched the keys to his rental and dashed out the door, a single thought echoing through his mind.

Please God, don't let me be too late.

Chapter 43

When Tyson arrived, he found the door to Skip's apartment wide open. He called Kavi's name, but was answered only by silence. Beneath his feet was something sticky, it looked like dried ice cream, and a broken bowl.

To his left was the living room. Tyson's heart sank when he saw his friend lying face down; you didn't need to be a doctor to see that he was dead. A pair of bloody footprints led from the rug by the couch to the front door. Tyson went to Skip's side, knelt down and turned him over. His body was stiff and it made a ripping sound as it tore away from the blood binding it to the floor. The black handle of a kitchen knife, one that looked a lot like something out of his own apartment, protruded from the top of Skip's head and a long deep gash had splayed open his throat. Tyson stared incredulously at Skip's right hand and the flap of skin bunched in his closed fist. It was difficult to tell exactly what part of her it had come from, but Tyson was certain of one thing: there had been a struggle and Skip had died fighting for Kavi's life.

Tyson's head fell into his hands as he wept. Skip was the closest thing to a real friend, and maybe even a parent, Tyson had ever had. The reality of it was almost too much to bear. She had been right under his nose the entire time, slowly guiding and manipulating his every move. Tyson pulled the knife out of Skip's head and flung it across the room.

The bitch wanted to be unplugged, didn't she? Wanted him to be isolated from anyone who might have helped him, anyone he'd ever loved, so that she might be the sole focus of his affections. And at first, maybe she wanted him back; but now, she wanted Kavi.

It isn't you your mother wants, but I'm sure by now you've already figured that out.

He knew it just as surely as he knew he was going to kill her once and for all. And this time there wouldn't be any hesitation. This wasn't some helpless old woman, lying in a bed filled with tubes and wires. She never had been. No, this was a monster.

He was mumbling to himself as he searched Skip's apartment.

Where did she take Kavi, Skip? Where'd they go? You gotta help me, ol' buddy.

On the kitchen counter was a copy of Frommer's New York State.

Why would Skip have his map book out?

Tyson held the spine and leafed through it with his thumb. The pages in the middle made an unusual clapping sound. He fanned through them again and heard the same noise a second time. Some of the pages had been torn out. It wasn't more than a few seconds before he identified them. P. 241-245. He flipped to the table of contents and suddenly he knew.

She'd taken him to Skip's cottage on Lake Harmony.

She wants you to find her, a little voice said, *so she can put that bag over your head and finish you for good.*

But if he knew Benda at all, he knew she would kill Kavi the minute he had served his purpose. Tyson ignored the voice and headed for his car.

Chapter 44

Tyson slowed the car to a crawl when he reached Skip's cottage. The house was dark and had a disquieting stillness about it that sent the flesh on Tyson's arms crawling. His initial impulse had been to go charging inside, swinging his fists at anyone that wasn't Kavi. But the hour long drive up—which he had cut down to forty minutes with the sort of reckless driving that could have landed him in jail—had given him time to think up another plan of attack. Back at his apartment, the TV news had left him with the impression that cops and crime scene techs would be swarming all over the cottage where the real Judy Stahl had been found. If he could swing by there first, maybe he could show up with the cavalry in tow. He was taking a real chance though, since for all he knew, the police were getting ready to pin him with half a dozen homicides.

Tyson's tires cut through the gravel as he sped down the road. Time was the other factor he was risking, since the slightest delay could cost Kavi's life. Tyson had no clue what she was doing to his son, but Dr. Hunter's words were still ringing in his head.

It isn't you your mother wants ...

And if Dr. Hunter's gaunt appearance was anything to go by, the boy wouldn't last long.

The two patrol cars and a crime scene technician's van in the driveway was all he needed to find the real Judy's cottage. Tyson pulled up behind one of the cruisers and bolted from the car without bothering to kill the engine.

The real Judy's place was a one floor bungalow. The front door was ajar and Tyson slowed as he approached. The silence was unsettling. The cottage was modern and whitewashed and inside he could see the lights were all on, but where were all the people?

He passed through a doorway into the kitchen and something sticky touched his face. He recoiled and slapped it away. He examined his hands and noticed heavy white filament. Looked like a spider web, but unlike one he had ever seen before. This was much thicker and when he tugged at it, the filament stretched but would not break. When Tyson passed through the kitchen and into the living room all the muscles in his body tensed. Suspended from the twenty-foot vaulted ceiling were the partially mummified corpses of two adult males and one female. Their bodies had been wrapped inside a swath of white filament, which covered them from the neck down. The skin on their faces looked like it had been vacuum sealed to their skulls. Something had sucked the life out of them.

Things were slowly falling into place. The Judy he thought he knew wasn't simply a product of his own haunted memories. She was a composite, the way the brother that he had never known, the one that had chased them out of his apartment building and killed Ruma, had been a mishmash of his memories and hers. He looked up at the ceiling again. One thing was certain: the version of his mother who had done this hadn't originated from him.

Two tiny marks on the far wall caught his eye. Bullet holes. And three more high above him. There had been a struggle and it looked as though the police had been shooting in all directions. But what exactly had happened? Had she been running on the ceiling?

A noise from the room next door startled him.

Slowly, Tyson backed out through the kitchen, suddenly feeling like someone who may have walked in on an intruder. He was acutely aware of the fact that he didn't have a weapon.

He searched the room, but couldn't find anything the police might have dropped during the struggle. He knew full well that sticking around to keep searching wasn't an option. Not simply because she might still be here, but because every minute Kavi spent in her presence brought him that much closer to death. She was going to use Kavi like some kind of recharging station, drain him for everything he was worth and then spit the kid out, just as she had done to Dr. Hunter.

Tyson snatched up a flashlight that had been left on the kitchen counter. He left through the front door at a brisk pace and stopped when he reached the first police cruiser. If seeing those bodies had convinced him of anything, it was that he needed a weapon.

The cruiser door was unlocked and he jerked it open. He found a shotgun inside the locked gun rack. He grabbed the handle and tried jarring it loose, but it wouldn't move.   The key must be inside the pocket of one of the dead cops, he realized with growing hysteria.

There isn't time. Kavi might already be dead.

He would have to think of something else. Heading back to his car, Tyson remembered something from Skip's letter. The cottage prep list. Yes, there was a weapon, he just wasn't sure if he'd be able to find it in time.

• • •

A few minutes later, Tyson stood in front of Skip's boathouse, rattling a locked door handle. He took a step back and slammed the heel of his boot against the space just above the knob and the door flew open.

He turned on the flashlight and followed the beam as it cut a path through the darkness. Tiny waves broke against Skip's Bombardier speedboat and it sounded like a wet hand slapping the lid of a coffin. Tyson tried to swallow, but his mouth was too dry. Inside a storage closet, below the snorkeling and scuba gear that Skip had loved so much, Tyson found what he'd come for. He reached in and took hold of the speargun. If a crossbow ever had a younger, gawky brother, this would have been it. Inside a leather case he found a half a dozen bolts. He'd have to make every shot count.

His hands trembled as he followed the directions on the handle.

Step one, lay the bolt in place. Step two, reach out and pull the wire to your chest until it clicks into the groove. The process required two hands and Tyson had to set the flashlight on the bench beside him while he worked. His teeth ground together and the muscles in his forearms burned as he attached the wire to the metal release lever.

Tyson then slung the bag of bolts over his shoulder and followed the tip of his speargun out of the boathouse and up the damp stony path that led to Skip's cottage.

He had almost reached the front entrance when he realized his dilemma. The speargun, at nearly a meter in length, might be too cumbersome for going room to room. But what other option did he have? He slid the flashlight into his pocket. The door knob turned freely and he pushed his way inside, feeling more and more like the terrified child he had once been, pushing his way into the room where the monster lived. But this time the monster was real.

The cottage was a void of impenetrable blackness. He fished the light out from his pocket and switched it on. The beam swept back and forth across the room. He was in the solarium. White sheets clung to the furniture like the discarded skin of ancient spirits. An archway led from the solarium into the kitchen. Heavy tendrils of spider silk crisscrossed the doorway. Tyson reached out with the light to swipe them aside, but instead the light snagged and wouldn't budge. Tyson grimaced as he wrenched it back and forth until finally the light came free. These strands were far stronger than even the ones he had found down the street at Judy Stahl's.

She's getting stronger, he realized. *With every kill she's becoming more and more powerful.*

A noise up ahead somewhere. Low and distant. A whimpering and he didn't need to see to know exactly who it was.

Kavi.

Tyson held the speargun out in front of him as he darted through the kitchen and toward the sound of Kavi's voice.

The room was so thickly covered with web, if he didn't know any better, he might have thought this was some kind of nest.

Or was it a nursery?

White everywhere. *Looks like a winter wonderland.* He frantically scanned frantically the shadows for Kavi. Where the hell was he? The pulse pounded in Tyson's neck. She was here somewhere, he knew. Hiding, waiting for the right moment to…

But so was Kavi and he could hear his voice, low and muffled as though something were in his son's mouth, preventing him from calling out.

A clump of bed sheets caught his eye. Tyson focused the beam of his flashlight on that spot in the corner. The pile was trembling, ever so slightly. And the shape was oddly human. Tyson cut across the room.

But those weren't bed sheets covering Kavi. His son's arms were splayed with that same heavy filament that now covered the entire cabin. Another bunch was covering Kavi's eyes and mouth. Tyson tore at the webs and gasped. His son's eyes were bulging with terror. That cherubic little face that used to look up at him with such adoration now looked drawn and gaunt.

An image of Dr. Hunter's tired, cadaverous face as it had been before he died flashed before Tyson's eyes. It wasn't blood she was after. She was draining their life force.

"Daddy?"

Kavi's voice sounded dry and brittle.

"Hold still, son, I'm getting you out of here."

Kavi shook his head. "She won't let us leave Daddy…"

Tyson put the speargun on the ground and began tearing wildly at the sticky webbing. "The hell she won't."

The strands coupling Kavi's arms to either wall were particularly strong. Tyson heard Kavi's sharp intake of air. He could see the terror in the boy's eyes as he peered at something over his shoulder. The angle of his gaze was steep. Which meant it was either very tall or…

As Tyson turned, he felt the hot needle pierce his left shoulder. Then a moment of blinding pain before he was lifted up off his feet and thrown against the far wall. He landed in a burst of agony. Across from him, at the other end of the room, now lay the flash light and, more importantly, the speargun. The beam from the light was pointing in his direction, casting a sick glow, making whatever was standing before it all the more gargantuan and grotesque. Tyson stumbled to his feet. His hand found the hole in his shoulder. Around the wound, his shirt was torn and already saturated with blood. The

279

creature was coming toward him. On its head was a patch of long brown hair and he knew right then that this wasn't some new nightmare. This was his mother. Not the young version that had been masquerading as Judy Stahl. No, this was the real her. Who she was on the inside.

Her legs were long and chitinous, bowing out widely until they touched the floor where they came to narrow points. Her belly was bloated and covered in giant pustules. As she staggered toward him, her new feet made a sickening sound, boring deep gashes into the floorboards.

She stopped, not ten feet from him and for the first time he could see her face. The sight sent a paralyzing chill coursing through his body. Her head looked like an inflated schoolyard kickball, except this ball was covered with eyes, short bristly hairs and a tiny mouth filled with sharpened teeth. Below, he could see the undulations of her dark glistening belly.

"Mommy's pregnant again, honey," she said and even in the dim light he could see the corners of her vile mouth turned up into a smile. "I've waited so very long for another chance to have a family. You're going to have brothers. Lots and lots of brothers. I love you so much. But after everything I've done I'm sure you already know that, don't you?"

"You're a liar! You don't love me."

The Brenda thing recoiled, as if in pain.

"Of course I do," she said pleadingly, drawing out the words into a hiss.

"I've learned a thing or two along the way and I know that just as you gave birth to me, I gave birth to you." The blinding pain in his shoulder was making Tyson's vision blurry and he forced his eyes open as they closed, fighting to stay conscious. "That monster inside you that I knew as a child became a part of the new and improved Brenda and when I cut you off from your physical body, well, the real you just started showing up in spades, didn't it? And now you've become on the outside what you always were on the inside."

He could see her eyes, all six of them, blinking.

To Tyson's immediate right was a block of cutting knives. If he could prevent her from seeing what he was up to, he might just be able to slide one of the blades free.

"You're in control now, just like when Alexander and I were young." He could see those leathery things she called lips quivering and he knew he had her, if only for a moment. His hand closed around the knife handle. He tried to nudge it out, but it wouldn't move. The angle was making it difficult. He remembered those two dead policemen and the bullet holes in the wall. Unless he could get the drop on her, he wouldn't stand a chance.

"Killing Kavi and me. None of it will undo what you've become now and that's the second chance you were really after, wasn't it? Now you're nothing more than a bloated dust mite. I'll bet this wasn't how you thought things would play out when you tricked me into cutting your life support, was it?" Tyson started laughing hysterically.

She didn't like that, not one bit and she was coming toward him now—a great looming bulk with clawed hands and a mouth full of razor blades.

The knife was still stuck.

She was so close he could smell her now. The odor was pungent, like a butcher's shop on a sweltering summer's day.

The edges of her forearm were serrated like the sharp side of a whale harpoon. It would slice through his flesh nice and easy, but when she pulled it out his insides would spill out onto the floor in a hot mess. She skittered toward him on her two insectile legs, her arm poised for the killing blow and suddenly Tyson knew what he must do.

"I love you."

She hesitated. It couldn't have lasted more than a second, but it was enough. Out came the kitchen knife and Tyson swung it through the air, cleaving Brenda's forearm in two. She looked down in disbelief as a foul black liquid pumped from the severed stump.

She shrieked, giving Tyson just enough time to swing back around and plunge the knife into her fattened belly. The blade made a wet sound as it broke her skin and tore at whatever monstrosity lay inside her. The knife was buried deep in her abdomen when Brenda swung her mangled stump into his chest and sent him flying across the room. The knife clattered onto the floor as Tyson hit the wall. The impact shook the entire cottage.

"Daddy? Daddy, are you okay? Please get up. Please!"

Tyson shook the fog from his head. He could hear the Brenda thing coming at him. Her breathing was labored and wheezy and he was vaguely aware that she was badly hurt, but hurt wasn't dead and dead was the only way they would be safe.

Kavi started screaming.

Lying not a foot away was the loaded speargun and the quiver of bolts. Tyson picked it up and fired. The spear brushed the side of her head, ripping out a handful of matted brown hair before the bolt thudded into the wall behind her.

Nine feet away.

Through the searing pain in his shoulder, Tyson scrambled to reload. With quivering hands, he fidgeted out another spear and set it in place. He swung onto his back and held the end in place with this feet while he drew the wire back.

Five feet.

He raised the gun and fired. The spear made a squishing sound as it punctured her chest, right between what might have once been a pair of sagging breasts. Brenda staggered back, wobbled, her feet cutting great holes into the ground as she tried to stabilize herself. Tyson was sure she was going to topple over. Any second now Brenda would fall face forward and be dead; but she didn't. She was still coming.

Three feet.

There wasn't enough time to load another bolt. His hands fumbled with the quiver. It was pointless. There wasn't enough goddamn time. Brenda cocked her good arm. It looked as though she was going to ram the needle point right down his throat.

Kavi was quiet. The boy could see what was about to happen and the terror of it had robbed him of his voice.

That smile was back on Brenda's face, as though she were admiring a fine piece of art, and in that freeze frame of time, what a tableau they would have made. Tyson on his ass, arms stretched out before him. Kavi, his body encased except for the small of his face. And the bloated thing before them that had once been Brenda, but which now looked less human than ever before. In slow motion she thrust her arm at Tyson's forehead.

There was a swooshing sound, followed by what sounded to Tyson like a ripe fruit being whacked against the wall. The Brenda thing let out a deep sigh. She shifted the bulk of her monstrous weight and turned.

Someone else was in the cottage with them; Brenda was distracted and for Tyson, that was all that mattered. He grabbed a bolt, slammed it into place and pulled back on the wire until it cut deep lines into his hands. Brenda was about to strike her new attacker when Tyson took aim and fired. The bolt tore through the air and sliced clean through the back of Brenda's skull, coming to a halt protruding from her forehead. She turned toward him and he watched in amazement as all six of her eyes rolled up to whites at the same time. She then collapsed on top of Tyson, her distended torso convulsing as the tip of the bolt tore a long, ragged gash into the wall as she fell. The horrible black blood pumping from her severed arm gushed all over him.

Tyson rolled her body off of him and suddenly became aware of two things. The first was that the kitchen knife he had pried free was now sticking out from the back of Brenda's neck. That one surprised him. The next one shocked him.

Chapter 45

"Well, Tyson, aren't you going to say hello?"

"Ruma?"

From behind him. "Mommy Mommy Mommy!"

"Yes honey," she said, stepping past Tyson. "It's going to be all right." She pulled at the steel-like webbing that covered Kavi. But she didn't need to pull very hard. Already white wispy ghosts were raining down all around them. Before long all of this, including Brenda, would begin to fade and then disappear completely.

"But I saw you… in the morgue."

She giggled softly and that hauntingly familiar sound brought tears to his eyes.

"You always were one to miss the point, even when it was staring you flat in the face," she said. He could hear her Bengali accent coming through loud and clear.

When Kavi was free, he leapt into Ruma's arms, sobbing. They hugged for some time before Ruma gently coaxed his arms from around her neck.

"I'm so sorry," Tyson said. "For everything."

She looked at him lovingly.

He felt a wave of emotion about to sweep him out to sea. "I never got a chance to tell you that. I was stupid. I was too wrapped up in my own bubble to see how much I was hurting the two of you. Can we start again? Wipe the slate clean like none of this ever happened?"

She smiled.

He pulled Kavi and then Ruma close to him and held them tight. He wanted nothing more than for this moment to last forever, but even now he could feel his throat begin to tighten. His lungs were closing up on him and he reached into his pocket for his asthma pump. Ruma's hand closed over his, stopping him.

She knew him better than anyone else, didn't she? He let the pump fall to the floor, but not before noticing Ruma's hand.

"You're wearing your wedding ring."

She looked at him as if he had suddenly lost his mind. "Of course I am. Why wouldn't I be?"

And suddenly Tyson knew and the realization felt like a giant boulder had come crashing down on his chest. Surely he should have realized it before. The resemblance was uncanny, she felt so incredibly warm and alive, but this wasn't the real Ruma. He remembered leaving Sunnybrook, the woman in the parking lot he thought was her. How quickly he had dismissed the idea. No, this Ruma was from that rosy little room in his mind where the ones he loved were kept safe and sound and timeless. There, the last eight months of his life was little more than a vague dream. It was from there that she must have crossed over, when he lost consciousness in Sunnybrook, only moments before his mother had stopped breathing for good.

"I love you," he whispered.

Tyson held both of them for a long time, wishing when he opened his eyes again that she would still be there.

Chapter 46

Nine months later

Tyson was stoking the fire when Kavi came in , thick wet snow caked onto his jacket and pants. He looked like the world's smallest Yeti.

"Cold out there, Buzz?"

"Yeah, Dad, it's sick."

Tyson raised an eyebrow. "Sick?"

"You know, Dad."

"So I take it you had fun playing? How's Billy from next door?"

A wide smile grew on Kavi's face. Even now after all this time, Tyson could still see shadowy lines under his son's eyes. "We're building a snow fort," Kavi said.

"Oh, sounds like fun. It's nice and toasty by the fire." Tyson helped Kavi out of his snowsuit. A teardrop of snot hung on Kavi's upper lip. He sneezed and half of it landed on Tyson's jeans. They both burst out laughing. Tyson pulled some Kleenex from his back pocket and wiped his son's nose and then the smear on his jeans.

"Don't worry, Buzz, won't be long now before this cold'll work itself out of your system."

Kavi sat by the fire, sipping at a mug of hot chocolate.

Tyson stood looking at his son, thankful. For a while, the police had been swarming around him like flies on shit. He must have been interviewed a dozen times. In the end, they had pinned the whole thing on Dr. Hunter. And it was at about that time that Tyson had seen an ad on Craig's List for a small country home on Lake Joseph. He didn't really mind that it was in the Catskills. He had also finally come to understand—and not just suspect—that while the Noxil might have opened that doorway between worlds, it was Brenda who kept it from closing.

She'd been obsessing over him for years, but it was only when Brenda slipped into that drug induced coma that she was really able to, as the old telephone commercials used to say, reach out and touch someone.

The conjunction of his mother's frightening new telekinetic abilities, along with his own adverse reaction to the Noxil, had created the perfect storm.

Of course, since then he still had the odd unsettling dream or two about that night at Skip's cottage. And yes, occasionally he woke up screaming, his hands grasping at imaginary spearguns, but it hadn't been long after the incident that his life had started returning to normal. That is to say, his dreams, good and bad, were finally staying in his head, where they belonged.

Both he and Kavi had started seeing therapists soon after Ruma finally disappeared. She had woken in the middle of the night to get Kavi a glass of water and vanished on her way back to bed. Tyson had called out to her more than once before he understood what had happened. Lying alone, he had wept quietly until morning.

Kavi looked back at him and smiled.

Tyson winked. "How's the hot chocolate, Buzz?"

"It's great," Kavi said through a foamy mustache.

On the mantel above the fireplace, two tiny

action figures stood staring at both of them. One figure was missing his left arm. The same toys he had found in his childhood lunchbox and kept, perhaps as a way to ensure that he would never again forget. Tyson yawned, looking forward to sliding into his warm bed for a good night's sleep.

Also by Griffin Hayes

Novels
Malice
Dark Passage
Hive Omnibus
Primal Shift (Season 1)

Novellas
Bird of Prey
Hive
Hive II
Hive III
The Neighbors
Primal Shift

Short Stories
The Second Coming
The Grip
Fatherland

Collections
Night Terror
Nightfall